SHERLOCK HOLMES

THE MONTANA CHRONICLES

BY

DR. JOHN. WATSON, M.D.

AS EDITED BY

JOHN S. FITZPATRICK

To Ann Maguire Swann
Thank you +
Best Wishes
John Fitzpatrick

RIVERBEND
PUBLISHING

D0964076

Sherlock Holmes: The Montana Chronicles
Copyright © 2008 by John S. Fitzpatrick

Published by Riverbend Publishing, Helena, Montana

ISBN 978-1-931832-96-0

Printed in the United States of America.

1 2 3 4 5 6 7 8 9 0 MG 14 13 12 11 10 09 08

Cataloging-in-Publication data is on file at the Library of Congress.

RIVERBEND PUBLISHING
P.O. Box 5833
Helena, MT 59604
1-866-787-2363
www.riverbendpublishing.com

DISCLAIMER

This is a work of fiction. In general, names, characters, places, and incidents are products of the author's imagination or are used fictitiously, and are not to be construed as real. Any resemblance to actual events, locales, organizations, or persons, living or dead, is coincidental. However, in three stories—The Tammany Affair, The Ghosts of Red Lion, and The Mysterious Woman—a number of the characters named in the story are based on actual people who lived in and around Anaconda, Montana near the turn of the century, although their use herein is completely fictitious. Many of the locales are also real, although the author "adjusted" geography and historical chronology a smidgeon to fit the story's plot. The reader should not interpret these writings to be historically accurate.

ACKNOWLEDGMENTS

A work of this type necessarily involves contributions from many people. First and foremost, I wish to thank my two long-time associates, Kay Haight for her outstanding secretarial assistance, critical insight and positive encouragement, and Barbara Effing for her copy editing. Jennifer McCord, Alan Joscelyn, Bill Beaman, Phil and Jean Green read early versions of the manuscript and offered many valuable suggestions for improvement. Chris Cauble and Janet Spencer at Riverbend Publishing did likewise, and I am very grateful to all of my reviewers for their assistance.

For favors big and small, thanks also go to Jerry Hansen at the Marcus Daly Historical Society, Anaconda, Montana; Lory Morrow, Rebecca Kohl, Katie Curey, and Brian Shovers at the Montana Historical Society, Helena, Montana; and Rodger Foster at Morrison-Maierle, Inc., Helena, Montana for helping fix a major IT problem.

John S. Fitzpatrick

DEDICATION

*To my parents Marcus (deceased) and Natalie Fitzpatrick,
from whom I learned the love of books and libraries.
Thank you for a gift which has spanned a lifetime.*

PHOTOGRAPHIC CREDITS

The author wishes to thank the following parties for permission to use photographs from their archives in this book.

MARCUS DALY HISTORICAL SOCIETY, ANACONDA

1. The Upper Works
2. Main Street
3. The Starting Line
4. B. A. & P. Passenger Train

MONTANA HISTORICAL SOCIETY, HELENA

5. Hearst Free Library
6. Reading Room
7. The Montana Hotel
8. The Tammany Bar
9. Tammany
10. The Red Lion Mine
11. The Red Lion Mill
12. Map of Southwestern Montana

K. ROSS TOOLE ARCHIVES
MAUREEN AND MIKE MANSFIELD LIBRARY
THE UNIVERSITY OF MONTANA, MISSOULA

13. Interior of the Opera House

WORLD MUSEUM OF MINING, BUTTE

14. The Southern Cross Mine

JOHN S. FITZPATRICK, HELENA

15. The Red Lion Tramway
16. The Boarding House

CONTENTS

 The Discovery

IT WAS MID-NOVEMBER 1994, just a few
days before Thanksgiving when the telephone rang and I heard the voice of Marian
Geil on the other end of the line. Ms. Geil was soon to retire
from her job, after serving 31 years on the staff at the Hearst
Free Library, in my hometown of Anaconda, Montana.

I became a "regular" at the library in 1961 when, as a
seventh grader attending the Junior High School across the
street, I began spending a part of my lunch hour in the library reading room pawing through the magazine rack or
checking out large stacks of very thin books, determined to
win the title for "most book reports written" in my reading
class. I lost the contest, second place actually, but found a
comfortable place in which to spend time and the start of a
book habit that would last into the present.

After identifying herself to me, Marian asked if I was
planning on coming to Anaconda to visit my parents over
the holiday. I replied in the affirmative and she asked me to
come by the library because she'd found something that I
would find "especially interesting." I prompted her for more
of a hint but all she'd say was "given your interest in myster-
ies you'll find it a special treat."

I was both perplexed and curious, so curious in fact, that I took the day off before Thanksgiving and arrived at the library just after 1:00 p.m. Marian took me to a small room in the corner of the building, which served as the library board's meeting room, the bindery repair shop, the librarian's office, and several other functions. We sat at a large oak library table, its smooth, black leather top glistening in the sunlight streaming through the window. There, she laid a thick envelope before me. The package was obviously quite old, the postage British in origin, and cancelled in September 1899. Marian then explained, "There is an old safe in the basement, which has been there for as long as anyone can remember, the combination lost. I've wanted to open it for years. I finally called the manufacturer and they sent out a man last week, who opened it. Inside, we found several old ledgers dealing with the library's finances in its early years, a Taft for President campaign button, and this envelope. Open it."

I did as I was told, carefully withdrawing a manuscript, typed on a fine bond paper. The title said it all. *Sherlock Holmes: The Montana Chronicles* by John H. Watson, M.D.

I was stunned, not just as a Holmes devotee of many years by then, but also as a Fitzpatrick, the fourth generation of my family to live in Anaconda. My great-grandfather had been Sheriff of Deer Lodge County back in the mid-1890s and it was somewhat of a family legend that he had worked on cases with Holmes and Watson.

"John," Marian continued, "if you'll look at this letter from Dr. Watson, he gave these manuscripts to the library to be published. Somehow they were forgotten, and it was never done."

"Well," I interjected, "you must see to it that is changed."

"My sentiments exactly," came the quick reply, "and that's why I asked you here. I'd like for you to edit the manuscripts."

I was flabbergasted. "You want me to edit John Watson, one of the great writers of his time? You can't be serious!"

"Yes, I am quite serious. This material needs editing," she answered. "It's not written in the same manner as Watson's other stories. Much of it just reads like a travelogue where he spends a lot of time describing the countryside and people he meets. If you look at his letter, Watson says as much."

So, that is how I came into possession of *Sherlock Holmes: The Montana Chronicles* or, at least, a reasonably good photocopied facsimile thereof.

Before I left that day, Marian showed me a filing cabinet where she planned to store the original in a drawer titled "Special Projects." She retired a few months later.

I took the manuscript home with me, fully intending to start working with it. After reading the document, I concurred with Marian's assessment. It needed work and I started the painstaking process of editing, trying to remove the extraneous material Watson had placed in the manuscript while faithfully keeping both the structure and pace of his tales, as only he could do so well. But, my literary career hit a snag. My regular job, managing governmental affairs in the minerals industry, fed me a steady diet of long workdays and travel. When I was home, I preferred to spend my free time with my family, instead of sitting at the table picking through 95-year old prose, even if it was John Watson's.

After a series of on-again, off-again editorial attempts,

I resolved to do the work during the summer vacation and stored my copy of the manuscript inside the cabinet portion of an end table, which resides in my home's front parlor. And once there, I promptly forgot about it. A year later, I discovered it was missing, the victim of aggressive house cleaning and lapsed communication between husband and wife. I raced to Anaconda to get another copy but the new librarian informed me that she had never heard of Holmes' *Montana Chronicles*. I subsequently learned that workroom had been thoroughly "reorganized" after Marian Geil's retirement, and if the manuscript was there, it had gone to the dump long ago. I spent several days dividing my time between rage and pouting over my own stupidity.

Then, about a year ago, in an effort to keep peace in the family, I agreed to clean out a whole series of files, mostly material pertaining to my work during the 1980s, which were stored in the basement of my home. I was taking my time about it, to the great consternation of my wife, when I rediscovered the Watson manuscript sandwiched between a file folder of political bumper stickers and a series of sociology bibliographies dating back to graduate school. I never asked how it got there. I was afraid I would be told.

The rest, as they say, is history. My work had begun.

John S. Fitzpatrick

Dr. John H. Watson
221-B Baker Street
London, England

September 19, 1899

Mr. Fredrick Clark, Librarian
Hearst Free Library
401 Main Street
Anaconda, Montana
United States of America

Dear Mr. Clark:

It's been longer than I care to recollect since my good friend, Mr. Sherlock Holmes, and I departed your fair community. In reflection, I've become quite fond of Anaconda. I treasure the many hours I spent in the library's reading room and the hospitality you extended to me as I labored at my task of chronicling Holmes' exploits.

I've enclosed with this brief missive copies of several manuscripts which detail Holmes' work in Montana. You are hereby authorized to publish and disseminate this work in the United States. Our mutual friend, Marcus Daly, has indicated that he will underwrite the cost of publication on the library's behalf.

The enclosed manuscripts are somewhat longer than those appearing under my name in The Strand. They reflect my natural writing style, which includes more description of my role in Holmes' cases as well as some narration about the sights and sounds we encountered during the investigations. However, the editors at The Strand insisted that such material be removed to give the chronicles a more singular focus on Holmes. I was tempted to follow that style here as well but ultimately concluded that life in America's premiere mining province, Montana, was so unique that readers everywhere would benefit from its description.

Again, thank you for your incomparable hospitality during my visit to Anaconda. I remain, Sir,

Very truly yours,

John H Watson

John H. Watson, M.D.

HEARST FREE LIBRARY—ANACONDA, MONTANA
Funded by the munificence of Phoebe Apperson Hearst, the library remains Anaconda's most important cultural institution. Mrs. Hearst's husband, George Hearst, was one of the original investors in the Anaconda Copper Mining Company.

READING ROOM—HEARST FREE LIBRARY
The main floor reading room as it appeared in the late 1890s. Dr.
Watson's letter to Librarian Fred Clark indicated that he spent
considerable time at the library drafting the case materials now
recognized as The Montana Chronicles.

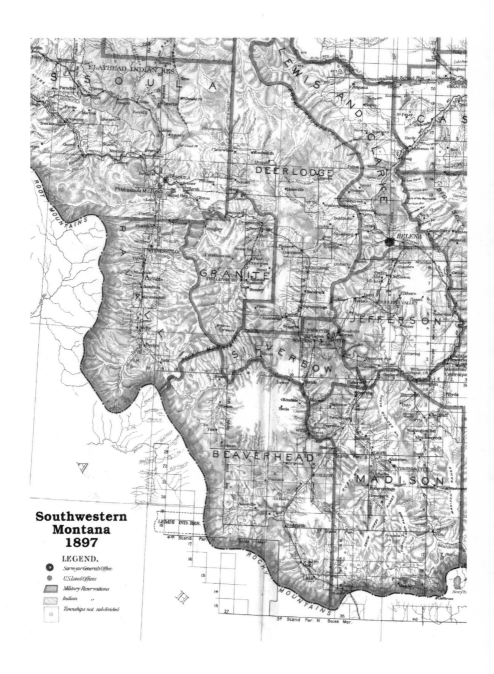

Southwestern Montana 1897

LEGEND.

Surveyor Generals Office

U.S.Land Offices

Military Reservations

Indian "

Townships not subdivided

8

The Opera House Murder

"Holmes, the cab will be here shortly. I trust you're as anxious as me to reach London."
My words echoed in the stillness of the second floor landing. There was no reply.

"Holmes," I called again. That was perplexing. We had just separated not ten minutes ago to complete our packing. The train for Chicago was to leave at noon, precisely forty-five minutes from now. We had journeyed to St. Paul, Minnesota in January 1896, a few short weeks ago, at the request of James J. Hill, affectionately nicknamed by his friends as the Empire Builder, to assist with a series of matters which I previously recounted as the Ice Palace Murders.[1] Mr. Hill's hospitality was incomparable, but it was time to return to London and the warmth of the British Isles. I know that sounds foolhardy, but once you've tried a Minnesota winter London seems almost Mediterranean.

I peeked my head into Holmes' room and called again. His luggage was beside the bed where his brown overcoat

---

1 John H. Watson, MD, *Sherlock Holmes and the Ice Palace Murders*, as edited by Larry Millett, Penguin Books, New York, 1998.

lay folded. "Can't be far," I assured myself, and retreated to the hallway.

"Dr. Watson, Mr. Holmes would like you to join him in the library."

I recognized the voice of Thomas, Mr. Hill's valet, and turned to see him standing outside my bedroom door. My puzzled look must have been obvious.

"Forgive me, sir," Thomas responded. "Mr. Holmes received a telegram a few minutes ago and rushed to the library. He asked that I come retrieve you."

Entering the library, I saw Holmes at Hill's desk examining a folio of maps. The Empire Builder was beside him, returning the telephone receiver to its cradle. "It's all arranged," I heard him say to Holmes.

"Holmes, we've a train to catch," I interjected.

"True, Watson, but not the one you anticipate. Mr. Hill has graciously loaned us the use of his private car for the journey."

"Splendid, but you needn't do that, Mr. Hill. Chicago is only a few hours ride. I am sure we'd be quite comfortable in one of your excellent coaches."

Holmes replied, "Watson, we're going to Montana. Rodgersburg,[2] Montana, to be exact."

---

2 Editor's note: A note was attached to the opening page of the manuscript, addressed to Librarian Fred Clark from Watson, which said, "You will immediately recognize that the name of Rodgersburg, Montana, is fictitious, but given the description of the city, our Montana readers will know exactly which community we visited. I am at a loss to explain the use of this stratagem to you, only to say that Mr. Holmes requested that I do so. By way of explanation he merely commented, "The criminal classes watch my work through your chronicles, Watson, as much as, and perhaps more so, than the law abiding among us. My exact whereabouts that year continues to be a source of discomfort to my foes, and what better way to keep them confused than by having your narrative of our exploits set in a far away place they can't find on a map. It will be utterly befuddling.""

I was stunned. "Montana! My God Holmes, are you daft?"

"Perhaps, but it's for a friend. I received a cable from Carleton Baines in London just a few moments ago."

"The Admiral?" I asked.

"Indeed," replied Holmes. "He writes:

> *Son Vincent being held for murder. Rodgersburg, Montana. Please help.*
>
> *Adm. Carleton Baines, Rtd.*"

Baines was an old friend who we'd last seen not quite two years ago at his estate near Chatham, England. Holmes had just solved the case, which I chronicled as *The Adventure of the Golden Pince-Nez*. We were at Chatham station preparing to return to London when we chanced upon the Admiral, who promptly invited us to his home for several days of good company and relaxation. Mycroft, Holmes' older, and somewhat more eccentric brother, previously had introduced the Admiral to Holmes and me. Mycroft and the Admiral were both engaged at Whitehall[3] in what can only be described as the Crown's most sensitive matters.

Besides being the most genial of hosts, the Admiral has a great fondness for firearms. His knowledge on the subject

---

Thus, in keeping with the intent of Watson's original manuscript, I have left the name "Rodgersburg" intact. To what extent he may have revised other names or places in the manuscript could not easily be determined inasmuch as many of the community's records were destroyed in a flood.

3 Editor's note: Whitehall is a street in the Westminster section of London extending between Trafalgar Square and Parliament. The street is lined with government buildings, including the British Admiralty. The term "Whitehall" is often used as a euphemism to refer to the British Government, much like Americans who say "Washington" or "DC" when referring to the U.S. Government.

is truly unsurpassed, and Holmes, Sherlock, that is, has frequently relied upon his expertise.

"Vincent," I muttered. "Is he the young man recently returned from South Africa whom we met at Chatham?"

"No, your memory is failing you, Watson, that was Royal," replied Holmes. "Vincent is the Admiral's second son, and apparently one from the prodigal branch. He emigrated to the United States in '85 after a bit of scandal involving Viscount Hardesty's daughter Miriam."

"I stand corrected, Holmes. But, pray tell what would a young man of means be doing on the American frontier?"

"Mining, most likely," added Hill. "That's what Montana is all about. Rodgersburg is a bustling little camp – silver mostly, some gold."

Over the next two hours, Holmes and Hill made ready our plans to travel west to the wilds of Montana. I took up temporary residence before the fire where I enjoyed one of Hill's Cuban cigars and a brandy, actually several brandies. Suffice it to say I was a bit unsteady on my feet when we finally departed for the station.

Our travel was quite comfortable, due in large part to the quality of Hill's liquor cabinet. From St. Paul we traveled northwest along a river valley populated by a mixture of small towns, farms, and woodlands before emerging onto the Great Plains and a long run across land so flat, I wondered how the water would drain away come spring. The unifying element linking each scene which rushed by the windows of our coach was snow, differentiated only by how high it was piled. I expressed the notion that we might see the great white bear of the north, but Holmes only chortled.

On the second day of our journey we entered eastern

Montana. I found nothing to differentiate it from North Dakota save that it started to snow, with the storm becoming progressively worse as we rode west. Late in the afternoon we pulled into a hamlet called Malta, a far cry from its namesake in the Mediterranean. I looked in vain for the station, but all I could see was a mound of snow with a stovepipe sticking out of the top. The train conductor interrupted our interlude, first by apologizing and then explaining that the track ahead was closed by snow drifts and we'd be delayed for several hours. Holmes invited me to join him on a walk about town, but I immediately demurred when I heard it was 22 degrees below zero Fahrenheit. He returned shortly before 10:00 p.m. and briefly reported spending the evening in the company of a gentleman named Pike Landusky and several miners from a place called Zortman, about 50 miles to the south. We both retired and I was briefly awakened by a slight jolt as the train moved forward, our journey resumed. A long night and day's journey took us through Havre, named after the great port on the north coast of France, where we turned south for Fort Benton, Great Falls, Helena – capital of the new state – and finally, to Butte, that great mining metropolis of the American west. Again, Holmes departed the car and I didn't see him again until breakfast.

It was the smell of fresh coffee brewing and Holmes talking with the steward which brought me out of my slumber and to the breakfast table.

"Watson, you're well rested, I presume?" asked Holmes with just a hint of mockery in his voice. Holmes requires much less sleep than I and he's fond of joking about my penchant for slumber.

"Indeed, and famished as well," I replied as I reached for the toast and bowl of strawberry preserves.

"Eat hardy, I am afraid the hard part of our journey is to begin. The sleigh will be here at eight. It's 62 miles to Rodgersburg."

"A sleigh," I stuttered dumbfounded.

"Indeed," said Holmes. "An ice flow damaged one of the bridges and the railroad line to Rodgersburg will be closed for several days."

The storm had broken during the night. It was a cold, clear February day, the sky a deep cobalt blue, the sun dancing off the billions of snow crystals which surrounded us on all sides. We took up residence in the back of the sleigh buried under a mound of blankets and buffalo robes. To my astonishment we made excellent time. I was fearful we would end up spending the night in some rough boarding house along the track, but after coursing through virtually impenetrable forest and a series of small mining camps too numerous to remember, we arrived in Rodgersburg. Again, I was taken by surprise, figuring it to be a clone of the small camps we had passed through during the journey. It was, in fact, a small city, amazingly lit with electric street lamps, which allowed me to quickly view the downtown stretched along a small stream I later learned was called Tower Creek.

We had rooms in the Rhyolite Hotel, a small establishment but clean and quite comfortable. I took leave of Holmes for an hour and took a hot bath to drive the cold out of my bones. When I rejoined him in the dining room after dinner he was seated with a big, dark-complected man wearing a silver star on the breast of a sheepskin coat.

"Watson," Holmes announced as he turned the visitor toward me. "Allow me to present Sheriff Keiley. Sheriff, Dr. John Watson."

"Good to meet you, Doctor," he answered with an accent I couldn't discern, but certainly not the brogue that characterizes most of the Irish, even those two generations removed from the Emerald Isle.

"Pray, join us for supper, Sheriff, and tell us what caused you to leave Wisconsin for the rigors of Montana," said Holmes.

"So it's true what they say about you, Mr. Holmes, that you know what's in a man's soul just by meeting him," answered the Sheriff.

"Not hardly, Sheriff. I only know what I can see and hear. You pronounce the 'th' sound as a 'd' which tells me you spent some time, probably in your youth, in New York. From there you went west to work in the lead mines of Wisconsin. It's all there in the way you wear your clothes and the inflection in your voice."

"You've got me dead to rights, Mr. Holmes. I've been in Rodgersburg for two years, and as Sheriff, just one," the lawman replied.

We were temporarily interrupted by a serving girl who placed large bowls of potatoes, beans, and meat on the table along with a loaf of fresh bread still steaming from the oven.

"What can you tell me about the crime Mr. Vincent Baines is alleged to have committed?" asked Holmes of the Sheriff, who had commenced eating the instant that food was placed before us.

"Not much to tell, Mr. Holmes. Mr. Baines is an actor and he shot Jasper Tompkins, another member of the troupe, on stage during the second act of *The Bandit Brothers.*"

"Never heard of it," I exclaimed.

"Very entertaining, it is, Dr. Watson," observed Sheriff Keiley. "The playbill calls it a melodrama."

"And you say young Baines shot Mr. Tompkins during the play in full view of the audience," interposed Holmes, returning us to the subject at hand. "No disguising one's actions in that."

"No," replied the Sheriff, "but it was cleverly done. In the play, the character played by Mr. Baines shoots the character played by Mr. Tompkins and he is dragged off stage. The audience didn't suspect a thing. The actors discovered the crime immediately when they saw the blood staining his shirt."

"And what was Mr. Baines' reaction to that?" asked Holmes.

"Said he was stunned, that it was an accident, someone must have put live ammunition into the gun instead of blanks."

"But you don't believe him?" I asked.

"No, I don't," said the Sheriff. "He's got motive. Mr. Baines and Mr. Tompkins were rivals."

"In what way?" asked Holmes.

"In every way," answered the Sheriff. "For who was the better actor, for one thing, but mainly, I think it was over Tess Carson, daughter of the local banker. The two of 'em have been contending for her hand the past several months."

"Most interesting," observed Holmes as he paused to secure another helping of potatoes.

"I don't know the lass myself," continued Sheriff Keiley, "but I heard she enjoyed the attention. I should also tell you that some of the town folk think robbery is behind the whole thing. There have been rumors about, that Tompkins had a lot of money."

"That is incredible! An actor, particularly one working out in the bush, a man of means?" I exclaimed.

"He was a regular visitor to the bank, and I am told it was to make deposits, not just look in on Tess Carson," replied the Sheriff.

"Miss Carson works there," said an astonished Holmes. "Isn't her father the banker?"

"Yes, Mr. Holmes, she works for him. Chief clerk, looks after the tellers."

"It's a big responsibility for someone so young, or at least I have presumed that she is a young woman, not a spinster."

"You're correct in that view. I believe Miss Carson is twenty-three, and well educated too. Not many men folk about these parts feel comfortable with a woman who can read the best books."

"Apparently Baines and Tompkins were the exception," I suggested.

"Let's assume so, Watson. Sheriff, I might want to look at Tompkins' residence. How should I get there?"

"Just go upstairs, sir. He lived in Room 301. In fact, the whole troupe lives here courtesy of Mr. Rodgers. All, that is, except Baines. Being a local fellow, he already had a place when he joined the theater."

The serving girl interrupted our conversation when she appeared at the table with a large basket containing food for the jail prisoners. The Sheriff excused himself with a comment about feeding Mr. Baines. Before he departed, Holmes made arrangements to visit the prisoner the next morning. After Sheriff Keiley took his leave, Holmes commented, "A good fellow, Watson, more like our English bobbies than some of those ruffians who called themselves police officers in St. Paul."

"How can you be so sure, Holmes?" I asked.

"I asked Hill for the pertinent information before we left Minnesota. The local stationmaster was most helpful. I received a full report when we reached Butte."

"So your deductions which so impressed the Sheriff were the result of a bit of reconnaissance beforehand," I said with a chuckle.

Holmes smiled briefly before continuing. "The Sheriff has a reputation for being an honest man. The judge appointed him to the position after he won a prizefight competition last summer. The finest pugilist in the county and a man beholden to no one."

With that Holmes drained the last of his coffee and announced that he was retiring for the night. I stayed in the dining room a bit longer to enjoy a second piece of chocolate cake and to read the local newspapers. A week old copy of the *Anaconda Standard*, apparently something of a regional newspaper, described the case against young Baines in considerable detail. Holmes would have his hands full. Everything seemed to point toward Baines' guilt.

I rose from a good night's sleep at 7:45 a.m. and drew back the curtains from my window. A thick layer of frost lined the window on three sides, but the corner of the pane was clear and I found myself looking out at a broad valley covered in snow. A saddle horse was tied to a hitching post about a half block away and the shadow it cast told me the sun was to my back. I was looking west. To the north was a line of low mountains, rounded in shape and covered by a rich, dark green canopy of pine forest. To the south were the icy blue spires of several mountain peaks reaching toward the sky like a line of gothic cathedrals. I assumed they must be the Rhyolite Mountains which our driver had spoken of last night as he guided our sleigh down a steep track.

The town of Rodgersburg was seated on a low bluff on the south side of the valley. To the southwest stood a complex of gray buildings, immediately recognizable as a large mine. Two tall, red brick chimneys belching a coal black smoke braced both ends of a long mill building where the ore would be crushed and the metal liberated from the waste rock. I had spent a summer in South Africa in the late 1880s where I acquired a gentleman's understanding of the mining business. Which is to say, I became conversant with the theories of geology, mining engineering, and metallurgy but, in fact, had no hands-on or practical experience. Nevertheless, it has stood me in good stead. Mining men the world over, whether it be coal miners from the English midlands, gold miners from the Rand, or lead miners in Germany all share one common trait. They love to talk mining. Anyone who can talk "mining" is their friend indeed. And I'd stake my personal reputation it's no different here in Montana.

After dressing I joined Holmes in the dining room and we were both delighted to meet Harriet Quigley, the proprietress. She was a most comely woman, a widow in her late thirties, I would guess, and quite vivacious. She had a manner about her that made you feel like you were the center of the world while you were visiting with her.

I complimented Mrs. Quigley on the comfort offered by her establishment and for the charm of the community, most notably the presence of electric lighting so far from the wellspring of civilization.

She laughed and chided me for my "metropolitan bias" as she put it, and went on to explain that "we owe it all to the mines."

"How is that, Mrs. Quigley?" asked Holmes, joining the conversation for the first time.

"The mining company needed electricity for the mine and to run the equipment in the mill. You can see it just west of the town," she replied as she pointed in the general direction of the smokestack I'd seen earlier. "So they built a dam across Tower Creek up by Quartz Peak to make a lake. Moonlight Lake, it's called, and they send the water from the lake down a pipeline to a building where they make the electricity."

"A generator," commented Holmes softly between bites of toast.

"Thank you, Mr. Holmes," replied Mrs. Quigley. "A generator. They had extra electricity so they strung lines all around town so people could have it in their homes and businesses. It's a godsend it is, gentlemen, and so clean. I hope to tell you, if I never saw another kerosene lantern for the rest of my life, it would be too soon."

Holmes broke out the smile he reserves for his most intimate acquaintances and Mrs. Quigley, obviously charmed, continued her explanation. "And when they're done making electricity with the water, they dump the rest in a reservoir just above the town and pipe it through the streets to all the buildings."

"You mean to tell us that the homes of common work-men have both electricity and running water?" I questioned in disbelief.

"Yes, Dr. Watson," came Mrs. Quigley's reply, "and it gets

better than that. Rodgersburg doesn't have outdoor privies. When they put in the water lines they put in a sewer system too. In Butte and Helena, only the rich folks get indoor plumbing. Here, everybody's got it, all because of the mining company. Mr. Rodgers saw to it when he owned the mines."

I wanted to hear more about the town and this Mr. Rodgers who Mrs. Quigley had referred to, but our conversation was interrupted by the ringing of a bell.

"Excuse me, gentlemen," said Mrs. Quigley. "I must answer the telephone."

I was stunned. A telephone in a common hotel. The next thing Mrs. Quigley will be telling me is that they are common fixtures amongst the shopkeepers and working class. The state of my disbelief must have shown on my face because Holmes quietly observed, "Watson, perhaps the most unique feature of the American republic is its capacity to democratize everything. In Europe, we tend to hoard the advancements of civilization for the upper classes. Not here." With that he folded his napkin, set it on the table, and departed while I sat and watched Mrs. Quigley talk on the telephone from her desk in the far corner of the room.

Holmes was right, of course, about the spirit of American democracy, but there was more to it. Even a robust commercial center like St. Paul, from which we'd recently departed, lacked many of the modern conveniences that the town of Rodgersburg seemed to take for granted. I surmised that it was the mines and the great wealth they produced which funded the richness of life in the community.

Mid-morning found Holmes and me in a cell in the Rhyolite County jail, face-to-face with the accused, Vincent Baines. He favored his mother, being thin and fine-boned with a full head of sandy brown hair and a bookish look about him. At the foot of his bunk a pair of spectacles rested on a Bible, which he hurriedly moved to provide a place to sit. I would have taken him for a bookkeeper or, perhaps, a teacher but never an actor.

After we were introduced and a pause to answer questions about his family back in England, young Baines blurted out, "I didn't do it, Mr. Holmes. I didn't shoot Jasper," to which Holmes raised his eyebrow. "I mean, I shot him, sure, but I didn't mean to. The shooting was part of the show and the gun was supposed to be loaded with blanks. But it wasn't. It had real bullets, but I didn't put them there."

"According to the Sheriff," stated Holmes, "you were responsible for loading the firearms."

"True," replied Baines, "and I did, just before the first act. But I loaded both pistols with blanks, not live ammunition, and I left them in their holsters with the other props on the right-hand side of the stage. Someone must have reloaded my pistol after the curtain went up."

"Who could have had access to the firearm?" inquired Holmes.

"Everyone. The whole cast and stagehands are backstage at various times during the play," responded Baines.

"Any with a chance to be alone with the pistol?"

Baines paused to ponder Holmes' latest question, rubbing his forehead and face while his eyes danced around the cell. "Indeed, but it is not predictable. The actors and actresses are getting ready for their next scenes and they might not notice someone handling a prop. Two stagehands are about as well. I don't know." Young Baines seemed truly puzzled. "Let me think about it some more, Mr. Holmes.

I'll go through the play in my mind, step by step."

"Thank you, that would be helpful. Now, pray, tell me about your relationship with the victim, Mr. Tompkins."

"I only met him last June. He joined the troupe back then. Jasper was a professional actor from St. Louis, not like me. I am just an amateur. We've appeared in four productions together."

"Four productions!" I exclaimed in disbelief. "In a town so small."

"Mr. Rodgers, the owner of the Opera House, made his fortune in the mines," replied Baines. "He's very partial to the theater and organized our troupe, as he puts it, 'to provide a bit of merriment' and help the town through the winters. We do a new production every eight weeks or so and in the summer we take our shows on the road to the other mining camps in the area."

"Interesting," answered Holmes in a monotone, clearly disinterested in the history lesson, "but what about your relationship with Mr. Tompkins?"

"Sorry. We acted together, but that's about as far as it went. He favored a more conservative lifestyle than I, quite content to stay in his room and read."

"And you prefer the company of your fellow men," responded Holmes.

"I've lived in Rodgersburg for several years, Mr. Holmes. I worked in the mines for a short period, and then in the Mercantile before I became an actor. I know a large number of people and I am not adverse to having a drink with them or attending the town's other social activities."

"And that includes keeping company with Miss Tess Carson?" asked Holmes.

I though I saw a faint blush on Baines' face as he nodded in agreement.

"And I understand Miss Carson was also keeping company with Mr. Tompkins," pursued Holmes.

Baines nodded again, clearly discomfited by Holmes' inquiry, but said nothing. We waited. Holmes got up from the bed, walked to the barred window, gazed out for a few seconds and then reached into his coat pocket for his pipe. After filling the bowl and putting fire to the tobacco, he turned again to young Baines and with his look said, "Tell us more."

"Tess, I mean Miss Carson," stammered Baines, "met Jasper at the bank. She works there. There were rumors that he had a lot of money, but personally, I don't think it was true. Since then he's been a guest in her father's home and she's been seen in his company on several occasions."

"And that means she's been seen less in your company," retorted Holmes.

"I suppose," answered Baines in almost a whisper, "but she'd never marry him. I know she's drawn to his intellect but, for heaven's sake, he's an actor."

"Which distinguishes him from you in what way, Mr. Baines?" probed Holmes.

"I am not an actor, I mean, not really. This is just a temporary post. I'll return to business. I am ambitious and will make something of myself. Albert Carson, Tess's father, has his eye on me for a spot in the bank."

"And might that spot disappear if you lose the hand of fair maiden?" Holmes asked mildly.

"Uh, no," exclaimed Baines. "Mr. Carson was opposed to Jasper from the start. He'd never consent to a match between Jasper Tompkins and his daughter."

"Mr. Baines," I interrupted, "if you're concerned about making something of yourself, return to England and claim your inheritance."

Baines turned to me with a start and gave me a look that I could only interpret as anger mixed with incredulity as he replied, "Ah yes, to the manor born, claim your lineage. Never, Dr. Watson. I came to the United States to be a free man, and for me that is life without titles, testaments, and inherited leisure."

"And money," I snorted in return.

"Inherited money, as well," answered Baines. "I am a student of Herbert Spencer and Walter Baghot[4] and plan to earn my place in society, not simply claim it based on the deeds of some long forgotten ancestor. And please, I would appreciate it if you'd not mention my background around Rodgersburg. No one knows from where I come."

"It's too late for that," observed Holmes. "The American frontiersman lives by his wits, and while he may not know your family, when he sees you being aided by a consulting detective from London, I am sure he'll understand you are a man of means and not the son of some humble shopkeeper."

Baines seemed startled by Holmes' simple observation and, as he shook his head in dismay, responded, "Well, leave the townspeople to their imagination."

---

4   Editor's note: Spencer and Baghot were two English social theorists who wrote during the late 19th Century. Both attempted to extend the postulates used by Charles Darwin to describe evolutionary biology, to the social realm. That is, just as competition between and among animal organisms and species causes evolutionary change through survival of the fittest; competition between human beings, groups, nation states, etc. drives the social evolution or progress of human societies. This "school" of social theory later became known as Social Darwinism.

We continued the interview with young Baines for another half hour but little of substance was gleaned from the conversation. For my part, I was puzzled by Baines' attitude. Holmes is masterful in his observations of human behavior, and I pride myself on being equally proficient in understanding human emotion, a faculty developed through my years of medical practice. Yet, I found Baines an enigma. On the one hand, I could clearly see that he was emotionally attracted to Miss Carson, and that alone was sufficient to ascribe motive in the killing of Jasper Tompkins. At the same time, while he was fiercely independent I didn't sense that he had the constitution to coldly kill his rival in full view of a packed playhouse.

As Holmes and I emerged from the jail we were greeted by a stiff wind from the North. Holmes surprised me by commenting on the cold. He's generally impervious to the weather and I wondered whether he was coming down with a chill. Together, we braced ourselves against the weather and started the six-block walk back to our hotel. About halfway there, Holmes took hold of my arm and stepped me into a recessed doorway marked only by a small, brightly painted sign proclaiming "Noodles." The small café seated ten at three tables. To my surprise, the proprietor was Chinese, and to my delight he served tea.

Good tea is hard to find in the western United States. The Yanks prefer coffee followed, it seems, by whiskey and beer in about equal measure. I hadn't had a good cup of tea since leaving the British Isles and was anxious to learn if my fortune had changed.

I ordered the Darjeeling, as did Holmes. As the tea steeped in the pot near my right elbow, Holmes gazed toward the frost-covered window lost in thought. I poured us both a cup and was overjoyed by the full-bodied, robust nature of the brew. It was not, however, a Darjeeling, an Oolong for certain, possibly Formosan Oolong. If there's one thing a cultured Englishman knows, especially one who has been to India as I have, it's tea.

Holmes pulled a pencil and some paper from the inside breast pocket of his coat and started to write. I motioned to the proprietor, who subsequently introduced himself as Jack Tao, and we were soon engaged in an animated conversation about tea. He readily admitted that the tea was from China, not Darjeeling, and added, "Americans think tea from India, so why confuse? I have lady customers and the young Englishman you come to help. Like you, he knows tea and, he discovered little ruse."

"Why do you assume we've come to help Mr. Baines?" I asked.

"It's around town. Rodgersburg is a small place. The arrival of famous person like Sherlock Holmes and his friend can only mean one thing. You here to investigate Opera House murder."

Holmes gave Mr. Tao a broad smile while I quietly agreed that his assessment was correct. Mr. Tao looked directly at Holmes and said, "Mr. Baines look like a clerk, Mr. Holmes, but he a hard man, angry man." With that he excused himself and left us to our tea. Holmes briefly quizzed me regarding my assessment of Vincent Baines but offered little in return. Finally, he handed me three pieces of paper and asked that I take them to the telegraph office while he sought out Albert Carson, the local banker and father of Tess Carson. We agreed to meet back at the hotel in time for the midday meal.

The first of Holmes' telegrams was to Admiral Baines back in England. It said:

Reached Rodgersburg. Met Vincent. Heard story. Situation difficult. Will advise.

Holmes

The other two dealt with matters unconnected to our current adventure but surprised me nonetheless. I hadn't realized that Holmes was looking into matters on behalf of the Crown[5] here in the United States.

Holmes returned to the hotel at 11:45 a.m. and promptly shared the details of his visit with the banker. "It's most interesting, Watson. Mr. Carson thinks quite highly of Master Baines but did not fully corroborate his story."

"How so, Holmes?"

"Carson seems to bear no ill will toward Mr. Tompkins, notwithstanding the actor's profession. To the contrary, he was quite impressed by the man's background and educa-

---

5   Editor's note: Regrettably, Watson does not provide any additional information in the Montana Chronicles regarding the nature of Holmes' case. My curiosity was aroused, however, and I contacted the British Museum in London which has possession of Watson's files. I was fortunate to make the acquaintance of archivist Chester Bowles who had extensive experience with Watson's papers. He subsequently provided me with a copy of a letter written by Holmes to his brother Mycroft in June 1896. A passage therein states, "Notwithstanding my travels to the western United States, I am glad that I was able to contribute to the effort to resolve matters with the Vatican. I unabashedly admit that I have been astounded by the repercussions from the incident. Hopefully, His Holiness has learned that the Germans cannot be trusted in such matters."

Holmes was referring to Pope Leo VIII. It also would appear that Holmes was still involved in resolving matters related to the sudden death of Cardinal Tosca in 1895. Watson subsequently mentioned the case in his narrative entitled *The Adventure of Black Peter* and also in *The Hound of the Baskervilles*, but the case was never chronicled.

tion. His father was an Anglican priest and Tompkins graduated from Harvard University with a classical education."

"Odd breeding ground for an actor," I commented in reply.

"Apparently, Tompkins was drawn to it by his wife who was an actress and discovered that he had a flair for it as well. His real forte, however, appears to be writing. He has written a number of stage plays. While not high art, they have been commercially successful. Tompkins authored *The Bandit Brothers* in which he met his fateful end."

"And what became of Tompkins' wife?"

"Carson reported that she died of consumption about five years ago. Since then, Tompkins has moved around the west with one company of touring actors after another until he landed here in Rodgersburg."

"Was Miss Carson attracted to Mr. Tompkins?"

"According to her father, yes, but in an intellectual, rather than an emotional way. He didn't seem overly concerned about a match between the two. As you now might have gathered, there was a great deal of difference in their ages. Miss Carson is twenty-three and Mr. Tompkins was in his early forties, her father thought."

"Most intriguing, Holmes, but of course, young Baines wouldn't see that," I offered offhandedly. "What did the good banker say about our client?"

"He observed that Baines has a good head for business, is a diligent worker, and is well regarded by Clyde Rodgers, the town's founder and benefactor," answered Holmes. "Furthermore, he didn't mention bringing Baines into the bank as the young actor reported."

"That sounds a little impersonal, too objective an assessment for a man courting one's daughter," I contended.

"True," responded Holmes. "That was my reaction as well. Having come from rather humble stock himself, Mr. Carson would appear to have an exaggerated opinion of good breeding. Suffice it to say, he does not know of Baines' breeding although, as we discussed earlier, our presence has convinced him there is more to Baines' background than meets the eye."

"If I might offer a conjecture," I interjected, "the father thinks Baines is a little too coarse for his daughter."

"Possibly, quite possibly. He did mention that the attraction between Tess and Vince, as Carson calls him, is based on music. He said that Tess played the piano and has an excellent singing voice. Mr. Baines is also an accomplished vocalist and plays several instruments. That is how they met, at a holiday songfest about two years ago."

Holmes paused to pour himself a short glass of water from the pitcher atop the dresser and said, "Let us continue this discussion later. Mr. Carson was kind enough to invite us to his home for luncheon, where we'll have a chance to talk with his daughter. It's about a ten minute walk and, if we leave now, we can be right on time."

I reluctantly dressed to face the cold once again. A light snow was falling when we reached the street. Fortunately, the Carsons lived south of the hotel and the wind was at our back. We arrived promptly at 12:30 p.m. The Carsons' home was quite modest, particularly given his position in the community. It consisted of five rooms on a single level, scarcely larger than our flat on Baker Street but cheerfully decorated and comfortably warm.

After taking our coats, Mr. Carson quickly ushered us into the dining room and introduced us to his wife Kathleen and daughter Tess. Carson was of medium build and balding. His wife was a full-figured woman who was prematurely gray, but most affable. Tess was tall like her mother, but very slender, much too slender in my view, with light brown hair and piercing green eyes.

Our repast was simple but quite filling, consisting of a beef stew with several root vegetables, grits, and fruit pastry for dessert. Our host explained that he was a Southerner by birth and grits were his last remaining connection with that life. I'd never eaten them before. Corn meal mush isn't a staple in the English diet. I sampled some with butter and more with cinnamon and sugar. As usual, Holmes ate whatever was before him without complaint or comment.

Mrs. Carson directed our luncheon conversation. She had previously read several of my accounts of Holmes' detective exploits and quizzed us about several cases. I hate to confess, but her memory was better than mine and she brought up several issues I'd long forgotten, although Holmes could remember as if it were yesterday.

The elder Carsons excused themselves after dessert, he to return to the bank and she to attend to some household shopping, leaving us in the company of Tess. I started on a second piece of pastry while Holmes initiated the interview with Miss Carson. I expected him to come straight to the point, as was his forte, but instead, he inquired about her education. "Miss Carson, I could not help but notice how you held your coffee cup. You grasped the handle like a proper English lady being served high tea. I take it you attended finishing school."

"Indeed, Mr. Holmes. How perceptive of you," answered Miss Carson with a slight blush. "We came to Montana when

I was six years old and lived in several mining camps before settling here in Rodgersburg. Most of my youthful companions were boys and I learned to do the things that boys learn – how to trap, fish, shoot, and make things with their hands. When I was twelve, my father suddenly took cognizance of the fact that his daughter was more like a son, and he decided that I needed to spend some time back in New England embellishing my social graces and, hopefully, find a suitor who is not so 'rough around the edges' as father is prone to say."

"And yet you came back to Rodgersburg, apparently without the suitor," continued Holmes.

"Yes. While I greatly benefited from the education I received, my father's wealth was insufficient to attract the type of suitor my parents envisioned. Instead, I found myself keeping company with men and women alike who were keen of mind and full of spirit, but alas, they generally were of lesser means than I."

"Most interesting," replied Holmes. "I trust that some of these people you describe as keen of mind and full of spirit were actors."

"Correct again, Mr. Holmes. I am most impressed with your insight. I have heard that your powers of observation and deduction are seemingly without limit."

"Oh, quite to the contrary, Miss Carson. I simply recognize what others see and fail to recognize. And, in this instance, I understand that you were well acquainted with the two most prominent actors in the troupe performing at the Opera House." Miss Carson was poised to respond, but Holmes quickly continued, "I daresay that actors are not the kind of company you would have kept, had you spent your youth exclusively in Rodgersburg."

"Mr. Holmes," answered Miss Carson, adopting a coy manner. "Whatever can I say?"

"I also understand, Miss Carson," continued Holmes, "that you were romantically involved with both the victim, Mr. Tompkins, and his accused killer, Mr. Baines."

She looked Holmes right in the eye and calmly responded, "As you have so delicately observed, Mr. Holmes, I kept company with both gentlemen, but neither had captured my heart."

"But, perhaps you had captured theirs," answered Holmes.

"If so, it was unknown to me. Neither made any declaration of love, although I do concede that Vincent hinted at his affection for me," she replied.

"And Mr. Tompkins," inquired Holmes, "what were his intentions?"

"I don't know," answered Tess. "Our relationship was purely intellectual. Jasper was a very well read man, had a vast number of experiences in life, and was a brilliant conversationalist. If he felt something special for me, he kept it hidden from my view. As you can imagine, Mr. Holmes, Rodgersburg is hardly a cultured place and Mr. Tompkins was a cultured man. He was invited to all of the best homes in the community and his company was sought out by anyone who wanted to talk about something other than the weather, horses, and mining."

"Miss Carson, do you believe that Mr. Baines found Mr. Tompkins a sufficiently dangerous rival that he would kill him?" I asked, while Holmes nodded in agreement.

"Perhaps, Dr. Watson. Vincent has exhibited a temper from time to time, but it is hard for me to see him as a murderer."

"And why is that?"

"Because Vincent lacks resolve, Doctor. He is the most agreeable of men, but he can't ever seem to commit to anything. He's held several jobs in the short time he's been in Rodgersburg, always flitting from one thing to another."

Holmes rejoined the conversation by asking, "Is it possible that Mr. Tompkins had other enemies who might wish to see him dead and were willing to use Mr. Baines as an unwitting accomplice?"

"Not that I am aware of. Please understand that's a question I couldn't possibly answer. I've only known Jasper for a few months. Indeed, he's been in Rodgersburg less than a year."

"How about Mr. Baines? Does he have any enemies?"

"Vincent has mentioned difficulties with other members of the cast from time to time, but it never sounded very serious—artistic differences, from what I could tell. Wait ... there's no love lost between Vincent and Frank Hardaway. Hardaway was in the audience the night Jasper was killed. I know because he was quoted in the newspaper about how he witnessed the whole thing."

"Who is Frank Hardaway?" I asked.

"Just a guy around town. He used to be a miner," answered Miss Carson in reply.

"What is the reason for the bad blood between Hardaway and Baines?" followed Holmes.

"I don't know the details. You could ask my father, but it goes back a couple of years when Vincent was working at the mine. Hardaway was discharged and Vincent had something to do with it," replied Miss Carson.

"There is also a rumor about town, Miss Carson, that

Tompkins was a wealthy man and killed for his money."

"Well, Mr. Holmes, thankfully that is a subject on which I do not have to speculate. Mr. Tompkins had an account at father's bank with a modest balance, $262.00 to be exact. I know that because I waited on him the last time he was in the bank."

Holmes prolonged the conversation with Miss Carson much longer than I expected. He kept coming back to her relationships with Mr. Tompkins and Mr. Baines from different angles, but with the same result in every case. Miss Carson insisted there was no relationship between herself and Jasper Tompkins and that she had no special feelings for Mr. Baines, although it was likely that he was attracted to her.

I confess that I was impressed by Tess Carson's relaxed demeanor. She answered every one of Holmes' inquiries fully and dispassionately, and I was convinced of her veracity.

It was half past two when Holmes and I departed the Carson residence to make our way back to the hotel. The snowstorm had abated, the sun was shining, and the air crisp. I don't know of anyplace else on earth where the weather seems to change so abruptly. Certainly not London. There, whatever weather we're experiencing seems to stay around for several days at a time.

As we walked toward our lodging we made several stops. Holmes purchased a new pair of gloves from the haberdasher. At the stationers, we both purchased some writing paper while I picked up two books to sustain me in the evenings. *The Adventures of Huckleberry Finn* sounded lively and I was familiar with several of Mr. Twain's other works. *Moby Dick* looked intriguing, but the name Herman Melville meant nothing to me. Being a bit of an anglophile, I haven't read much American literature. Our last stop was the tobacconist where Holmes replenished his supply and I purchased, after much discussion with the shopkeeper about the merits of finely distilled spirits, a bottle of California brandy. I hoped it would be the perfect complement to my literary acquisitions and add to the pleasure of a winter evening by the fire.

Upon returning to the hotel, Holmes seemed unusually anxious to discuss our foray in the Carson household. Normally, his reserve is overwhelming and I have to pry the information from him. In the course of our discussion I observed that Tess Carson was a fetching young woman, to which Holmes replied, "Fetching . . . I leave that to your judgment, Watson, but I am perplexed by her mood."

"I daresay, Holmes, I thought her the picture of equanimity."

"Again, I agree, Watson, and that is what I find so perplexing. Miss Carson has just lost two friends or, at least, two companions, one by murder, and the other quite certain to be hanged. Nonetheless, she did not seem saddened by the whole sorry affair. I find that troubling."

"Holmes, I believe you've misread her character completely. We are not dealing with an Englishwoman, particularly one of noble birth, given over to her emotions. Egads, man, we're on the very edge of the American frontier. The women here are made of sterner stuff. I am sure she feels a great loss but also manages her grief, at least publicly, with strangers. You can't be delicate and survive out here."

"Perhaps," responded Holmes, "but recall this morning when I paused briefly to visit with Sheriff Keiley after our conversation with young Baines."

"Certainly. I wondered what that was all about," came my reply.

"Well, I asked the Sheriff who had visited Baines since his arrest. Four people, excluding ourselves. Mr. Rodgers, the Opera House owner and, if Mr. Carson is to be believed, Baines' patron as well, made one appearance. Mr. Anderson, Baines' lawyer, has been there three times. Carol Carmody, an actress with the Opera House troupe, has been to the jail daily. She's been accompanied by another one of the performers, Beth Allen, on four occasions. Tess Carson has never visited her admirer. Not once."

"Surely, Holmes," I started to say, but was interrupted by a knock at the door. It was the young lady who had served us supper the night before with a telegram for Holmes. He read it quickly, thanked the young woman, and reached for his coat.

"Watson, I must leave momentarily. I should be back in time for supper and then we can catch the performance at the theater."

"The theater," I mumbled in surprise.

"Indeed. Didn't you see the playbill when we passed by earlier today? *The Bandit Brothers* is reopening tonight. It's our chance to investigate the scene of the crime. And all we have to do is cross the street."

"Now, there's irony for you, Holmes. We travel close to 5,000 miles and the scene of the crime is across the street from our lodgings. If we could only be so fortunate in Britain . . . ."

"Instead of having to slog our way through the streets of London in a downpour," interrupted Holmes, saying precisely what I was thinking. "There are times, my good friend, when I think you've lost your sense of adventure." Then he laughed.

I was about to protest, but Holmes' jocularity got the better of me and I chuckled as well.

The curtain went up promptly at 7:00 p.m. We procured seats about eight rows back but could have sat anywhere inasmuch as only about forty people were in the audience. *The Bandit Brothers* is a story of two young farmhands who disguise themselves and rob the home of a nearby rancher. The robbery is botched, a man killed, and the rancher's daughter taken as a hostage so the bandits can make their escape. The "good" bandit brother falls in love with the young lady and wants to free her. The "evil" bandit brother objects, the two quarrel, and the "good" brother shoots the "evil" one. The good bandit frees the young lady, surrenders to the law, and is to be hanged for his part in the robbery when the young lady realizes that she loves him in return and saves the "good" bandit from the scaffold.

Clearly, it was not high art, but the actors were capable and kept the audience engaged throughout the play. Jasper Tompkins had played the "evil" bandit and Vincent Baines the "good" one.

During the intermission Holmes observed that Tompkins' classical education had served him well. The set design for the play was positively Shakespearean.

I was baffled by his comment and my befuddlement must have shown.

"Watson," he asked, "how does the set design for this production compare with the show we saw with Mr. Hill in St. Paul?"

"There's no comparison," I replied. "The production in

St. Paul had several very elaborate backdrops, superlative costumes, and numerous props. Here, hardly anything is on stage but a couple of props and the actors. Oh, sorry, Holmes, now I see what you mean, just like classic Elizabethan drama. The playgoer creates the setting in his imagination. Nothing but actors on stage." I was about to ask Holmes why that was important, but we were summoned to our seats for act two.

The shooting of the "evil" bandit brother took place about ten minutes into the second act. I don't know why, but I had presumed that this incident would consist of a single shot being fired. As such, I was totally unprepared for the melee on stage. It was a firefight. The two actors traded several shots across the floor before the "evil" bandit fell mortally wounded. Throughout it all, Holmes watched the events unfolding before our eyes as only he could, meticulously cataloguing the performance of the actors and categorizing every nuance and sound.

The play ended happily at 8:30 p.m. as the "good" bandit and the rancher's daughter were united, in love, proving again that good triumphs over evil. If only life were so clear-cut and simple, I thought. Notwithstanding the banality of the show's plot, I was thoroughly entertained. The actors were excellent and I briefly wondered what I would have seen had not one male lead been killed and the other in jail. Holmes motioned that he wished to return to the hotel. His eyes had that detached look and I could tell he was pondering the evening's events.

Holmes and I met for breakfast the next morning but little was said between us except that I should enjoy the day while he took care of some other matters. I assumed he was talking about the affairs of state alluded to in yesterday's telegrams. I didn't press the issue but was puzzled how he could be of service to the British Crown while ferreted away among the snowbanks of western Montana.

The day was spent pleasantly. I wrote a long letter to Mrs. Hudson, caretaker of our lodging in London, in which I briefly recounted the events of the past several weeks. Mrs. Hudson has a special fondness for Holmes and worries incessantly about our well being whenever we're on a case. After catching up on my correspondence I made several no-

INTERIOR OF THE OPERA HOUSE
This photo taken near the turn of the century shows the interior of the Opera House as Holmes and Watson would have seen it.

tations in my journal about the Ice Palace case recently concluded in St. Paul, as well as our current adventure. About 2:00 p.m. I ventured forth for a walk about town. Rodgersburg was a surprisingly clean and well-ordered community, far different from the typical mining camp whose roughness is exceeded only by its impermanence. The business district was quite extensive for such a small town and I gathered that it served as the mercantile center for the many mining districts spread throughout the surrounding mountains.

Most of the town's commercial buildings and many of its homes were built of brick, which perplexed me given the abundant supply of freestanding timber on the slopes above town. The mystery was solved soon after I turned east from the railroad station and discovered the local brick works. I visited briefly with the manager who informed me that all of Montana's major cities had a brickyard and a brewery, "two things essential for civilization," as he phrased it.

Around 4:00 p.m. I visited, for the second time, Mr. Tao's noodle parlor for a cup of tea. As I passed the window of a neighboring saloon, I was startled to see Holmes in conversation with a rough looking man, both with large schooners of beer before them. I thought it wise not to intrude. Holmes would explain things when it was time.

Mr. Tao had just delivered a second pot of tea when Holmes came through the door and exclaimed, "Watson, I thought that was you in the street. Excellent meeting you here. I have one more matter to attend to before supper, but I would really appreciate you joining me at another performance of *The Bandit Brothers* this evening."

"Certainly, but why? We've seen it once."

"True, Doctor, but only from the perspective of the audience. I have made arrangements to sit backstage where we can see it from the perspective of the actors." With that he turned and retreated into the street.

While I thought a second trip to the theater a redundant and profitless enterprise at the time Holmes asked for my company, I quickly saw the wisdom of his reasoning. Backstage is another world and the activities of the actors and stagehands, which are largely screened from the audience's view, are often frenetic.[6]

Inasmuch as there were no chairs or benches about, we stationed ourselves atop a table with a full view of the area on the right-hand side of the stage. The pistols used in the gunfight were hung in their holsters from pegs on the nearby wall. The actors made their entrances and exits from the stage and I mentally tried to track who might have had the opportunity to substitute live ammunition for the blanks which young Baines claimed were loaded in the guns. Over the course of the forty-minute first act, it seemed as if every member of the cast had been alone with the pistols and had sufficient time to reload the firearms if that were their intent.

If Vincent Baines were correct in his claim that someone else had reloaded his pistol, the suspect list included nine people. I mentioned as much to Holmes at intermission and he concurred with my theory. He then asked that I take up a new post backstage on the opposite side of the hall, stage left, for the balance of the performance. It was

---

6   Editor's note: At this point in the original text Watson temporarily digresses to discuss Holmes' earlier experience as a Shakespearean actor where "Holmes gained familiarity with both costuming and greasepaint, two skills which helped make him a master of disguise." See also the work of Holmes biographer W. S. Baring-Gould, *Sherlock Holmes of Baker Street*, Popular Library, New York, 1963.

much less lively on that side of the theater with fewer actors gracing the stage from that wing. My only observation
of note was the relationship between the back door and a
set of stairs, which accessed the basement. One of the actresses used the stairs and then appeared on stage via a trap
door set behind a prop. A similar stairway was on the right
side of the stage, although no one used it while Holmes
and I were there. It appeared that anyone knowledgeable
about the theater's design could have entered the building
through the rear entrance and crossed the hall beneath the
stage to where the pistols were hung, unnoticed by either
the audience or the performers.

At the conclusion of the play, it took me several minutes to find Holmes, then closeted with the blonde-headed
actress who played the heroine. She was actually a fairly
plain sort of woman except for her very ample bosom. She
was very amiable and reminded me of Mrs. Kathleen Carson with whom we had lunched the previous day. Holmes
doesn't seem to notice such things, notwithstanding his
claim that he recognizes what others do not, but I have
observed that American women are more open and independent than their sisters in the British Isles, and I find it
quite refreshing. I was about to step back from the doorway
when Holmes introduced me to Miss Carol Carmody, the
faithful visitor to Mr. Baines' jail cell. I had intruded upon
Holmes' interview with Miss Carmody, but he waved me to
a seat and returned to his conversation.

"Miss Carmody, Mr. Baines has suggested that someone
reloaded his pistol at some time during the performance.
It appears to me, having just witnessed the play again from
backstage, that the entire cast had access to his gun."

"That's not true, Mr. Holmes, and please call me Carol. I, for one, did not have the opportunity. All of my entrances occur stage left. And, as you've no doubt noticed, one can't walk around the back side of the stage without being seen."

"True, thank you for correcting me on that point, Miss Car . . . Carol," sputtered Holmes, the informality sticking to his tongue like paste. Holmes was somewhat taken aback by the directness of her answer. Apparently, she'd given some thought to who had access to the pistols during the first act of the play and was anxious to establish her alibi. I didn't mention the possibility of crossing under the stage. Holmes needed to be briefed on that point first.

"Well, Carol," ventured Holmes, "I understand that you frequently visit Mr. Baines at the county jail."

"Yes, every day, if possible," she replied.

"That's very thoughtful of you, but also something very uncharacteristic for a casual friend," replied Holmes.

"We're more than just friends," Carol said unsteadily, as if expecting a rebuke.

"Lovers, perhaps," said Holmes matter-of-factly.

"No!" came Miss Carmody's sharp reply. Holmes just stared at her while I shifted in my seat waiting for her explanation.

"I like Vince very much but, I am embarrassed to say it, he has his sights on another woman."

"I trust that you're referring to Miss Carson," said Holmes. Miss Carmody nodded dejectedly. "So notwithstanding the unrequited nature of your feelings for Mr. Baines, you are standing by him. Very noble . . . ah, Carol. But tell me, don't you find his continuing allegiance to her a bit disconcerting?"

"It's not the first time a man made himself a fool over a woman, Mr. Holmes. I trust it won't be the last," she said stoically and then continued. "Miss Carson seems to have abandoned Vince to his fate. It hasn't gone unnoticed by him."

"So, perhaps, he is slowly beginning to appreciate who his real friends are," observed Holmes. "I only hope there will be time to allow that friendship to mature."

"I am counting on you, Mr. Holmes. We both are," she replied.

Holmes was discomfited by Miss Carmody's remark. We hadn't found anything yet that supported young Baines' claim of innocence. If anything, everything pointed to him as the guilty party. Holmes turned away from her while he knocked a wattle of burnt tobacco from his pipe and asked, "Miss Allen frequently accompanies you on your visits to Mr. Baines. What is her interest in his situation?"

"Why don't you ask her?" replied Miss Carmody. Holmes turned and I looked up given the impertinence of her answer only to discover Miss Allen standing in the doorway.

She stepped into the room and said to Miss Carmody, "I wondered where you had gone. Entertaining distinguished visitors from Europe, I see."

"Mr. Holmes, Dr. Watson, may I present Beth Allen, my roommate and my accomplice in affairs of the heart."

I stood to take her hand while Holmes murmured a greeting. Miss Allen looked at Holmes and said, "So you want to know why I visit the jail, Mr. Holmes? It has nothing to do with Mr. Baines directly, though I hope he will be exonerated. My interest, if you will allow me to be so bold, is Sheriff Keiley. I find him a most attractive man."

Holmes remained expressionless, but I felt myself wince. I couldn't get over the forwardness of these American women. I wondered if the younger generation of British women was so bold. I could tell that Holmes was momentarily put off by Miss Allen's reply, so he replied with a most conventional question. "Miss Allen, do you know of anyone who might want to kill Jasper Tompkins?"

Beth Allen paused, looked toward Carol Carmody and meekly said, "I'm sorry, Carol," paused again, turned back to Holmes and, in a hushed voice said, "Only Vincent Baines."

Holmes raised his eyebrow and asked, "Over Miss Carson?"

"I heard them argue," replied Miss Allen, "the day before Jasper was killed."

"Go on, please tell us what you heard," answered Holmes.

Miss Allen was clearly uncomfortable having to undermine Baines' alibi in front of her friend who was clearly in love with the young man. She started haltingly, "I had just returned from the Opera House where I had picked up the skirt from one of my costumes for mending and, as I passed by Jasper's door, I heard Vince's voice. He was angry and I heard him say, 'You are too old for her, Jasper, step aside and spend time with her father. At least he's your contemporary.'"

"Did Tompkins reply?" asked Holmes.

"Yes," responded Miss Allen, "I'm afraid I eavesdropped a bit."

"Pray, tell us what was said," I responded, and then felt somewhat embarrassed by my own outburst.

"Jasper said, 'Vince, I offer Miss Carson education, refinement, and security. You offer hard work and adventure. It's a clear contrast and I don't intend to surrender the field of battle at your request. Perhaps you should take your arguments to lady fair. Convince her and I will gracefully withdraw.'"

"What did Mr. Baines say to that?" I asked.

"I don't know," replied Miss Allen. "He started to speak but I heard someone coming up the stairs and moved on to my room."

Holmes seemed oddly detached, as if he were scarcely paying attention, although I knew better. He retreated from the conversation, leaving me to elicit what I could from the ladies which, I daresay, was of little substance. By happenstance I made a small comment about Tompkins' shameful death, to which Miss Allen replied, "It's no loss, Dr. Watson. He was a shameful womanizer and a cheat."

I was caught completely by surprise but somehow found my tongue to ask how she knew that.

"Because, Dr. Watson, Jasper Tompkins was my father. He abandoned my mother at age 18 when he learned she was carrying me." That comment got Holmes' attention, but he allowed me to continue.

"And did Mr. Baines know that?"

"No, he did not. No one in the company, until now, knew of my relationship with Jasper, not even Jasper."

"Which no doubt had something to do with the way you so harshly rejected him when he made advances to you last summer," laughed Carol Carmody.

"That was disgusting," retorted Miss Allen.

"Perhaps your animus toward Mr. Tompkins fits you as a suspect for murder," I observed.

"No, I didn't kill him," she quickly replied.

Holmes interrupted and asked, "Miss Allen, you said that Jasper Tompkins didn't know that he was your father. Did you plan to tell him?"

Yes . . . when the time was ripe," came Miss Allen's slow reply. She seemed discomfited by the question and I could tell from the flicker of Holmes' eyes that he had read her response as I had.

"And when was that likely to be?" asked Holmes quickly.

"I . . . I don't know exactly. After I got to know him better and had a chance . . ."

"To see how much money he might have?" asked Holmes pointedly as he interrupted Miss Allen's halting explanation.

"Mr. Holmes," came Miss Allen's sharp retort. "That's monstrous for you to even suggest such a thing!"

"But he was reputed to be a rich man!" countered Holmes just as forcefully.

"I wouldn't know that," replied Miss Allen, her eyes fixed to those of Holmes, her resolve evident.

I wondered who was going to be the first to blink and, surprisingly, it was Holmes. "Watson, I see no reason to detain the ladies any longer. Carol, Miss Allen, thank you for your cooperation. Please excuse us. If I think of anything else, perhaps you would favor me with another conversation."

"Of course, Mr. Holmes," they both chimed. With that Holmes hurriedly departed the room and I struggled to catch him in the hall.

"Holmes," I asked, "aren't you cutting off the discussion prematurely? I suspect Miss Allen may have had more motive for killing Tompkins than young Baines."

"Indeed, Watson, but I am afraid any more conversation

right now might just confuse things. Both ladies are accomplished actresses. I am not sure either of us could tell when they were lying or telling the truth."

"But Holmes!" I tried to protest.

"Trust me, Doctor, we'll revisit both ladies, but now I want to return to the hotel and have a look at Tompkins' room. It seems this case is long on talk and short on facts. Let's see if we can find something to steer us toward a conclusion."

It took a few minutes to reach our rooms in the hotel. We shed our outer garments and quietly climbed the stairs to the third floor. Room 301 was just to the left of the stairwell and faced both the street and Opera House. I twisted the knob on the door. "Holmes, it's locked."

"No matter, Watson," he whispered, and reached into his breast pocket removing a small kit from which he selected a pick and with a couple gyrations of the hand, we were in the room. Holmes crossed to the window and drew the curtain and I turned on the electric light. It lit the room brightly and revealed a lodging which appeared to have been occupied for some time. In addition to the bed and dresser, two tables were next to one another by the window, and a straight-backed chair with a black leather seat faced a typewriter. Several piles of books and folios of paper surrounded the writing machine. I started to rummage through the piles and discovered that the folios contained scripts which Tompkins authored. There was also a well-worn copy of *The Aenid*, a compendium of Shakespeare's writings, some Sophocles, Homer, Cervantes in French, and several other luminaries of the theater. While I marveled at the breadth of the deceased's taste in reading, Holmes was carefully examining the contents of the closet. I took hold of a script entitled *The Mother-In-Law* and moved to the bed to stay out of Holmes' way. I was starting Act I, Scene III, when I heard Holmes exclaim, "Most interesting, indeed."

"What's interesting?" I asked, my curiosity getting the best of me.

"The top drawer of the dresser has clearly been rummaged through. It lacks the order of the two lower drawers and the closet. There are several envelopes here, two of which are empty. The others contain past acting contracts. I am inferring, of course, but it appears that someone came here looking for something, found it quickly, and departed. That individual may have been wearing a dark brown garment. I've retrieved a fiber of that color from a sliver in the dresser's top edge."[7]

Holmes placed the fiber onto a piece of clean, white paper, carefully folded it, and put it in his pocket. I think that was the first piece of hard evidence we'd found in the case thus far, but I wondered if it meant anything. Then Holmes offered, "The only thing that I can recall being dark brown is the skirt worn by Miss Allen's character in the play. How about you, Watson?"

"You're half right. I believe the character portrayed by Tompkins also wore a dark brown coat at the start of the first act."

---

7 Editor's note: In the original text Watson goes on at some length discussing Holmes' belief that "the study of textiles is essential to the art of detection." Holmes observed, "It is not possible for man to commit mayhem without leaving something of himself behind for the careful observer. Frequently, it's a piece of his apparel which will rip or slough off with the most casual of contact." Once again, Holmes preceded his time using techniques which are now a routine part of sophisticated crime scene investigations.

"Right you are, Watson. Good observation," said Holmes as he turned out the light and we quietly made our exit.

The sound of church bells brought me back to my senses. It was already Sunday. I'd lost track of the time. We had stayed in Tompkins' room past midnight and I was exhausted by the time I had crawled in between the sheets.

Holmes was in an expansive mood at breakfast where I finally got the time to tell him about the stairway to a basement beneath the stage. He quickly noted that if my observation was correct, then Miss Carmody had to be numbered among the suspects as well.

"Our problem, Watson, is that we've only got one plausible culprit, Baines. He and Tompkins were rivals for the affection of the same woman, a point well established on several fronts by now. Initially, I dismissed the robbery theory, but after visiting Tompkins' room last night I am beginning to give it more credence. The only problem is finding a suspect."

"And we have the matter of Miss Allen's relationship to Mr. Tompkins," I offered.

"Indeed," replied Holmes. "She certainly seemed angry enough to plot murder and she had the opportunity to reload Barnes' pistol. Unfortunately, so did every other member of the cast, which, if we add Miss Carmody to the list, narrows it down to ten people."

"What do you plan to do now?" I asked.

"Go to church, Watson. Mr. Rodgers invited us to share his pew when I visited with him last night before the performance, and there's a luncheon to follow."

Holmes never ceases to amaze me. I'd been with him to countless places, but church wasn't among them. Theology wasn't high on his list of interests. He must anticipate finding out something related to the case, but heaven knows what.

We arrived at the Episcopal Church promptly at eleven. The service was traditional, the choir well rehearsed, and we were in an adjoining meeting room for lunch by a quarter past twelve. My assignment was simple – enjoy myself, mix with the natives, and send to Holmes anyone who was in the theater the night Baines shot Tompkins. I found several and they were delighted to be referred to the famous English detective.

As we departed the luncheon Holmes talked about how he wasn't going to take long trips in the future unless he brought his violin. He claimed to miss the music's calming influence. As I was about to enter the hotel intending to spend some time with the books I'd purchased two days back, Holmes abruptly turned and said, "Watson, it's time to inspect the theater. Mr. Rodgers was kind enough to provide me with the key."

Upon entering the building through the front doors one encountered a ticket booth sitting as an island in a short hallway. From there one passed into the lobby with toilets to the right and a bar to the left, where a patron might quench his thirst between acts, a feature which no doubt contributed to the ribaldry of the audience and the financial well-being of Mr. Rodgers.

The auditorium was three stories high with seating for approximately 150 on the main floor and half again as many seats in the balcony which covered the back third of the room. There were two boxes at ground level and two more above them slightly lower than the balcony on both sides of the stage for a total of eight. A heavy deep purple velvet curtain hung from the proscenium covering the stage.

The building was dark when we entered, and cool. I wasn't looking forward to an afternoon spent under such circumstances, especially when it was so bright and blue outside. We made our way to the staircase near the back door where Holmes tried several switches before finding the one that illuminated the stairwell and basement. Holmes made his way down the stairs, slowing examining the handrail, stairs, and sidewalls. At the bottom a long corridor extending the length of the building toward the street greeted us. To the left was the building's foundation and to the right a wall with three doors which opened into two dressing rooms and a wardrobe storage area. At the end of the hall was a heavy door which opened to a passage beneath the street entering the basement of the Rhyolite Hotel.

"Well, that explains it," I said to Holmes.

"What's that, Watson?"

"Why I've never seen any of the acting troupe in the lobby of the hotel. They must go down the stairs and cross to the theater through the tunnel."[8]

"Seems rather elementary, now that you mention it, Doctor."

Holmes and I retraced our steps to the area beneath the stage. One small globe attempted to illuminate an area at

---

8   Editor's note: Watson failed to mention it but readers during his day would have recognized the tunnel as a steam tunnel containing steam pipes emanating out from a central heating plant (boiler) which heated several buildings at once. Such installations were common in commercial areas during the last half of the 19th Century and first part of the 20th. Central heating plants were cheaper to install, required a single place of storage for coal, and could be manned more efficiently than smaller boilers located in each building. The practice began to die out in the 1930s when natural gas began replacing coal as the preferred fuel for space heating.

least fifty-by-thirty feet, without much success. The dim-ness was exacerbated by the shadows cast from the various theater props, which were stacked against the walls and piled in islands across the floor. The stairwell leading up to the right side of the stage was visible, but there was no clear path from one side of the stage to the other. Holmes timed me as we experimented with how long it would take to get from the left side of the stage, through the basement, reload Baines' pistol, and return. It took me about two minutes start to finish, which fit easily, in Holmes' estimation, with how much time the actresses had between their stage ap-pearances in the first act.

"And," I observed, "an absence from the stage wings could be easily explained as a quick trip to their dressing room." Holmes made no reply.

As we started to climb to the back stage area, something caught my eye and I called out, "Holmes, does this merit our attention?"

To the side of the stairwell I had spotted two footprints in the dust. Judging from the size of the shoe, they belonged to a woman.

"Capital observation, Watson," he replied and then began a meticulous examination, not of the footprint but of the wall at the entrance to the stairwell. A few seconds later he reached up and pulled something from one of the boards. "Look, Watson, another strand of dark brown thread. Someone appears to have stood here waiting. But for what?" Holmes mused. With that he pulled over an empty packing crate and upended it to cover the footprints. "Watson, I believe we're done here."

It was half past three in the afternoon when we departed

the theater and separated. It would be getting dark in an hour, so I took advantage of the free time to walk about the town and enjoy the sunlight. It had warmed up considerably and the snow on the roofs was melting. I continued to be impressed by Rodgersburg. Its residential areas consisted of small, but neatly appointed houses which demonstrated a permanence or, at least, a belief in the future that escaped most mining camps.

Holmes did not join me for dinner. The serving girl reported that she had seen him leaving through the back door of the hotel just after five. His continuing absence gave me time to enjoy an after dinner brandy or two and delve into *Moby Dick,* meeting Captain Ahab and his tale of the great white whale.

At breakfast, Holmes asked me to contact the local photographer whose shop we had seen up the street and make arrangements for him to photograph the footprints we'd found in the basement of the theater the day before. I set about that task promptly and by 10:30 had also accomplished my second mission, which was to search through the theater's dressing rooms and wardrobe storage for anything dark brown. Miss Allen's brown skirt was hanging in the women's dressing room as expected, but I also found numerous articles of brown clothing in wardrobe storage and an orange and brown flag.

With nothing to do pending Holmes' return, I decided to take a walk once more. That decision lasted for about two blocks where I spotted a sign announcing the Apex Saloon and beneath it the word 'poker.' I prefer whist or bridge, but enjoy some light gambling from time to time. One evening in St. Paul, Holmes and I had joined one of

Mr. Hill's weekly games. It was most interesting to watch Holmes' concentration pitted against Hill's confidence and resolve. Suffice it to say I knew I was overmatched and smart enough to keep my losses to a minimum.

I emerged from the Apex at 4:00 p.m., twelve dollars richer and a bit light headed from the several schooners of beer which I had quaffed during the game. The prospect of a light dinner and an early bedtime looked very appealing.

At dinner Holmes quickly sized up my situation and asked, "I do hope you'll be able to accompany me to the theater again tonight, Watson. I need one more look at the gunfight scene."

"Wouldn't miss it, old boy," I said through a yawn. There is something about drinking in the afternoon. When I am finished, all I want to do is sleep.

That evening our seats for the performance were in the second balcony where, I am loath to say, I fell asleep during the first act. The report of gunfire jolted me to my senses and I discovered that I was alone. Holmes must be traipsing around the theater taking measure of his theory of the crime. I yawned, stretched, yawned again and settled back into a slumber until jostled awake by a smiling Holmes to a background of the audience's applause, truly music to my ears. "Well, Holmes," I said in greeting. "It seems like a great time to go to bed."

"Watson, you disappoint me. How about a spot of tea first?"

Not one to let my friend down, I readily agreed and soon found myself closeted with Holmes at Jack Tao's noodle parlor. Holmes had invited Tao to join us. The great detective is not one for idle chat, and I wondered how Mr. Tao fit into the investigation. I didn't have too long to wait.

"Mr. Tao," started Holmes, "I see that your establishment is directly across the alley from the Rodgersburg Bank. I'll bet you see a lot of activity over there."

"Yes, I see and hear too, Mr. Holmes." Tao had trouble with the 'l' sound and it came out sounding like 'Howmes.'

"And you know Miss Tess Carson."

Tao nodded in reply and said, "Everybody know Miss Carson."

"I understand she has many admirers," asked Holmes, but it was clear from Tao's expression he didn't understand.

"Men friends," said Holmes quietly.

"Ah, so. No, not so many, I think. One old man, like her father. I see them many times," responded Tao.

"Ever see her with the young Englishman?" asked Holmes.

"No, never with him. Just the old fellow."

"Where did you see them?"

"In back by bank, over by fence."

"Watson, perhaps you didn't notice, but there is a vacant lot to the side of the bank with a tall wooden fence around it. I noticed a table and some chairs, as well."

"Yes, yes," exclaimed Tao. "Mr. Carson like to eat lunch outside when weather good."

"How about Miss Carson?" asked Holmes.

"I never see her eat there. Just there at night with old man."

"What were they doing, Mr. Tao?"

"Talking, holding, how you say it, embrace."

"Yes," answered Holmes, "embrace, holding one another. Did they kiss?"

"Oh, many times," reported Tao.

At that point Holmes turned to me and observed, "Miss Carson's relationship with Tompkins seemed to be a bit more than intellectual, Watson."

I had no reason to doubt Tao. He had no reason to lie. My stomach tightened as I reflected on our lunch with the Carson family a few short days ago. I'd seriously misjudged the young lady. I looked back at Holmes and nodded in agreement.

Holmes turned back to Tao and asked, "Did you see Miss Carson and the old guy, as you call him, recently?"

"Before he die, two maybe three days. I go out in alley, hear noise behind fence, like crying. I look. They there together. I hear her say, 'you can't leave me now,' and he starts to laugh. Then I come back inside."

"Was that the last time you saw them?"

"Him sure, but I see Miss Carson and father in bank, three nights, a few days ago. That not right. Mr. Carson never come to bank at night."

"What were they doing?" probed Holmes.

"Working, writing in their books."

"Thank you, Mr. Tao. You've got great ears and eyes." Holmes then pulled a $20 gold piece from his pocket and placed it on the table before Tao. "Perhaps you would be so kind to now take those eyes and ears to sleep."

Tao palmed the money, smiled at Holmes, and said, "Gentlemen, I must ask you go. Time to close and go bed."

We pulled on our coats, stepped outside, and I turned toward the hotel, but Holmes took hold of my shoulder and whispered, "This way, Watson. We're going to do some banking."

I started to reply but Holmes motioned for me to be

quiet. We rounded the corner east of Tao's noodle parlor and stepped into the shadows at the mouth of the alley.

"Holmes, are you daft?" I questioned quietly. "There's bound to be some type of alarm, even if you can succeed in penetrating the door."

"We're not in London, Watson. There's no alarm that I could see and the door has a common lock. I stopped by this morning to visit with Miss Carson and, as our hoodlum friends are wont to say, cased the place."

"But for what reason?" I stammered.

"To look at the books. I doubt the Carsons are going to surrender them voluntarily. I've a premonition, which Mr. Tao just strengthened. Quickly now."

We moved down the alley staying close to the back wall of a dry goods store until we met the fence Tao had described earlier. There were no lights in the noodle parlor. True to his word, Tao had gone to bed. Holmes pulled into the narrow yard between the bank building and the dry goods establishment and, once again hanging in the shadows, moved toward the street and the bank's front door.

"Stay here and keep a look out until I call for you," said Holmes. "Whistle if you see anything awry." Holmes stepped around the corner and moved to the bank's recessed doorway. Apparently, the lock wasn't as common as Holmes assumed. After about two minutes of waiting, I spotted a man emerge from another doorway farther down the block. I whistled softly, heard Holmes' reply, and then moved back toward the alley where I pressed myself against the wall of the bank so I would not be seen. A few seconds, later a man walked by slowly, without even casting a glance in my direction. By the time I returned to the front of the building I heard Holmes call my name. After checking the street carefully, I quickly joined my compatriot inside the bank. Holmes posted me by the tellers' cage and asked me to stand lookout once again. The words were hardly out of his mouth when, through the front window, I spotted another man stopping to light a cigar. I looked back to see Holmes disappear through a doorway while I ducked down behind the tellers' counter. The man crossed the street, stepped up to the back doors, shook them to see that they were locked, and disappeared from view. It was the town's night watchman on his rounds.

Holmes rejoined me a minute or two later to tell me to get comfortable but stay awake, it might take him some time. He was gone about thirty minutes. In the meantime, several people walked by the bank but no one paid it any heed.

"Watson," Holmes whispered in a light voice, "I think we might safely return to our lodgings. Part of the mystery is solved."

We encountered no problem returning to the hotel, but Holmes refused to answer my entreaties about what he had found. As we parted company in the hotel corridor, he said, "Doctor, tomorrow I shall ask Sheriff Keiley to exhume Mr. Tompkins' body. As a medical man I would appreciate your handling the autopsy."

I was dumbfounded at the thought and weakly waved my hand to indicate my allegiance.

Holmes had no trouble convincing the Sheriff of the advisability of his idea. But reopening a grave in frozen ground was no small task. By noon the body was laid out on a plank stretched between two sawhorses next to the grave and I pulled out a scalpel from the small medical kit I keep for travel. The autopsy consisted of me removing the bullet which had extinguished Jasper Tompkins' life. It had penetrated the right ventricle of his heart and come to rest in muscle tissue next to his backbone.

As the gravediggers returned the corpse to the grave, Holmes asked the Sheriff to host a small gathering at the jail in the afternoon at 5:00 p.m. He also requested that Sheriff Keiley gather up young Baines, Carol Carmody, Beth Allen, Tess Carson and her father for the meeting and closed by saying, "I think we can bring this little matter to a close and see justice done."

About ten minutes before the appointed hour Holmes and I entered the foyer of the Rhyolite County Jail. Misses Carmody and Allen were already there, standing near the steam radiator against the far wall. Sheriff Keiley saw Holmes and announced that he would get the prisoner. With his departure, Miss Carmody quickly stepped over to Holmes and asked, "Can you free him, Mr. Holmes? He is innocent, isn't he?"

"All in good time, dear lady. Please be patient. It will be revealed soon, but not before the other guests arrive," answered Holmes.

Sheriff Keiley returned with young Baines wearing leg irons, the sight of which discomfited the ladies in attendance. The Sheriff sat Baines at a long table and invited the four of us to step around a counter which divided the room and join Baines.

The tension in the room was palpable as we sat quietly waiting for the Carsons to appear. They arrived about ten minutes late with Albert Carson begging our pardon for their tardiness. There was a moment of awkwardness when Tess Carson stood facing Vincent Baines. Perhaps sensing that we were watching her, she reached out and embraced him affectionately and said, "You poor boy."

Soon thereafter we were all seated, all that is except Holmes, who paced back and forth near the head of the table. Finally, "Thank you all for coming," uttered Holmes. "I asked you here so that hopefully we can clear up the little matter of Jasper Tompkins' murder. After thorough examination, I believe that Mr. Baines is innocent of that foul deed."

Our guests engaged in a collective gasp. The Sheriff and the Carsons appeared perplexed. In contrast, Misses Allen and Carmody both drew broad smiles.

"Then who might be the guilty party?" interrupted the Sheriff in his Irish brogue tempered with a Wisconsin accent.

"Allow me, Sheriff, and I will answer your entreaty," responded Holmes. "When Watson and I first arrived here in Rodgersburg we were greeted with three alternative theories of the crime. The first, of course, was that Mr. Baines shot Mr. Tompkins, his rival for the attention of Miss Carson. The second theory, as advanced primarily by Mr. Baines, is that someone else reloaded his pistol with live ammunition and used him as the instrument of Tompkins' death. The third theory centers on the premise that Tompkins was a wealthy man notwithstanding his profession. Mr. Baines killed him, again innocently, so someone else, as yet unnamed, could gain access to his wealth. Just recently Watson and I became aware of a fourth potential explanation based on the theory that his death was arranged by a daughter long since abandoned who discovered him here in Rodgersburg."

Holmes' final statement caught several of my tablemates by complete surprise and they began looking at one another. Beth Allen acted surprised as well while Carol Carmody blushed, if ever so faintly.

"I must admit that I didn't think too highly of the robbery theory initially, but then I made two conflicting discoveries. First, when I questioned Miss Carson, Tompkins' banker, about his wealth, she quickly dismissed the notion by pointing out that his account only contained $262.00 which is a nice nest egg for a working man, but hardly suffices as wealth. But then, Watson and I discovered that Mr. Tompkins' room had been searched and the contents of at least one envelope, most likely money, had been removed. In searching Tompkins' room I also discovered a dark brown fiber attached to the dresser, suggesting that the thief wore dark brown. Miss Allen wears a dark brown skirt in her role in *The Bandit Brothers*. It also turns out that she is Mr. Tompkins' daughter."

Miss Allen immediately became the focus of everyone's attention. Miss Carson gasped, and Vincent Baines shook his head in disbelief. Miss Allen started to protest but Holmes cut her off, saying "I'll have more to say on that point later."

Sheriff Keiley glanced at each one at the table in turn as if to ask, "Are you the killer?"

"At first I was intrigued by Mr. Baines' theory that someone had reloaded his pistol with live ammunition. But," continued Holmes, "my belief in the plausibility of that theory quickly vanished once I'd witnessed the gunfight in the play."

"But, Mr. Holmes," interjected Baines.

"Sir, allow me to continue," responded Holmes. "I made several observations which were inconsistent with Mr. Baines' theory. First, the pistols and holsters used by Baines

and Tompkins were virtually identical. How could someone substituting live ammunition for a blank be sure they
were inserting it in the right firearm? And, there is the little
matter of the gunfight itself. Like my assistant Dr. Watson,
I too thought the shooting scene consisted of a single shot
but, in fact, it was two men trading volleys across the stage.
Neither actor truly aimed their pistol. If one of the pistols
contained live ammunition, there should be several bullet
holes in the set not to mention several casualties among the
cast. But that wasn't the case. Mr. Tompkins died of a single
shot to the heart and the chance of that happening as a result of Mr. Baines' shooting is implausible."

About that time a door in a back room opened and the
voices of two men could be heard. Sheriff Keiley excused
himself to join the men who had come in from the cold.

Holmes continued, "This past Sunday, Dr. Watson and
I attended services at St. Mark's Church and afterward had
the opportunity to meet many of your neighbors at a luncheon. I talked with several who were in the audience the
night Tompkins was killed. While all admitted to seeing
the shooting, not a single one could recall seeing any blood.
How could that be, I asked myself. Tompkins' character
wore a white shirt and blood would have been visible instantly after he was shot."

Holmes paused for dramatic effect and heightened the
tension in the room by stopping to light his pipe. "Well,
there is one way for that to happen. Tompkins was shot after he was already down on the floor feigning death from
the mock gunfight in the play. Recall that scene for a minute. Tompkins falls down behind the water barrel after being shot by Baines' character, only Baines doesn't know he's

been shot and squeezes off a couple more rounds. In the meantime, the real killer shot Tompkins from somewhere high above him, most likely the near box of the second balcony or the catwalk above the left side of the stage. The discharge from that firearm wasn't noticed by either the cast or the audience."

"Sounds preposterous to me, Holmes," said the elder Carson. "Hitting something with a pistol at fifty feet or more is no small task."

"True, Mr. Carson," answered Holmes, "but I never said Tompkins was killed with a pistol. He wasn't. This morning, Dr. Watson and I exhumed Tompkins' body with the aid of two of the Sheriff's deputies and we recovered this from his chest cavity."

The Sheriff returned to the room and nodded to Holmes who, in turn, pulled out the slug which I had removed from near Tompkins' spine and put it on the table. "This is a 30-caliber bullet, most likely from one of Mr. Winchester's pump action rifles like the one the good Sheriff is now holding in his hands. Every firearm leaves its own distinct signature on the bullets it shoots, and we can compare this slug with another shot from the rifle to determine if they came from the same gun. It's an emerging technique in the science of fighting crime, called ballistics, which is taking hold in Europe, though not common knowledge in the United States. I learned all about it from an old friend of mine, an Admiral retired from the Royal Navy." Holmes' indirect reference to Baines' father brought a mile to Vincent's face, which he quickly extinguished and, likely, was seen only by me.

When I heard Holmes' explanation, my immediate

reaction was skepticism, but I stifled any comment in that regard. I had long ago learned that he doesn't make statements of that type unless they are true. Besides, I didn't need to say anything as once again Albert Carson expressed his incredulity, a feeling shared, I am sure, with others at the table. "That's preposterous, Mr. Holmes. A rifle of this type is mass-produced. Every one is the same," claimed Carson.

Holmes shrugged and said, "Sheriff, with your assistance."

Sheriff Keiley handed Holmes the rifle he was holding. Then one of the deputies entered the room carrying two 30-caliber pump action Winchesters which appeared to be identical to the rifle Holmes held in his hand. A second deputy entered carrying three canvas bags of something which he placed on the floor near Holmes' feet.

"Please explain what we have here, Sheriff," said Holmes.

"Gladly, Mr. Holmes. The rifle you hold is one my deputies recovered from the suspect's premises. The two held by Deputy Meehan belong to the Sheriff's Department. The three sacks which you requested contain sawdust."

Holmes thanked the Sheriff and then laid out four sheets of paper, labeling one for each of the three rifles and a fourth for the slug recovered from Jasper Tompkins' body. Then he put one of the sacks of sawdust on a chair, cocked the rifle he was holding, and shot it into the sawdust bag. The roar of the rifle going off in such a confined space was deafening, and the smell of cordite filled the area.

As an old military man I should have prepared myself for the impact of Holmes' display by covering my ears, but I did not and consequently found myself temporarily deaf, my hearing replaced with a sharp, high-pitched ringing.

The Carsons appeared to be similarly overcome. In contrast, Miss Allen appeared to be conversing with Miss Carmody and the Sheriff who was standing between them. I saw Holmes turn to me and say something I couldn't comprehend. He just snickered and waited for a brief period. Finally, I heard. "Watson, would you please extract the slug from that bag of sawdust while I ready the next rifle?"

"Certainly," I replied, and left my seat to do as requested. I quickly found the slug a few inches into the sawdust and placed it on the paper labeled 'suspect's rifle.' Holmes, I think in pity for me, instructed us to cover our ears and then repeated the exercise with the next two rifles while I retrieved the spent bullets. When I returned to my place at the table, Holmes pulled out his magnifying glasses and examined each of the slugs in turn, resting the slugs on their side. Then he motioned to the Sheriff to join him at the head of the table.

"Sheriff, please examine each of the slugs, then remember what you saw until after Mr. Carson and Miss Carmody have done likewise." The Sheriff carefully examined each of the slugs, rolling them over in his hand and looking again. Carson and Miss Carmody followed the same process.

"Tell us, Sheriff, what did you discern in your examination of the bullets?" ordered Holmes.

"The bullet from Tompkins' body and the one marked 'suspect's rifle' have two small lines on the side about an eighth of an inch apart."

"And the other two bullets?" asked Holmes.

"They've got marks on them too, but not the same as the first two slugs," answered Keiley.

"Is that your opinion as well, Mr. Carson?"

"Yes, I don't believe it but all three guns leave a different mark."

"And you, Miss Carmody?" continued Holmes.

"I don't know much about guns, but I agree with the Sheriff," she replied.

Holmes took the floor again and pronounced, "I trust that we can now all agree this rifle is the weapon which killed Mr. Tompkins, not some shot fired from Mr. Baines' pistol on stage." No one spoke but there were nods of agreement from several in the room. "And, now that we've established that Mr. Baines did not shoot Tompkins, perhaps you could free him from his leg irons."

In the meantime, the two deputies cleared the room of the rifles and sawdust bags and placed another cloth bag in front of Holmes. I wasn't surprised that no one had asked Holmes where the murder weapon was found. He could be quite intimidating. His confidence, reasoning and grasp of the facts caused people to defer to him even though he spoke with a soft, relaxed tone.

Holmes opened the bag and pulled out a piece of paper which I recognized as one of the photographs taken by the stairs in the theater's basement. Holmes handed it to me and asked that I pass it around for all to see. When it had been returned, Holmes said very matter-of-factly, "The murderer's shoe prints discovered near the base of the stairs in the basement of the theater."

I watched the expression of those assembled at the table and the glances they gave one another. "It is my considered opinion," opined Holmes, "that the perpetrator started in the basement of the theater, waited at the foot of the stairs until the opportune time, then climbed to the catwalk and fired upon Mr. Tompkins as he lay on the stage. It's also my belief that the assailant was dressed like a member of the cast so he could move about the wings and basement of the theater without raising suspicion. The only thing I don't know for sure is whether Tompkins' room in the hotel was robbed before or after the murder. When was it, Miss Carson, before or after you killed him?"

There was an outcry from those at the table, the loudest complaint coming from her father who yelled, "Are you insane, Holmes?"

"Not hardly, Mr. Carson. Unless you want to admit to the murder."

"What . . . I . . . murder? That's preposterous. I liked Tompkins."

"Well, then, it's your daughter. The shoe prints found in the basement of the theater match those of her brown boots, the same boots she wore last week during our dinner at your home. More importantly, the murder weapon was found in your bank. So, sir, it's either you or your daughter."

Surprisingly, Carson said nothing, his eyes moving between Holmes and his daughter. Finally, he turned toward her as did everyone else in the room. Tess Carson sat there impassively for several seconds staring at Holmes and then said, "Yes, Mr. Holmes, I killed Jasper Tompkins. We were lovers. He promised to marry me and take me to San Francisco. Instead, he abandoned me."

Our silence continued and then Miss Carson began to sob. "And he didn't even have a good reason. Just that his acting contract was about to expire and he had decided to go to Denver. He said, 'Tess, it's been fun.' When I asked what was to happen to me, Jasper just laughed and then told me to 'side-step over to young Baines. He is too much in love to care that you're used goods.'" At that point, Tess Carson broke down completely.

As you can imagine, the next few minutes were a state of pandemonium. Beth Allen exhaled a great sigh of relief, Carol Carmody rushed to Vincent Baines' side and drew him into her arms, and Albert Carson stayed in his chair, stunned to hear that his daughter had killed a man, while Tess Carson was taken to a jail cell. Soon, her father would join her. Along with finding the rifle at the bank, the deputies brought in the ledger books and Holmes showed the Sheriff how the Carsons had cleaned out Tompkins' account and transferred the money to theirs. It was quite simple, really. Tess recopied the ledgers for the Tompkins and Carson accounts, deleting deposits and withdrawals from Tompkins' funds and inserting them into her father's. Then they reconciled the general ledger for the bank. But their cleverness got the best of them. The bank's other accounts showed the handwriting of several different tellers. The Tompkins and Carson accounts showed only Tess' writing. Carson was reluctant to admit his complicity in draining Tompkins' bank account but, he finally confessed to his perfidy as well. Tess had told her father that Tompkins had no kin and now that he was dead, she reasoned why should his money, which exceeded $25,000, be left to the county. It was the perfect crime of opportunity and apparently, Albert Carson didn't want to miss the opportunity before him. He was, however, innocent of Jasper Tompkins' murder.

Holmes and I closed out the day by having a quiet dinner at Jack Tao's noodle parlor and then walking to the telegraph office where Holmes cabled Admiral Baines back in

England. He wrote:

> *Case closed. Vincent exonerated. Met girl. Staying on.*
> *Expect grandchildren.*
>
> *Holme*s

We departed Rodgersburg three days later, after the bridge had been repaired and the railroad line reopened. At Butte we once again boarded Mr. Hill's private car for the trip back to St. Paul. From there we would make our way to the east coast and find a steamer back to England.

I had just settled into my chair with one of Mr. Hill's excellent brandies in hand, hoping to finish *Moby Dick* when Holmes took the chair beside me, filled his pipe, and said, "Two more successful adventures for your archives, eh, Watson?"

"Indeed," I replied after sipping the brandy. "But you know, Holmes, I didn't think you were up to your usual game out in Rodgersburg. I don't think I've seen you work a case so intensely in a long time. Were you distracted by events in England?"

"Perhaps a bit preoccupied, Watson. Fortunately Inspector Lestrade is safely looking after that matter. Just a little case involving the misappropriation of a gold shipment from South Africa."

"And Mr. Baines' problem?"

"It simply took me several days to develop a theory of the crime but I still lacked a suspect. It was the discovery of that dark brown fiber in Tompkins' room which allowed me to conclude it was Miss Carson."

"You say, conclude. So you thought of her as a suspect earlier?"

"Recall our lunch at the Carson household, Watson. I

had gone to the bank to see Mr. Carson and while I was there I watched the ebb and flow of customers being served by the bank's teller staff. Miss Carson sat at a desk behind the tellers outside her father's office and never interacted with the customers. But that afternoon when I mentioned the rumor about Mr. Tompkins being wealthy, she was quick to point out Tompkins only had $262.00 in his account. I found that very curious. I realize bankers generally know the status of their biggest accounts, but here was a woman who denied any relationship with Tompkins, yet knew to the penny what Tompkins had to his name."

"But that didn't lead you to murder."

"No, it didn't," responded Holmes. "That was a matter of literally stumbling into it by blind luck."

"Oh?"

"The night we entered the bank, you spotted the night watchman on the street and I stepped through a doorway which turned out to be the ledger storage room. The rifle was in there hanging on the wall above the ledger cabinets, and it got me to thinking."

"But how did you know it was the murder weapon?"

"I didn't, but it prompted me to think about how Tompkins could be shot from the upper reaches of the theater."

"Wasn't it risky just to assume that the rifle would give up a spent bullet with the same characteristics as the one we pulled out of Tompkins?"

"Yes, if I had merely assumed it. I went back to the bank again later that night after we'd returned to the hotel and I tested the rifle. You can't believe how long it takes to air out a building to get rid of the cordite smell after you pull the trigger. Digging up Tompkins' body was done to confirm the facts. I also searched Miss Carson's desk where I found a dark brown dress folded in the bottom drawer, and that's when I knew Tess Carson killed Tompkins. I had the who and the how and Jack Tao suggested the why, but we needed Miss Carson to confirm the facts. "

"And to think, all this time I was thinking it was your skill at deductive reasoning."

"With a little science and subterfuge, Doctor. Science whenever possible, and subterfuge when required," answered Holmes with a smile before lighting his briar.

The Tammany Affair

"Montana!" I retorted, hardly believing my ears. The very sound of word gave me goose bumps, not from fear mind you, but from cold. Montana and Minnesota, interchangeable in my mind as the two coldest places on Mother Earth. We had visited both states the previous year in the winter of 1896. Spring was well advanced in London and the very thought of going back to the American North Country, where I doubted it ever warmed up, chilled me to the bone. "Holmes, what on earth could be of interest to you in the American backwoods?"

"A cable from Marcus Daly, my dear Watson. You recall meeting him at Mr. Hill's home during our recent sojourn to St. Paul."

"Indeed, the miner," I replied.

"He's a bit more than a miner," said Holmes, clearly annoyed at my lack of recall. "Mr. Daly operates the largest copper mines on earth."

"Oh yes, the company with the quaint name. Some kind of animal."

"A snake," admonished Holmes.

"Yes, a snake, Cobre Mines. No, that's not it."

"No, Watson. Cobre is Spanish for copper. It has no connection to its reptilian namesake the cobra," said Holmes, his face the very portrait of exasperation. "Daly's company is the Anaconda."

"Ah, yes," I replied. "A copper mining company in the Montana mountains named after the great constrictor of the Amazonian jungle. How novel."

"Watson, the issue before me is Mr. Daly's life, not the name of his company. He has been repeatedly threatened and the local police have been singularly unsuccessful in finding the perpetrator of these threats. Since Mr. Daly contacted me at Mr. Hill's suggestion, I trust that I can count upon both your able assistance and companionship."

Initially I demurred, but Holmes was persistent and, alas, I was won over by the promise that Montana's summers were both warm and dry. Notwithstanding the trials I had endured in the Afghan Wars, I was very partial to the climate in that part of the world. Hot and dry, the perfect tonic for the little touch of rheumatism I was feeling with more regularity these days.

In short order we made our way to Southampton for passage across the Atlantic on the *Majestic*, a White Star liner. The voyage took seven and a half days, one day longer than scheduled due to rough weather in the mid-Atlantic. I don't have very good sea legs and was happy to be back ashore. Holmes, as usual, was unfazed by the heaving and pitching of the ship, calmly smoking his pipe and devouring several books. We arrived in New York on June 26 and, on reaching our New York hotel, Holmes telegraphed Daly to report on our progress and received an entreaty in reply asking that we reach Montana with all possible haste. Two arduous days of travel by rail brought us to St. Paul, Minnesota, and the home of James J. Hill, President of the Great Northern Railway Company. Hill met us in his dining room for a late night repast.

"Well, once again we are indebted to you for your hospitality, Mr. Hill," I exclaimed as I filled my plate with a large slice of pot roast.

"I am so pleased to see you both," answered Hill, "And, delighted as well that you have chosen to assist my good friend Marcus Daly."

Holmes, who rarely ate after 7 p.m., broke with tradition and ladled rich brown gravy over a generous helping of potatoes while he questioned Hill.

"Mr. Daly seems quite distressed. What do you know about the nature of these threats against Mr. Daly's life?"

"Very little, Mr. Holmes. Marcus was here about six weeks ago. He wants to expand the scope of his company's railroad operations to the Pacific Coast and came to approach me about investing in the company. Over dinner that evening he mentioned the threats and reported that neither the local police nor a detective agency in his employ had been able to get to the bottom of it."

"And that's when you suggested he contact Holmes," I interjected between mouthfuls of the roast.

"Indeed, but Marcus seemed reticent. He said he felt foolish asking a man to come all the way over from England to protect a horse."

"A horse!" I said, astounded. "Holmes has come to protect Mr. Daly."

"Not quite, Watson," Holmes said. "I hope you will

forgive my little ruse. Mr. Daly cabled me asking for help in protecting his racehorse, Tammany."

"My God, Holmes, have you gone daft? Is this what your talent now merits, a little ruse to get me across the Atlantic?"

"If I had told you that we were going to Montana to protect a horse, you wouldn't have come, dear friend, notwithstanding how much I've come to rely upon you."

I didn't immediately respond to Holmes. I was irritated over the childish ploy that he'd used to get me to join this latest expedition but secretly pleased by the compliment he just paid me. Normally, Holmes wants for no man's company and there is little he can't accomplish if left to his own devices. "Surely you jest, Holmes," I finally muttered in reply.

"Watson, you're an old military man. You've forgotten more about horseflesh than I'll ever know. I expect you'll be critical to the investigation."

Hill briefly recounted the facts of the case as he knew them. Mr. Daly maintained a stable of fine racehorses, among which a stallion called Tammany was the most accomplished. Daly was planning on racing the horse in several contests along the east coast of the United States later in the summer. In early April he received a letter warning him not to go. It was followed by two subsequent missives, each more aggressive and threatening in tone. Each of the letters was postmarked in Butte, Montana, where Daly's mines are located. The final note threatened that Tammany would be destroyed if the horse left its stable in nearby Anaconda, the town to which we were headed. According to Hill, Daly had his share of enemies, but they were business or political rivals and gentlemen in their own right. None would stoop to harming an innocent animal in a conflict with the Copper King.

Both Holmes and I were exhausted by our travels and I slept soundly in the gigantic featherbed our host provided, covered only by a cotton sheet. At dinner, Hill had remarked how favorable the weather had been lately and I reveled in the warmth of the evening breeze that blew silently into the bedroom.

Promptly at 9:45 the next morning, Holmes and I alighted from our carriage at the train station after giving Hill our profuse thanks for his impeccable hospitality once again. Holmes had made arrangements for us to take the Northern Pacific in lieu of Hill's Great Northern Railroad. When I protested that we should patronize the railroad service offered by our friend, Holmes quickly assured me that Hill took no offense. "Besides, Watson," added Holmes, "We shall see some new country this way and get to Butte a day sooner."

The coach to which we were assigned was quite comfortable. Holmes lit his pipe as we were leaving the station and sat back to peruse the bundle of newspapers Hill's butler had provided when we left the house.

I was fascinated by the portraits painted by the landscape as we trundled west. What a stark contrast to the monotony of the snowfields we'd seen on our previous trip. The field crops formed a mosaic of green interrupted only by the freckle of a white house or red barn as we flowed down the track.

The hours melted away as I watched the American Midwest unfold before me, its agricultural bounty more magnificent than I could have imagined. The United States was truly the breadbasket of the world.

After crossing the Missouri River between Bismarck and Mandan, North Dakota, it became noticeably drier. Grain was replaced by grass and it was already turning brown from lack of moisture. Cattle, then sheep, became ever more common as we continued our westward migration.

Late in the afternoon of our second day aboard, the conductor advised us that we would be pulling into Glendive, Montana, where the train would exchange engines, reprovision the dining car, and change crews. He invited us to stretch our legs for a bit and tour the town, there being "no danger we'd walk too far."

Holmes and I did just that, and after strolling the wooden sidewalks and peering in the occasional shop, we found ourselves bellied up to the bar in Dion's Place across the street from the train depot.

Holmes rarely imbibes but when he does, he tends to indulge his adventuresome nature and tries whatever is produced locally, which, in this case, led to the two of us enjoying a schooner of Dion's beer. Secretly, I would have preferred a glass of madeira or port, but one look at the saloon told me that asking for some would have been a frivolous gesture, indeed.

The barkeeper, a tall, cleanshaven fellow with sandy hair answering to the name of Mick Devlin, hailed us as if we were old friends and engaged in an animated conversation about the state of life on the great plains.

Whether it was the warmth of Devlin's demeanor or the opportunity to commiserate with someone other than me, I don't hazard a guess, but Holmes was positively effusive in his response to Devlin and quizzed him intently about the town, politics, railroading, and sheep ranching. Suffice it to say, it was a most interesting half hour. Devlin left the saloon in the care of one of the patrons and walked us back to the station where he shook our hands and invited us to stop and see him on our return trip.

After lighting his pipe, Holmes commented, "There's no pretense about these Montana folk, Watson, such a refreshing change from the English aristocracy."

I was about to take issue with Holmes' comment but realized it would be for naught. Instead, I turned to gaze out the window as the train gained speed and our coach settled into a rhythmic sway. We'd be in Butte by morning.

We reached Butte promptly at 8:00 a.m. The sun was already high in the sky and I could tell that the chill I'd experienced the last time I was here[9] was about to be burned out of my bones. The air was still and a smoky pall from the smelter chimneys and powerhouses at the mines hung just above the city like a gray, gauze umbrella.

The streets were already full of wagons, the modern arteries and corpuscles of commerce. During our previous visit, I was both impressed by the size of Butte and its energy. During a military and medical career which has carried me halfway around the world, I've had the opportunity to visit many mining camps. But Butte was no camp. It was a thriving metropolis, the result of the good Lord concentrating an unbelievable abundance of mineral wealth in one location. Butte's only rival to the claim of Mining Capital of the World was Johannesburg,

---

9   Editor's note: Watson and Holmes traveled through Butte on their way to Rodgersburg, Montana, to solve the case chronicled as *The Opera House Murder.*

South Africa. I hoped that our stay in Montana would provide us with an opportunity to spend considerable time here.

As we stepped down from the car to the station platform a tall, thin, balding man in a black suit walked toward us slowly, finally stopping in front of me and inquiring, "Dr. Watson?"

"Indeed," I replied.

"Mr. Daly sends his regards and requests that I accompany you and your companion to his rail car for the balance of your journey to Anaconda. Please follow me, gentlemen."

We walked toward the station until meeting another locomotive on an adjacent siding with the initials *B.A.&P.* and the number *9* stenciled on its side. Behind the tender stood a single coach with the train's conductor standing adjacent its back steps. Following our guide, Holmes and I entered the car and faced the Copper King, Marcus Daly rising from his chair to meet us.

"Mr. Holmes, Dr. Watson, so good of you to come." His handshake was powerful, the mark of a man who first worked and then realized wealth in later life. "If I may, let me introduce you to Sheriff John Fitzpatrick, Mr. William Thornton, our mayor, and Mr. J. B. Losee, who is President of the Anaconda Racing Association. You've already met Tavary, my secretary."

"Gentlemen, the pleasure is ours," answered Holmes while I nodded in assent.

"Come join us for breakfast," answered Daly.

While we took our chairs at the dining table, Tavary appeared with a tray containing plates full of fried bacon, eggs, toast, and fruit preserves. Holmes had eaten earlier and limited his intake to coffee. But I was famished, as was

Sheriff Fitzpatrick, and together we made short work of the victuals spread before us.

Holmes also surprised me. Characteristically he likes to display his powers of deductive reasoning to a prospective client but did not. Instead, he simply asked Daly to "Tell us about your little problem, kind sir, from the beginning."

Daly finished a swallow of coffee, wiped his mouth with his napkin, pursed his lips while in thought and answered, "I can't be sure it's the beginning of this series of events, but back in February someone broke into the horse stables on the stock farm. Nothing was stolen and none of the animals were bothered. Perhaps the groom who discovered the break-in drove off the intruder before he could finish what he was about to do. I don't know, but we didn't have any more trouble and I kind of forgot about it until April 2nd when I received the first note."

"What did it say?" asked Holmes.

"Let me show you," answered Daly. With that he reached into his breast pocket, retrieved a thin leather folder and extracted an envelope from which he withdrew a single piece of paper and laid it before Holmes. Pasted to the sheet of paper were several words cut from a newspaper which read

> Take Tammany East
> The Horse Dies

"And this was postmarked from Butte?" inquired Holmes.

"Indeed, Mr. Holmes. And that is puzzling in itself because the note is constructed from words cut from the Hamilton newspaper. The type is distinctive," answered Daly.

"Hamilton? I am afraid the good doctor and I are not familiar with it."

"It's a small town in the Bitterroot Valley west of Anaconda. It's where my stock farm is located," responded Daly. He paused to take a bite of toast and sip from his coffee cup.

Sheriff Fitzpatrick, sensing that I could use another morsel or two to tide me over, wordlessly passed me the plates of griddlecakes and bacon. While I replenished my plate, Holmes stared into his coffee cup for what seemed the longest time before finally asking, "What were your plans for the horse this summer?"

"Initially, I had no plans, but in March I was visited by Dr. Hiram Alborn and Benjamin Stolz, two business associates of my partner, James Ben Ali Haggin. Both gentlemen are horse aficionados and knew of Tammany's past exploits. They encouraged me to take him back east for the racing season. I asked Mr. Losee here for assistance, and we found six races which appeared suitable for a horse of his disposition."

"When did you plan to leave?" asked Holmes.

"Mid-April. We made arrangements to board Tammany at a farm near Baltimore for the duration of the racing season."

"But you never left," observed Holmes.

"Indeed," replied Daly softly, "After receiving that first threat I thought it advisable to bring Tammany to Anaconda. I am better able to look after him here."

The train moved steadily through a narrow canyon. I saw the name *Durant* on a small station house and suddenly we broke free of the mountains and entered a large valley. Several plumes of smoke were visible in the distance which I assumed, correctly as it turned out, to mark Daly's great copper smelter in Anaconda. Sheriff Fitzpatrick nudged me and pointed to a group of buildings about a mile distant. "That's Finlen, Dr. Watson. Marcus and I enjoyed our first business venture there. We raised horses and mules which we sold for use in the mines of Butte."

"And profitably so, Dr. Watson," commented Daly. "That was well before my life became so complicated with the demands of the copper business."

Holmes brought us all back to the business at hand by asking, "Mr. Daly, when did you abandon your plans to take Tammany back east?"

"Not until nearly the first of June after I received the third threat. Pardon me. I should have mentioned this before. Right after we brought Tammany to Anaconda, I received a second letter." With that Daly reopened the leather folder and pulled out two more notes, again constructed from words cut from a newspaper. The first said

> Race in Anaconda,
> Race in Butte.
> Death Lies East of the Divide.

"Divide?" I was puzzled by that description.

"Continental Divide, Dr. Watson," said Thornton, speaking for the first time since we had left Butte. "You crossed over it when you came over the hill into Butte. It refers to the highest point in the mountains and determines which ocean a river drains to. Rivers west of the Divide enter the Pacific Ocean; those east, the Atlantic.[10]

---

10 Editor's note: The Continental Divide enters Montana from Canada, in Glacier National Park, and follows the main chain of the Rocky Mountains south until it reaches Butte. There it abruptly turns to the west and is described by the high peaks of the Anaconda Range, lying approximately six

"The second note said
   Good Decision
   Don't Change Mind,
   Or Else."

"When were these notes received?" asked Holmes.

"April 23 and June 7," replied Daly.

"And, I note that the type style is different from that of the first note."

"Yes, Mr. Holmes. These two were crafted from type set by my own *Anaconda Standard*."

"But postmarked from Butte?" said Holmes as if it were a rhetorical question.

"Yes," came Daly's terse reply.

"Who would have known about your plans to take Tammany back east for the racing season?" I asked while Holmes paused to pour another cup of coffee.

"Practically the whole world, Dr. Watson. Mr. Durston, the editor of the *Anaconda Standard*, ran the story first and then sent it out to all of the State's newspapers as well as the *New York Times, Chicago Tribune, St. Louis Post,* and a number of others."

Holmes continued to question Daly, but for my part, I temporarily lost interest in the investigation as the train drew up to the outskirts of town and I was able to get a view of Daly's great smelter on the hillside, its chimneys perched on top a low-lying ridge connected by brick flues to the buildings below. What a magnificent expression of man's ingenuity. A few short minutes later we pulled into the station and

---

miles south of the city by the same name. The Divide proceeds west where it intersects the Bitterroot Mountains and turns south once more. It forms the border between Montana and Idaho until it reaches Yellowstone Park.

I was able to look up the main street of Daly's town of Anaconda. After disembarking, Daly suggested that we walk the
two blocks to the lodging he had arranged at the Montana
Hotel. I later learned that Daly owned the hotel as well.

It was a beautiful day, the sun arcing west from the
eastern sky, itself a rich blue interrupted by an occasional

THE UPPER WORKS—ANACONDA, MONTANA
The Upper Works was the first of three copper smelters built by the Anaconda
Copper Mining Company in Anaconda. Originally constructed in 1884 to
process 500 tons of ore per day, it was already too small the day it opened.
A second smelter, the Lower Works, whose smokestacks can be seen in the
distant background, was opened in 1889. Both smelters were salvaged in the
early 1900s after the company opened the new, Washoe Smelter, on a hillside
across the valley. Today, the remnants of the two original smelters have been
incorporated into Old Works, a Jack Nicklaus signature golf course.

wisp of cloud. It was already too warm for a coat and I felt a trickle of sweat trail off my forehead to my right cheek. Mr. Thornton and Sheriff Fitzpatrick, both men of robust stature like myself, also seemed to be noticing the heat.

Under a lamppost at the corner of Park Avenue and Main Street, we said our goodbyes to Mr. Thornton, whose office was in the bank building catty-corner from the hotel. The Sheriff also excused himself, but not before Daly garnered a promise that he would join us for dinner at seven.

After the Sheriff stepped away, Daly commented to Holmes, "A most reliable man and good friend, the Sheriff. I wanted to bring him into my company but he refused. His father was killed in a lead mine back in Wisconsin and John wants nothing to do with the enterprise. A pity."

MAIN STREET —ANACONDA, MONTANA
This view, taken about 1889 at the corner of Commercial Avenue and Main Street, looks south toward the Deer Lodge County Courthouse. The photo shows the commercial vitality of Anaconda at that time. The B.A.&P. railroad depot and Whatley's Café, much favored by Dr. Watson, were located in the block behind the photographer.

"We all find our rightful place in our own way," responded Holmes in a comforting way. One could see that Daly truly felt a loss by not having his friend involved in his business. "And he continues to serve you through his office," Holmes continued.

"Aye," answered Daly. "He looks after the whole of Deer Lodge County, which covers almost 5,000 square miles, and he operates a fine stock ranch and dairy out on Nevada Creek about 70 miles north of here."

The three of us mounted the front steps of the hotel to enter the lobby. I was impressed by its grandeur from the outside, a four-story brick structure built in a "u" shape with four conical cupolas crowning the roofline at the front corners of each wing. The interior of the lobby was done in marble and dark wood. I observed a door on the left leading to the bar and made a mental note to sample their wine list later that evening. After registering with the clerk on duty, Holmes and I shook hands with Daly, who departed for his office a block farther down Main Street. The bellman showed us to our rooms on the second floor overlooking Park Avenue. Holmes advised me that we were to meet Daly again at 2:00 p.m. in his office and that I should look to my own luncheon inasmuch as Holmes needed to prepare several telegrams.

After unpacking my bag and getting settled I intended to walk about the town and then investigate the fare of one Whatley's Café, whose opened door we'd passed on our way from the train depot. The aroma of bread fresh from the oven had lodged itself in my cranium and inspired the need for a visit of longer duration. As I re-entered the hallway, I heard the soft melody of a piano coming from the doorway at the end of the passage. Whoever was at the keyboard was accomplished, indeed, and with the music of Mozart acting as a magnet to my curiosity, I set forth to investigate.

I entered a drawing room extending across the front width of the hotel wing with a magnificent grand piano pushed near the window at the southern corner of the room. The pianist was a woman of uncertain age with auburn tresses cascading down to her shoulders. I stood in the doorway watching her play, she unmindful of anything save the music issuing forth from her hands. Eventually, she saw me leaning against the doorjamb and beamed a smile across the floor in my direction. She also bid me to enter with a quick wave of her right hand and I delightfully complied by taking a seat in a Queen Anne style chair tastefully upholstered in maroon and gold.

Suffice it to say, I was soon introducing myself to Miss Margaret O'Sullivan, a most comely woman in addition to being such a proficient musician. I complimented her talent and was rewarded in turn by her playing several more pieces by Brahms, Beethoven and Bach. After a weak protestation on her part, I managed to convince Miss O'Sullivan to join me for lunch at Whatley's. She ate little but favored me with a full hour of engaging conversation. I learned that Miss O'Sullivan was originally from the east coast, some little town in New Jersey across the river from New York, where she later studied music and worked professionally for a short time. She was relatively new to Anaconda herself, having just arrived the year previous so that she could be closer to family who had made the migration west previously. Most of our conversation was, in fact, about me. Miss O'Sullivan was captivated by my relationship with Mr.

Sherlock Holmes and I regaled her with several tales of our exploits together. When I sat with Miss O'Sullivan it felt as if we were the only two people in the world. I felt extraordinarily content.

After finishing a hearty slice of apple pie, Miss O'Sullivan was gracious enough to allow me to walk her home. Along the way, she gave me a brief history of the town and pointed out several of its more prominent buildings. I found the simple lines of St. Paul's Catholic Church on the corner of Park and Cherry Streets most elegant.[11] After saying goodbye, I quickly returned to the hotel to find Holmes seated in the lobby enjoying a pipe and reading the current edition of the *Anaconda Standard*.

"Good to see you, old boy," said Holmes as he looked up over the top of the newspaper. "I feared you'd miss out meeting with Daly."

"You know better than that, Holmes. I am never derelict when duty calls," I responded.

"True," answered Holmes with a smile breaking out over his face, "But never before have I seen you confronted by such a delightful diversion."

There are times when I just hate Holmes' deductive reasoning, most typically when he applies it to me. "I surrender, Holmes. Pray, please tell how you know of my 'delightful diversion' as you choose to characterize it."

"Well, for one thing, your face was positively aglow with a big smile as you came through the hotel doors, Watson." Holmes folded the newspaper on his lap and knocked the tobacco ash from his pipe into a nearby spittoon. He faced

---

11   Editor's note: The church was constructed in 1888 and demolished in 1980.

me sternly and continued. "Your demeanor upon entering the building was at variance with your normal professional persona. It reminded me of the time when you first met Mary Marston. And, there's a bit of a bounce and skip to your walk."

"I protest, Holmes. There is no bounce and skip to my walk. I am the very picture of equanimity."

"What is the delightful creature's name, Watson, and what did she do to play such music with your heart?"

"Holmes, I swear there are days when . . . ." I stopped mid-sentence. Holmes' chortle had turned into a full belly laugh, a sight most uncommon in the detective. He'd gotten my goat, and all I could do was admit my folly. Soon I was laughing as well and described my luncheon with Miss O'Sullivan.

"She gives music lessons to youngsters at her home, Holmes, and is the organist at St. Paul's Catholic Church," I explained as I took the chair beside him.

"And how does a woman so fair come to live in a rough frontier town like Anaconda?" asked Holmes.

"To be near family," I explained. "I gathered that her parents are deceased and a city like New York is no place for a young woman to be alone."

We lingered for a few moments longer in conversation and then departed to see Mr. Daly with Holmes ribbing me one last time about the bounce and skip to my walk.

Daly's office was in a two-story brick building at the corner of Main and Third Streets, a block south of our lodgings. A small brass sign to the right of the doorway said "Anaconda Copper Mining Company."[12] We were met by Daly's secretary, Tavary, and advised that the copper baron had been detained at another meeting. Tavary showed us to Daly's office and offered us coffee while we waited. The office was simply furnished with an oak rolltop desk shoved against a wall fronted by a large oak table with leather top on which there were several stacks of papers. I sat in a black leather chair while Holmes paced around the room looking out the windows, checking the contents of a bookshelf and examining the painting of two horses overlooking a wooden post and rail fence.

We had been there but a few minutes when Daly burst through the doors, spied Holmes analyzing his artwork and commented, "Admiring my art, Mr. Holmes? It's my favorite."

"Indeed," said Holmes as he turned to face the mining man. "I trust that one of the stallions depicted here is Tammany."

"No. These two are Tammany's stable mates. That's Inflexible on the left and Hamburg on the right. I've commissioned a portrait of Tammany, but it's not quite finished. Gentlemen, please excuse my tardiness." Daly set a briefcase atop the table, removed his coat and tie and sat down firmly. "Please also excuse my temperament as well. There is something about spending time with lawyers that turns my good humor most foul. I am involved in yet another lawsuit with that insufferable Mr. Heinze, not a matter for you to concern yourself with."

But we did talk about Mr. Heinze at length. It seems that Heinze, like Daly, owned several copper mines in Butte. According to Daly, Heinze was less the industrialist and more a common thief. Apparently, Heinze went about Butte look-

---

12   Editor's note: At the time, the corporate offices of the Anaconda Copper Company were on the second story of the *Anaconda Standard* building. The structure currently houses Anaconda's Elks Club (BPOE #239).

ing for small fractions of land located between the mining claims of other companies. He would then sink a mineshaft on his land and, once underground, would mine into the ore zones of adjacent mines and extract their ore. Under the apex theory of mining law, a miner was entitled to follow and continue to mine a vein that apexed, or reached the point closest to the surface on his land, even if the vein flowed under a claim held by another. Heinze got rich by

THE MONTANA HOTEL
ANACONDA, MONTANA, CIRCA 1898
Holmes and Watson resided here during their stays in Anaconda. The salon where Dr. Watson met Miss Margaret O'Sullivan was located on the front of the north wing (i.e. right side), second story.

claiming the veins he mined apexed on his property while he relied on the uncertainties of geology and the protocols of the legal system to prove otherwise. In the meantime, he kept mining, smelting, and selling copper taken from the veins of his competition.[13]

When we at last returned to the matter which caused us to cross the Atlantic and journey two-thirds of the way across North America, our conversation with Daly was brief. Holmes obtained the names of the horse's trainer and groomsmen and a list of persons Daly thought most likely to be involved in a threat against his horse. Arrangements were made to visit the stables in Anaconda where Tammany was currently housed.

After departing Daly's office, I turned toward the Montana Hotel but Holmes led me across the street to a less imposing structure labeled the Commercial Hotel.

"Sheriff Fitzpatrick keeps a room here, Watson, and I promised we'd stop by to get his view on the case."

Holmes and I found chairs in the corner of the small lobby while the young woman working at the desk went to fetch the Sheriff. He joined us moments later and offered us cigars which, after being set to match, filled the room with a most pungent aroma. Holmes heartily approved and complimented the Sheriff on a most excellent choice of cigar.

"Thank you, Mr. Holmes, but I claim no special talent in selecting fine tobacco. Marcus' man Tavary introduced me to this smoke and I've favored it ever since."

---

13   Editor's note: This event in Butte's history is commonly referred to as the Apex War and is well described in C. B. Glasscock, *The War of the Copper Kings,* Grosset and Dunlap, New York, 1935, and Reno H. Sales, *Underground Warfare in Butte,* the Caxton Printers, LTD, Caldwell, Idaho, 1964

THE TAMMANY BAR
MONTANA HOTEL, ANACONDA, MONTANA
The Tammany was Anaconda's premier watering hole in the late 1890s.
The hotel was radically remodeled in the 1970s, leaving little of the original
structure intact. The Tammany back-bar was sold at auction and transport-
ed to Seattle. In 2006, it was located in storage and purchased by Anaconda
dentist Dr. Jill Robison, who plans to restore the Tammany Bar room.

"Well, again, thank you," answered Holmes and, after pausing to exhale, opened the conversation about the case. "What do you make of these threats against Mr. Daly's horse, Sheriff?"

"I'm not sure what to believe, Mr. Holmes," replied the Sheriff while he flicked the ash from his cigar into the spittoon. "I've proceeded as if the threats were real, but there's been no hint of foul play or any harm done to any of Marcus' horses."

TAMMANY
*The wooden mosaic of Marcus Daly's favorite racehorse as it appeared on
the floor of the Tammany Bar.*

"What motive could anyone have for threatening the
horse?" I asked.

"That's troubling to me as well, Dr. Watson." The
Sheriff scratched the side of his head near his ear and
shook his head no before responding. "I can only think
of two plausible motives. First, someone simply wants
to hurt Marcus and harming one of his thoroughbreds
would be tantamount to attacking a member of his
family. Second, someone wants to keep Tammany off

those racecourses back east. Maybe they favor another horse that would be racing."

"Interesting conjecture, Sheriff," replied Holmes. "It's very similar to my own thoughts about the case thus far, but a couple of things confuse me. If someone wanted to simply hurt Mr. Daly, why wouldn't they just kill or maim the horse? Why send the threatening notes?"

"You've got a point, Mr. Holmes. Perhaps someone is just trying to badger and worry Marcus."

"My other concern, Sheriff, has to do with your second theory about keeping Tammany off the east coast racing circuit. It's hard for me to believe that someone living in Montana would care about such races. I emphasize the point, living in Montana, because Mr. Daly's notes were written here and mailed locally."

The Sheriff digested Holmes' words thoughtfully, then shook his head no again and said, "I am not sure I can agree with you on that point, Mr. Holmes. There are a number of well-to-do men in these parts, particularly in Butte, who watch and wager the eastern racing circuit."

"Anyone in particular come to mind?"

"I can think of three," said the Sheriff as he shifted in his chair to more squarely face Holmes. "Mr. Betancourt, Colonel Smitham, and Mr. Heinze. All three of these gentlemen are involved in racing and are generally opposed to Mr. Daly in business."

"Betancourt," mused Holmes. "What can you tell us about him, Sheriff?"

"He's originally from Kentucky, Mr. Holmes. Felix came to Butte about six years ago and established himself in the furniture and household goods business which has done very well. I understand his father was a successful business-man in his own right. His Union sympathies stood him very well during the Civil War and he was a major purveyor of supplies for the Northern armies fighting in Kentucky and Tennessee."

"They say an army marches on its stomach," I injected, "and those that supply them march frequently to the bank."

"Well put, Watson," commented Holmes with a smile. "What are Mr. Betancourt's political sympathies, Sheriff?"

"He's allied with Mr. Heinze," came the Sheriff's quick reply. "They own a stable together, but the horses are indi-vidually owned." The Sheriff paused a moment and shook his head once again. "I almost forgot," he continued. "Sy-son, another of Marcus' horses, badly beat Betancourt's stal-lion Alabaster last year in a claiming stakes[14] where Alabas-ter was the clear favorite. It cost Betancourt a lot of money and I've heard that he's still upset about it."

"Interesting," replied Holmes, but judging from the in-flexion of his voice, it wasn't. "What can you tell us of Colo-nel Smitham?"

"Colonel?" I asked, more as a comment.

"You're right, Doctor. Military titles aren't much used by Americans. Smitham was a Union cavalry officer who stayed in the service and fought in the Indian Wars under General Sheridan. He passed 60 years of age a while ago, I am guessing. A most taciturn fellow."

"Retired?" asked Holmes.

"Not fully. He's an agent for William Andrews Clark, Marcus' main rival."

---

14 Editor's note: A claiming stakes is a horse race where the horses are offered for sale for a specified price to eligible buyers.

"Yes, I've heard of the man, but Watson has not. Perhaps you might detail the essential points of his character."

"I called Clark, Marcus' rival but it's more than that. There is deep animosity between the two. Like Marcus, Clark is a successful mining man and has numerous other business ventures as well. He arrived in Butte just after I did, in 1872, and purchased the Original, Colusa, Gambetti and several other mines. He built the first stamp mill in the city and started the Colorado and Montana Smelting Company later on. Then he got involved in the Moulton Mining Company, the Colusa-Parrott Company, Butte Reduction Works, and the United Verde Copper Company in Arizona."

"How did the man find time to sleep?" I wondered out loud.

"That's not the half of it, Dr. Watson. Clark's also got mercantile interests around Montana. He's involved in banks, railroads and real estate all across the country."

"So why the enmity with Daly?" I asked.

"No one knows how it got started, not even me, and I am as close to Marcus as any man alive. One story has it that Clark heard about Daly's plans to build his smelters at Anaconda, swooped in, bought up the property and then took a tidy profit on the sale of the land to the Anaconda Company, but I don't believe it. No doubt there was some conflict in their business dealings which set the stage for the rupture, but I am not privy to what that might be."

"Rupture?" I asked, puzzled by the term.

"Indeed, a very public break in their relations in 1888. Clark got himself nominated as the Democratic candidate for Territorial Delegate to Congress. In a state full of working men, that's tantamount to election and Clark expected to win easily. But, he didn't. Daly threw his support to Thomas Carter, the Republican who won."

"Clark felt betrayed," I commented wryly.

"That would be putting it very civilly, Doctor. In fairness to Marcus, his support of Carter had more to do with business than it had to do with Clark. He sensed, correctly, that Benjamin Harrison would win the Presidency and a Republican senator, beholden to Marcus, would do the Anaconda interests more good than Clark. Since then, it's been one contest after another and the Clark-Daly feud colors everything in Montana politics."

"Sheriff, pray please tell the Doctor of the Capital fight," injected Holmes.

"Through the early 90s Marcus was pretty successful in holding Clark's political ambitions in check. In 1894 the State voted to select a permanent place for the State Capital with the contest coming down to between Anaconda and Helena."

"Since I haven't seen anything approaching a Capitol building in your fair city, I gather than Anaconda came off second best."

"To be sure," replied the Sheriff as he exhaled a stream of cigar smoke. "Clark threw his money and prestige behind Helena and in the end, prevailed. Marcus told me he spent over $2 million to get Anaconda selected but it was all for naught.[15]

I was astounded by what I had just heard. Daly's demeanor was hardly that of a rich man, although I appreciat-

---

15 Editor's note: For additional information on the Clark-Daly feud, see Michael P. Malone, *The Battle for Butte*, University of Washington Press, Seattle, 1981, and C. B. Glasscock, op. cit. 1935.

ed that he was successful. Now I hear that his wealth rivals, if not exceeds, that of most of the British nobility.

Fortunately, Holmes broke the silence. "Given the magnitude of Mr. Clark's win in the Capital fight, would he stoop to threaten Daly's race horse?"

"I truly doubt it, Mr. Holmes," answered Sheriff Fitzpatrick. "Mr. Clark's mind is firmly and perpetually focused on business and politics. There's not a shred of frivolity in the man's soul and I've never heard of him participating in racing in any way."

Holmes continued, "You mentioned that Colonel Smitham was Clark's agent."

"Aye, he is."

"What is Smitham's connection to horse racing?"

"Same as Heinze and Betancourt. Smitham has a farm east of Butte near the village of Whitehall where he stables a half dozen thoroughbreds." The Sheriff paused to draw on his cigar and after exhaling commented, "Smitham's horses are an inferior bunch. You'll usually find them racing at county fairs in little towns like Missoula and Bozeman where they're competing with the mounts of local ranchers."

"I am surprised he can afford a stable of thoroughbreds irrespective of their value," answered Holmes.

"It's his wife's money. Her father and brother were both railroad men in the Midwest and died tragically many years ago. Mrs. Smitham was their only heir."

"And that leaves us Mr. Heinze," said Holmes. He stood up, tossed the stub of his cigar into the spittoon next to the Sheriff's chair and gazed out the hotel window momentarily. "I already know of his relationship with Daly. What can you tell us of his racing interests?"

"He's a sportsman in the fullest sense of the word," replied the Sheriff. "Heinze is involved in racing, sponsors prize fights from time to time, and fields a baseball team in the local league. He's a very popular fellow with the miners."

"Even though he jeopardizes their jobs by stealing ore from the other companies?" I asked.

"Indeed. The men recognize Heinze for the man that he is, a rascal who lives by his wits and outsmarts his rivals at every turn. I would hope that you would never repeat this to my friend Marcus, but Heinze is the most affable of men. He's got a good word for everyone and when Heinze is in a saloon, his money is the only money that buys a drink."

"Is Heinze capable of threatening Daly's horse?" I asked the Sheriff.

"Capable, certainly," he replied, "but I think it unlikely. Heinze has been back in New York since the first of March and I don't think he would craft a stratagem like the threats against Tammany unless he could be here to see their effect. Heinze would take great pleasure in Marcus' anxiety as he watched him at the bar of the Silver Bow Club."

"Did you talk with either Betancourt or Smitham about the threats against the horse?" asked Holmes quietly as he rested himself against the windowsill.

"I tried," answered the Sheriff, clearly discomfited by the question, "but I don't have jurisdiction in Silver Bow County. When Smitham discovered the purpose of my mission he excused himself and refused to talk with me anymore. Betancourt was more talkative but mostly he was trying to draw information out of me."

"What's your conclusion, Sheriff?" asked Holmes as he

once again returned to his feet and looked down on the law enforcement officer.

Fitzpatrick smiled back at him and said, "I don't believe any of the three are involved, but if I had to pick one it would be Betancourt. The entire chain of events is too imaginative for Smitham but well within Betancourt's ability."

"Thank you for your analysis, Sheriff. Your thoroughness is to be complimented."

With that remark Sheriff Fitzpatrick seemed to both puff up and relax. At that moment the young woman who had staffed the hotel desk appeared before us with a pitcher of beer and three glasses on a tray and commented, "I know it's a little early in the day for you, Sheriff, but given the heat, I thought you might like a little cool refreshment." She set the tray on a small table next to Fitzpatrick as the three of us chimed a collective thank you.

I stepped up from my chair and poured us each a glass. Holmes took a long drink and began questioning the Sheriff anew.

"What else did you do during the investigation?"

Fitzpatrick wiped his mouth with his shirtsleeve. "I inspected the horse to insure that it hadn't been trifled with, put one of my deputies on duty at the race track to assist with security, tried to trace the threatening letters back to their point of origin, and interviewed the employees who care for Tammany."

"And what did you discern?" questioned Holmes as he polished off his beer and motioned to me to refill his glass.

As I did so, the Sheriff replied, "The horse is fine, well fed, watered, and exercised, completely fit to race. I had no luck with the letters. The paper was a common variety and none of the stationers in either Butte or Anaconda could remember selling any to unusual customers. The people at the post office didn't remember anything out of order."

"And the staff?" asked Holmes.

"Tammany is cared for by Hans Steinbeisser, the trainer, and two grooms, Cyrus McGuire and 'Little' Pat Connors. Little Pat is a former jockey and doesn't weigh but a hundred pounds. Hans and Little Pat have been with Marcus for years; Cyrus came out here about two years ago. Supposedly, he worked for various breeders based around Belmont Park in New York."

"Did any of them report anything unusual?"

"Except for the break-in at the stable at the stock farm last February, no. Steinbeisser is beside himself with worry. And, he's angry as well, very unhappy at being denied a chance to race Tammany on the eastern circuit. Hans is very proud of the horse and considers him to be the mightiest thoroughbred on the continent."

"What about the grooms?"

"Nothing very helpful," answered Fitzpatrick through a yawn. "They may know something about horses but neither of them seemed capable of talking about the situation. The only thing they seemed to know or understand was what they did personally on any given day. It was very frustrating, especially conversing with Cyrus. It was like he'd never talked with another human being before, never once looking at me face-to-face and mumbling so low I could hardly hear him."

"Sheriff, he must be good with the horses," I observed as I drained my schooner of beer.

"You're right on that point, Dr. Watson. I expressed my

frustration with Cyrus both to Marcus and old Hans and they both laughed at me for my impatience. They also both confirmed that Cyrus had an uncanny ability with horses, almost a sixth sense. Marcus said that McGuire can spot a horse in heat at 400 yards. Marcus has Cyrus looking after the breeding for the stable."

"Sheriff, pardon me momentarily. I must ask that young lady …"

"Anne Mitchell."

"Yes, Anne, to please bring us some more of that beer."

"Capital idea, Watson," chimed in Holmes.

"It's called 'Rocky Mountain' and it's brewed right here in Anaconda," answered Fitzpatrick proudly.

After Miss Mitchell refreshed our glasses, Holmes continued the interview with Sheriff Fitzpatrick. By the time I had finished my third beer, I confess that my mind was wandering in and out of the conversation although I noticed that Holmes' disciplined mind was suffering no lapse of focus.

Holmes' concluding question to the Sheriff was right to the point. "Could any of Daly's stable hands be involved in this affair?"

"I don't see how, Mr. Holmes. Steinbeisser has been Marcus' friend for almost as long as I have and Tammany is like his child. He couldn't be complicit in this matter. Little Pat, by all appearances, is a model citizen. He lives with his wife and two children at the stock farm. When they were here in Anaconda they were good churchgoing people and, most unusual for an Irishman, Little Pat is not a drinking man."

"That leaves McGuire," observed Holmes while setting down his beer glass.

The Sheriff shook his head no again, something akin to a nervous tic, I fathomed, his obvious distaste for the man evident. "Mr. Holmes, I have to believe Cyrus innocent. He's incapable of the crime. The man is a complete illiterate; he can't read or write a word."

Holmes and I stood, shook hands with the Sheriff once again, and started for the exit when Holmes turned back to Fitzpatrick. "Sheriff, I may have need for one or two young men to run some errands for me. Could you recommend a couple of lads?"

"Three of my sons, Edward, John and Joe, are in town with me for a few days. Will they do?"

"Perfectly. Perhaps you could send them around to my room this evening."

Holmes had his Baker Street Irregulars back in London and was about to recruit a new legion. I wondered what was on his mind, but I knew better than ask. I'd simply be advised, "All in good time, Watson."

Holmes and I returned to the hotel where we both bathed and readied ourselves for supper. We were again meeting Daly, Mayor Thornton, the Sheriff, and J. B. Losee.

We ate in the hotel dining room and the meal was excellent. We all ordered large T-bone steaks, the flesh of which was both savory and delicate. My comment to that effect prompted a discussion between Holmes and Thornton on the relative merits of grass versus grain fed beef. I mentally sided with Thornton. Grass fed was superior.

The case per se was not discussed during the meal although Daly and Losee talked extensively about racing, Daly's horses, and to a small extent about Daly's stable hands.

As we parted company for the evening, Daly gave me a

wide smile and said, "I've also heard, Dr. Watson, that you made the acquaintance of one of Anaconda's young ladies. I would hope that a sophisticated man of the world like yourself won't lead her astray."

I was caught off guard and felt a blush rise up my neck as I responded, "This is the second time in a matter of just a few hours that I've been found out. I bow to the powers of your deductive reasoning. You're certainly a match for Holmes."

"I think not, Doctor," answered Daly with a grin that had also infected Thornton and Losee. "Deduction had nothing to do with it. I visited with my daughter Margaret, who is a dear friend of Miss O'Sullivan. It seems you made a very positive impression indeed."

"Hear, hear," shouted Thornton softly. It was a fitting end to a most interesting day.

I slept very well indeed, waking only once to pull another blanket over my torso. Holmes was waiting for me in the dining room of the hotel at 7:30 a.m., drinking tea and reading the *Anaconda Standard.*

"An excellent publication, Watson. No *Times*, of course, but truly excellent for such a small metropolis."

"Yes, I am acquainted with it from our trip to Rodgersburg last year."

"Ah, yes, I'd forgotten."

"Holmes, you forget nothing," I replied somewhat peevishly. "What direction will you be taking the investigation today?"

"I think it would be more efficient if we divided our initial efforts. Daly has arranged for me to meet with the manager of his stock farm and I want to talk with Betancourt and Smitham in Butte. If you would be so kind, I'd like to have you visit the stables at the racetrack. Get me an assessment of both the horse and the stable hands."

"If that is your wish."

"And one other thing, Watson. You are to introduce yourself not as Dr. John Watson but as Sherlock Holmes."

"Surely you jest. Me masquerading as you? I'll be found out instantly."

"You underestimate your abilities, old boy. Even so, I only need the ruse to function for a few hours. If my theory of the case is correct, that's all the time I'll need. Shall we say 6:00 p.m. for dinner?"

With that Holmes departed. I am frequently amazed by his investigative methods and from time to time they fail to bear fruit, but that is the exception, hardly the rule. If he wanted me to be Sherlock Holmes, so be it. Perhaps I should buy a pipe.

The cab driver let me off at the gate outside the racetrack at about 9:30 a.m. and I proceeded in the direction of the stables to the right of the grandstand. It was an impressive facility to be found in such a small town. There were three long wooden stables and one smaller facility constructed out of brick, which I correctly assumed was Daly's stable. Nearing the stables I met two young men leaning on a fence and watching a horse being exercised on the track. I inquired as to the location of Tammany's stall and was directed to the opposite end of the red building immediately before me and was then advised that it was Tammany out on the track. I kept company with the two lads for another quarter hour. Together we watched the horse and I listened to them talk, mostly about horses and fishing, apparently not quite yet at the age where the fairer sex begins to captivate their attention.

Tammany was a strong, powerful animal. His brown, shading to black coat, glistened in the sun. The exercise groom who I assumed was Little Pat Connors seemed to melt into the back of the stallion, the two functioning as one. They rode by us several times, once at a sprint and I was impressed both by the spirit of the horse and the skill of the former jockey astride his back. They ended the workout and returned to the stables.

At the stall I met Hans Steinbeisser, Little Pat, and Cyrus McGuire and promptly introduced myself as Sherlock Holmes.

As horses go, Tammany lived like the king he was assumed to be in Daly's stable. His stall was about four times larger than those of adjacent horses and it stretched across the width of the stable, north to south, giving the horse the opportunity to bask in both the noonday sun or take shelter from it on the lee side of the building. Most astounding, however, was the wallpaper.

Indeed, a horse stall wallpapered with Irish green and copper velvet. The opulence Daly showered on his horse was in stark contrast to how he treated himself.

After seating me at the small table in the center of the room, Steinbeisser offered me a cup of water.

"It's fresh from the well, Mr. Holmes, and very cold."

The sun was well into the sky and the heat of the day was building rapidly, so I accepted the trainer's simple act of hospitality. Setting the cup before me, Steinbeisser continued.

"I am glad you're here to help with this mystery. I swear I haven't slept a full night through since that first note was

THE STARTING LINE

The starting line, a portion of the grandstand, and one of the stables at Anaconda's racetrack is shown in this photograph circa 1900. The racetrack was located where the western addition to the Anaconda town site was constructed in the 1950s. Several of the streets in that part of town were named after Marcus Daly's stallions including Ogden, Hamburg, and Tammany.

received. I am afraid to take my eyes off the horse, afraid of what might happen if I am not on duty."

"I trust that you have several men to help out," I offered in reply.

"Not really, Mr. Holmes. Just three, my two grooms-men and O'Brien, the Sheriff's deputy. O'Brien works the night watch. But he's a drinking man, so I am not put at ease much, even when he's on duty."

"Have there been any problems?"

"Nothing aside from the letters." Steinbeisser momentarily excused himself and went into the stable area where I could hear him talking with the grooms about another horse called Ogden. He quickly reappeared, apologized for his departure and muttered something about breeding horses in a timely fashion, but he talked so rapidly I didn't fully fathom what had been said. Still thinking I was Holmes, Steinbeisser continued. "I told you that there weren't any other problems, but that isn't true. It seems like nothing has gone right since that first note was received."

"How so?" I asked in reply, trying to squint just a bit as Holmes is apt to do when interrogating a witness. Steinbeisser paused for several seconds and I sensed that he was internally torn over what and how much of Daly's business he should divulge to me. I waited, sipping some water from the cup he had provided me while he collected his thoughts.

Steinbeisser resumed speaking almost in a whisper. "It's been one problem after another since the stable break-in. About three weeks later there was a fire in the big storage barn. Cyrus found it and set off the alarm. We put it out before there was much damage."

"Mr. Daly never said anything about any fire."

"It's because he doesn't know. I didn't tell him, Mr. Holmes," answered Steinbeisser, clearly discomfited by what he was revealing.

I was astonished by what I was hearing but said nothing other than what my probing glance would convey.

"I didn't say anything, Mr. Holmes, because I think Cyrus set the fire." Steinbeisser's face had become red, and a small bead of sweat appeared aside his left eyebrow. "Pardon me, Mr. Holmes," Steinbeisser continued. "I don't mean it the way it sounds. Cyrus is prone to melancholy, particularly in the winter when the skies turn gray. It's like he gets discon-

nected from the world around him and he gets terribly forgetful. I don't think he meant to start the barn fire on purpose,
more like he kicked over the lantern and didn't even realize
what he had done until the room filled with smoke. Then he
discovered the fire. Fortunately, I was just coming around the
corner of the barn when he sounded the alarm."

"Had he been drinking, Mr. Steinbeisser?"

"Probably, Mr. Holmes, but I never observed it at the
time. Mr. Daly has great respect for Cyrus' way with horses,
but if he knew Cyrus had set the barn on fire, he'd be vio-
lently angry. Mr. Daly also knows all about Cyrus' taste for
the drink and would send him packing, I am sure."

"And you, too, for protecting him," I quickly added.

Steinbeisser nodded glumly.

"I am not here to investigate or judge your loyalty to your
employer, Mr. Steinbeisser," I said, sternly attempting to fully emulate the Holmes I was portraying, "and I'll say nothing to Mr. Daly unless I believe your actions have harmed
him. I suggest, kind sir, that you examine your heart. Perhaps your loyalty would be better served looking after Mr.
Daly's interests rather than those of Mr. McGuire."

I stopped to ponder my next move. What would the
real Holmes do in this situation? Steinbeisser's description
of Cyrus' bouts of melancholy were no surprise to me. It's
a common affliction in the British Isles, particularly during the winter when the fog sets in and many folks try to
lift their spirits with liquor, which only seems to make the
symptoms worse. It sounded like McGuire was an extreme
case, however, perhaps bordering on dementia. Steinbeisser
didn't need a medical lecture. Instead I asked, "You mentioned other problems?"

"Indeed. We lost two of our better brood mares to broken legs this spring and our breeding program has been a disaster. Mr. Daly wants to breed a superior racehorse. He's searched the globe for the best stallions and mares."

"Like Tammany," I interjected.

"Aye, but it's not worked at all. Not a single mare has become pregnant by the seed of our great stallions. It is unfathomable."

I am puzzled, Mr. Steinbeisser. Do you believe any of these events are related to the threats Mr. Daly received against Tammany?"

"I can't see how, Mr. Holmes," answered Steinbeisser. He stopped pacing around the room for the first time and took up a seat opposite me at the table. "No, it's just a run of bad luck."

Steinbeisser then went on at great length to describe the circumstances of how the two mares broke their legs, followed by a longer discourse on the procedures used to breed racehorses, but my attention lapsed and my mind wandered while I maintained an interested face, occasionally commenting at the appropriate time as Steinbeisser released his pent-up frustration. Mercifully, at noon the smelter blew its steam whistle and I excused myself from Steinbeisser's presence on the pretext that I had another luncheon engagement.

Re-entering the hotel at half past the hour, I met Miss O'Sullivan in the company of another young woman who was quickly introduced to me as Miss Margaret Daly. After a few moments of conversation I had obtained a commitment from Miss O'Sullivan to join me for dinner. Holmes would understand. We were business companions to be sure, but we were men first.

Dinner was delightful. I had looked for Holmes several times during the afternoon and again after returning Miss O'Sullivan to her home, but it was for naught. My report of the conversation with Steinbeisser would have to wait until morning. No matter.

My sleep was deep and uninterrupted, much like it had been before the untimely death of my wife Mary Marston. She was a tonic for my soul and Miss O'Sullivan seemed to have the same effect on me. As I made ready for breakfast I found myself wishing that Holmes wouldn't be in any rush to get back to England after he solved the case. Maybe my earlier, rather harsh evaluation of Montana had been premature.

In London it was Holmes' and my practice to breakfast promptly at 7:30 a.m. and, true to form, I found him seated at the dining room table as I entered the room.

"You look well rested, Watson. I trust you found something pleasant to do this evening past, notwithstanding my absence."

I studied Holmes for a second before answering. "You don't, old boy. Look well rested, that is. Given that smidgeon of lamp black below your left eye, I am given to believe that you were on another of your nocturnal prowls."

"Very observant of you, Doctor," replied Holmes as he wiped the offending ash from his face with a napkin. "I took the liberty of examining Mr. Daly's stables last night."

"You must tell me about it."

"In due time, Watson. Pray tell me about your visit with Mr. Steinbeisser."

Over the next twenty minutes I relayed the substance of my conversations the day before. Holmes was most interested in Steinbeisser's description of Cyrus McGuire's character and we discussed the medical aspects of his apparent condition at length. Taking advantage of a pause in the conversation while Holmes spread some marmalade on a slice of toast, I asked, "Holmes, notwithstanding your explanation yesterday, I am most curious as to why you would send me out posing as you. I've never thought of myself as an imposter."

"You're much too hard on yourself. Your acting skills are quite well developed and who better to portray me than you? Nobody knows me as well as you."

"True, Holmes. But again, why?"

"I had every confidence that you would elicit any valuable information from Steinbeisser that could be had and I couldn't very well talk to Steinbeisser while I was in Butte talking to Colonel Smitham and Mr. Betancourt."

"Holmes, you're being evasive, a side of your character I consider peevish in this case."

Holmes chuckled. "Sorry, Watson. The purpose of my little ruse was to create some confusion regarding my persona here in Anaconda. I thought it might give me the freedom to visit the racetrack and stables without being recognized, which is where I was at last night."

"Oh." It was more of an involuntary reflex rather than a comment per se.

"Yes, Watson. Given what Mr. Daly had told us about this case, someone knows a good deal about his stable operation and that means they are watching it very closely. I figured a visit from a consulting detective might get some tongues to wag in the wind and provoke a response from the perpetrator of Mr. Daly's threats."

"And were you successful?" I asked, again marveling at Holmes' tactical approach to the problem at hand.

"Partially, Doctor. I posted myself in the shadows on the north end of the stable. Around 2:00 a.m. a figure stepped out from the tree line near that stream, I believe it's called Warm Springs Creek, and started toward the stables. I moved to better position myself and he must have seen me because he turned tail and quickly ran back toward the stream. I tried to follow but he knew the path and I did not."

"Did you get a look at him?"

"No, but I did succeed in chasing him all the way back to town. He disappeared in an alley just below the railroad station and I never saw him again."

"Now what?"

"We wait and watch." Holmes said it matter-of-factly and then shot a smile at me and nodded. "All the while for you to spend more time with Miss O'Sullivan, eh Watson?"

I tried to protest. "Holmes, we're here on business. Nothing more."

"Watching you linger over dinner last night, I was left with the strong impression that you had become just a bit intoxicated by the fine wine of feminine charm. That was me next to the wall, the gentleman who looked like a country parson."

"Confound you, Holmes, you and your disguises." I said it too loudly but before I could say more, he pushed back from the table and left me to the stares of the onlookers at the adjacent tables. In drafting my reports of Holmes' exploits I've tried to stay with the facts. Holmes, unbeknownst to his many admirers, has quite a sense of humor and he greatly enjoyed pulling my leg, particularly over my relations with the fair sex.

I had no idea what Holmes had planned for the day but since he didn't seem to require my services, I had time to catch up both my reading and writing. After updating my journal, I drafted short letters to Mrs. Hudson and Holmes' brother, Mycroft, to tell them of our travel. Mycroft, who rarely traveled more than a few blocks from his London lodgings was nonetheless quite interested in Holmes' cases, particularly those in alien lands, and seemed to enjoy my characterization of the natives and local culture. His amusement would know no limit when he discovered that we had traveled halfway around the world to deal with a threat to a horse. Mycroft was no fancier of the equine species, referring to them as a necessary evil. He thoroughly looked forward to the day when someone would come up with a small, practical steam engine for personal travel around the city.

I lunched again at Whatley's Café and then took a long walk around Anaconda. For an industrial city, it was surprisingly clean. The homes were small but well appointed, and I marveled once again at the richness of the American economy when a miner or smelterman could afford his own home. That was certainly not the case in the English midlands.

Three p.m. found me in the Union Beer Hall on Main Street, having a glass of draught with Sheriff Fitzpatrick whom I had encountered on a nearby street corner. He asked me to thank Holmes for employing his sons as lookouts at the racetrack. I didn't realize what he was saying at first but, after spinning through my memory of yesterday's events, I remembered the two boys watching Tammany being exercised. Young John and Joe Fitzpatrick were assigned the day shift. Their older brother, Edward, was at the track in the evening. Apparently, Holmes took up sentry duty during the dark of night.

I was about to leave the saloon when a small man entered the establishment and was heartily greeted by the proprietor. "That's Mr. Tuchscherer, the brewery owner," whispered the Sheriff. "One of the most highly regarded men in town." As the brewmaster always is in a town full of working men, I thought to myself. The Sheriff soon introduced me and I stayed to quaff another schooner of the amber ale while complimenting Mr. Tuchscherer on the quality of his brew.

The hotel desk clerk hailed me as I crossed the lobby on the way to my sleeping room, and gave me a note written in Holmes' hand. It said

> *Dine with me at seven. The game's afoot.*
> *S.H.*

The hotel dining room was empty when I arrived full of expectancy about what Holmes would reveal. The waiter seated me at a table abutting the wall in the back of the room and whispered that Holmes had been momentarily detained. Holmes and Daly entered the dining room together, paused to say something to one another, shook hands, and parted company with Daly entering a private dining room to the right while Holmes made his way to our table.

"Sorry, Watson," exclaimed Holmes as he pulled back the chair opposite me. "I stopped by Mr. Daly's office to advise him of the status of the investigation. During our conversation Daly received a call from his lawyer advising him that Mr. F. Augustus Heinze was due to arrive back in Butte. That seemed to set Marcus off and he excused himself for several minutes to bark orders at his underlings in the outer office. They're meeting now."

"I wondered," I replied. "Thornton and Tavary went into the side dining room a few minutes before you arrived."

"It's of no consequence to us. Our concern is the well being of the horse, not Mr. Daly's apex battles in Butte."

"You've reached a conclusion?" I asked, knowing full well that Holmes had solved the riddle. It was now just a matter of catching the perpetrator in the act.

"I have, Doctor, but I must admit that I am not as fully convinced of my theory as I usually am. Oh, and Watson, I do apologize for asking you to cancel your dinner engagement with Miss O'Sullivan."

I shook my head in dismay. "Duty calls, and please spare me the logic of your deductive reasoning by which you knew about our plans to dine together. Just tell me what you've learned."

"As you wish, Doctor, as you wish." At that point the conversation lapsed momentarily as the waiter filled our water glasses and took our order. Holmes looked tired, which was unusual for him. I swear the man can go for weeks on two hours rest per night. My constitution isn't nearly so hardy.

Holmes continued where he left off. "My trip to Butte was helpful, Watson. I was able to interview Colonel Smitham, Mr. Betancourt, and a horse trainer named James Hoepper who looks after Mr. Heinze's horses."

Holmes had an introspective look about him and spoke quietly. "The Colonel is certainly a taciturn man and has no appreciation for Mr. Daly. He also strikes me as a man without a shred of guile in his bones."

"Funny you should say that, Holmes," I interjected. I

visited with Sheriff Fitzpatrick earlier today and he offered a similar assessment, saying that the Colonel was a disastrous military commander who never had enough sense to try and sneak around the back of his enemy when he could engage in a frontal assault."

"Suffice it to say, Watson, while I believe Colonel Smitham has plenty of reason for wanting to hurt Daly, he wouldn't do it by threatening his horse. No, he's the kind who would simply have the horse killed."

"And Mr. Betancourt?" I probed.

"He struck me as cold, cunning, and at the same time with the capacity to be quite gregarious indeed, Watson. He reminded me of Sir George Burnwell from the case involving the Beryl Coronet."

"All the better to hide a sinister nature," I commented offhandedly, momentarily reflecting back to that investigation.

"My thoughts exactly, my friend," replied Holmes quickly. "But after sounding out Betancourt for better than an hour, I also realized that he was lazy. Betancourt wants the honors and acclaim of wealth, but doesn't have the steadfastness of purpose or vision of Marcus Daly or his rivals, Mr. Clark or Mr. Heinze, to be successful in his own right."

"So you dismissed both Smitham and Betancourt," I countered.

"Initially, and then I met Mr. Hoepper while posing as a horse buyer. A most congenial man, Watson, who showed me through Heinze's stable. It was most impressive. Mr. Heinze has a lot of horseflesh on the hoof. When it comes to race horses, he is no mere dabbler. Hoepper also knew a great deal about both Betancourt and Smitham and he wasn't hesitant to share his knowledge. It seems they formed a partnership to breed racehorses."

"In imitation of Daly," I retorted.

"Not according to Hoepper. He said Daly was imitating them. Hoepper reported that Smitham and Betancourt approached Daly about breeding their mares with Daly's great stallions but Daly turned them down. Several months later, Daly began his own breeding program on a scale far larger and more grandiose than anything envisioned by Smitham and Betancourt. And the plot thickens from there." At that point Holmes pulled out his pipe and tobacco pouch and began to prepare a smoke while I looked in vain for our waiter. The aromas wafting through the kitchen door had thoroughly aroused my stomach.

After lighting his briar, Holmes continued. "What was particularly galling to the partners is that Daly sold stud services from certain of his stallions, most notably Hamburg, to others but never to his rivals here in Montana. Here the story gets a little murky. Supposedly, Betancourt went to Spokane, Washington, and hired a horseman to act as a front for them in negotiations with Daly. Daly agreed to allow a breeding arrangement but somewhere down the line discovered the ruse that Smitham and Betancourt were playing on him. Daly switched studs and the mare supplied by Smitham and Betancourt ended up being bred with an ass."

"Oh my God, Holmes, so Smitham and Betancourt ended up being foster father to a mule." I could hardly believe what I was hearing and could just imagine Smitham's and Betancourt's anger and humiliation at being bested by Daly. He, in turn, would delight in telling the story to his miners and smeltermen over a cold beer. I was amused myself, but also puzzled as to why the copper magnate had not revealed the details of this escapade to Holmes.

"He did, Watson," came Holmes' sure reply, "when we met privately. Daly isn't crowing about his own chicanery because the mare was taken to Spokane after breeding and no mention of a 'racing' mule ever surfaced."

"Smitham and Betancourt hushed it up and are taking their revenge now."

"It certainly looks that way. What's more, a man by the name of Billy Farrell who is reported to be in Betancourt's employ has been seen hanging around the racetrack."

"By the lads you've got watching?" I asked.

"Indeed, and it turns out that Farrell lives in the Girton House on Front Street, and very possibly is the man I chased from the track last night."

"What's next, Holmes?" I asked, although I well knew the answer.

"We post ourselves at Tammany's stable tonight and trap the malfeasor." I relished the thrill of chase but was not looking forward to an all-night vigil in the horse stable.

Holmes and I got into position about 10:30 p.m. with me sheltered along the south side of the building behind a stack of barrels. Holmes took up residence on the north wall of the structure closer to the tree line and stream where he'd seen the nocturnal visitor the night before. It was a warm night and I was comfortable. Maybe too comfortable, because one minute I was staring at the three-quarter moon in the southern sky and the next thing I knew, Holmes was shaking me back to consciousness while the dawn broke over my left shoulder. "Sorry Holmes," I muttered.

"No matter, Watson. He didn't show. We might as well get back to the hotel and get some rest. We need to be back again tonight."

And we were, and through the weekend as well for six consecutive nights. By returning to bed at dawn and napping into the early afternoon, I managed to both keep up my strength and enjoy the companionship of Miss O'Sullivan almost daily. In contrast, Holmes became more sullen with each passing day. His inability to spring the trap was wearing on his nerves. His pallor was ghostly and I suspected that he was using cocaine to help him ward off exhaustion, though he had said nothing about it and I chose not to ask. Although I was well rested, I was feeling a bit melancholy myself having not seen Miss O'Sullivan the past two days. After the death of my wife Mary Marston, I doubted that I would ever love again, but I now found myself inexorably drawn to this young woman. Her presence literally buoyed my spirit and, in contrast, her absence seemed to diminish the entire day.

My thoughtful ramblings came to an abrupt end as the bellman next to me cleared his throat and brought me back to the here and now of the hotel lobby. I quickly apologized for my lack of attentiveness and asked him to find me a newspaper. I started to slip back into my mental fog when Holmes entered the front door and moved quickly toward my chair, after whispering something to the retreating bellman.

"Watson, it's good that you are a man of regular habit."

"You never cease to amaze me, Holmes. This morning when I left you in the hallway outside your room there didn't seem to be enough energy in your system to carry you to bed. Now, you're positively ebullient."

"I am, Watson, and it has nothing to do with sleep."

And everything to do with cocaine, I thought to myself. Holmes continued. "I underestimated our foe, Watson. I assumed that our presence in Anaconda would push him to seek a quick resolution to the Tammany affair, but I erred. He's gone underground, patiently biding his time."

We were temporarily interrupted by the bellman, who put a newspaper on the table near my right elbow and handed Holmes a pouch of tobacco.

"I came to this latest conclusion on Sunday but could not see Daly until this morning. The arrival of Mr. Heinze in Butte yesterday afternoon seems to have the entire Anaconda Company in an uproar."

"I suspected as much, Holmes. Both the *Anaconda Standard* and *Butte Miner* carried the story or, more accurately, carried several stories on the subject these past two days. It appears that Mr. Daly and his associates will get their day in court the first week of August."

"Yes," responded Holmes, "but Marcus and his lawyers aren't ready. They expected the trial to be scheduled in October. Suffice it to say, it's been difficult to get him to focus on the welfare of his racehorses when the ownership of his orebodies and ultimately the entire Anaconda Company is in doubt."

"You've a plan, I trust." It was a rhetorical question. Holmes always had a plan.

"At my suggestion, Mr. Daly gave orders to move the horses tomorrow afternoon to the safety of Sheriff Fitzpatrick's dairy ranch on Nevada Creek in the northern part of the county. There should be sufficient time to have that story work its way through the local rumor mill and force Mr. Daly's nemesis to show his hand."

"So one more night at the stables," I mumbled in a desultory tone as I pushed myself up from the wingback chair in which I had been camped.

"Not this evening, Watson. Steinbeisser and the grooms will be working late getting things ready for tomorrow. You should be able to enjoy Miss O'Sullivan's company once again and we'll both be able to get a good night's sleep."

I had taken a couple of steps when Holmes called back to me. "Watson, is everything all right between you and Miss O'Sullivan?"

"Indeed. Why do you ask?"

"I had assumed that you two were keeping company in the evenings but last night I saw her walking about on Front Street, hardly the neighborhood one would expect to see a refined lady."

"I've not had the pleasure of her company these past two evenings, Holmes. She said there were family issues that required her attention, a brother with a penchant for the drink, I believe."

"Sorry I intruded, old boy," answered Holmes.

Later that afternoon I chanced upon Miss O'Sullivan as I emerged from Finley's Confectionery. She apologized for her absence the past two evenings and with a flush of embarrassment on her face muttered something about her brother being better now. I quickly invited her to go with me this evening, explaining that Holmes and I would soon absent ourselves from Anaconda for several days while we saw to the safety of Daly's horses at Sheriff Fitzpatrick's ranch.

Together we enjoyed a pleasant evening, but Miss O'Sullivan was clearly distracted by her brother's condition of which she spoke briefly. I returned her to her lodging by 8:30

p.m. where, to my surprise and great pleasure, she embraced me and whispered how much she enjoyed my company.

Buoyed by the sweetness of her words, I coasted off to bed anticipating what tomorrow would bring. I didn't have long to wait, my slumber interrupted by Holmes shaking me and saying, "Watson, there's been a change of plan. We need to get to Daly's stables immediately."

I protested, albeit weakly, while I tried to gather my wits about me, and within a matter of minutes was dismounting from a surrey outside Daly's stables. Holmes motioned for me to follow him and we took up residence in the shadows of the board fence from which we could monitor three sides of the stable.

"I don't think it will be long, Watson," commented Holmes while I merely nodded in reply, too groggy to care. We'd been in hiding about twenty minutes when Holmes nudged me and said, "Over there, Watson. By the grandstand."

I looked in vain for several minutes but finally saw the figure of a man moving toward the stable in the shadow of the fence circumnavigating the racetrack. When he reached the stable he momentarily disappeared behind it emerging next to the north wall. Had we taken our customary positions of the past several nights, the intruder would have literally walked into Holmes' arms.

I felt Holmes' hand on my shoulder, a signal for patience, and I continued to hold in position waiting for his word to attack. The intruder then motioned with his left hand, a long, slowly drawn wave. We waited. Presently the door of an adjacent stable opened discharging another intruder leading a horse. The two made their way toward the first individual and then all three entered Daly's stable.

"Now, Watson, quietly," said Holmes as he sprang out of the shadows and ran toward the stable, me struggling to keep up. It was but a forty-yard dash, but I was winded by the time I met up with Holmes near the corner of the building. Together, we quietly slid toward the door of Daly's stable. Through a crack in the entryway, soft yellow lamplight could be seen from one of the stalls. Holmes slowly inched the door open while I said a quiet prayer that the hinges were well oiled. I'd left my faithful Webley revolver in the dresser drawer of the hotel in my haste to join Holmes for tonight's adventure.

Once inside the stable, we could hear the footsteps of both the equine and human species emanating from the breeding stall. We moved quickly to the door and Holmes asked, "What have we here?"

I immediately recognized two of the three horses – Tammany and one of Daly's mares named Aspen, the latter of which was being led from the stall by none other than Cyrus McGuire. His confederate dashed to a ladder leading to the hay loft above, but Holmes was quicker than he and caught him by the heels and pulled him back to the floor where he fell in a heap.

In my most menacing tone I told McGuire to drop the reins and go over to his associate and lie down on the floor. In the meantime, Holmes endeavored to pull off the hat and mask of the other intruder who fought vigorously. Once McGuire was settled in place, I entered the fray and grabbed Holmes' opponent in a bear hug from behind, and then the intruder let out a stream of curses the like of which I'd not heard since visiting London's docks.

I recognized the voice, and the smell, or perhaps better

said, the scent of cologne as it wafted up from the intruder's neck into my nostrils. My startling conjecture was quickly verified by Holmes who said, "At last we have the pleasure of meeting, Miss O'Sullivan."

I am at pains to admit this, but when Holmes said "Miss O'Sullivan," I felt a searing in my chest and a sense that all of the energy had drained out of my body. Still, I kept hold of her until Holmes was able to tie her hands and feet and stuff a rag in her mouth to stop the stream of invective directed our way. Holmes then sent me to wake Steinbeisser at the other end of the stables. I met him in the passage outside the breeding stall. He had been awakened by our brawl with Miss O'Sullivan, and I sent him to give the alarm. Holmes seemed to have things in hand so I slowly followed Steinbeisser back to his quarters and took the liberty of pouring myself a stiff drink from the bottle of whiskey which I had seen on his shelf during our previous meeting.

I lost track of events for the next hour or so while I tried to comprehend what I had seen in the stables versus what I knew in my heart. I searched for an explanation but all I felt was pain. Holmes would right my mind but no one would right my soul.

As I sank into a desultory gloom, I heard the sound of a saddle horse pound past the stable, followed a few minutes later by the squeaks and creaks of a buckboard.

"Watson, may we join you?" It was Holmes, accompanied by Daly and Sheriff Fitzpatrick.

"Forgive me, gentlemen," I replied. "I haven't been feeling well."

"I understand," said Daly in a comforting tone. "You've experienced the worst sort of wound, as have I."

My companions took seats around the table while Stein-beisser, who had followed them into the room, rounded up several mugs. Daly poured himself a whiskey and refilled my cup before passing the bottle on to the others.

"And where is Miss O'Sullivan?" I asked meekly.

"She and Mr. McGuire have been taken to jail," answered Holmes.

"Good," I replied. "I don't think I could face her just now."

"You won't need to, Watson. She specifically asked not to see you. After I had safely bound her arms and legs she asked to speak. I intended to question her about the crime but all she would say is 'tell Dr. Watson to forget me.'" Holmes paused a few seconds to let her words sink in. I felt a flush of embarrassment and replied with a half nod and grunt.

At that point Daly chimed in. "I trust you've fully un-raveled this affair, Mr. Holmes. Perhaps you can enlighten me."

"Indeed," answered Holmes as he searched his pockets for his pipe. "Miss O'Sullivan was not terribly communica-tive, but I took the liberty of removing Cyrus to another stall for a private chat and he was most forthcoming."

"Cyrus talked?" questioned Steinbeisser in an aston-ished tone. "I've worked side-by-side with the man for months now and never heard him utter more than a sen-tence or two."

"An orator he's not, gentlemen, but he communicates rather well once you know what to ask him."

"Please, Mr. Holmes." It was Daly again, clearly getting impatient. He was more interested in cutting to the chase than hearing one of Holmes' long expositions. Of course, it had no impact whatsoever on Holmes.

Holmes lit his pipe and exhaled a stream of blue smoke in my direction and then turned toward Daly and the Sheriff. "A most confusing case, Marcus."

Marcus. Holmes had taken to calling the copper baron Marcus. The informality of American life had infected Holmes. The only person he routinely called by first name was his brother Mycroft. If this kept up he'd be calling me John, and I'd be constantly looking about the room waiting for someone to answer him.

"The first point of interest," remarked Holmes, "was the fact that Mr. Daly received several threats to Tammany's well being but no overt actions were taken against the animal. To me, it suggested that someone wanted to keep Tammany in Montana for reasons unknown."

I was about to comment on the stable fire caused by Cyrus McGuire but held back when I saw Holmes shift a glance toward Steinbeisser.

"The next point of interest," intoned Holmes, "was the threats themselves. They all came from Butte but were drawn up using words from the Hamilton and Anaconda newspapers. Whoever was issuing these warnings of doom was able to closely monitor Mr. Daly's equine operations. That suggested, of course, one of Daly's own people, but I was persuaded by those who knew the individuals involved that could not be the case. So I shifted my focus to Mr. Daly's rivals." Holmes got up from his chair and began to pace about, more I suspect to stretch his back and legs than for any dramatic impact. "I also started an around-the-clock surveillance of the stable employing the Sheriff's three sons as my eyes and ears for the better part of each day. I was sure that my presence in Anaconda to investigate the situa-

tion would in some way stimulate a reaction from the perpetrator. I sent Watson, under my name, to meet with Mr.
Steinbeisser and witness the stable operations. His persona
being sufficiently different from mine was bound to cause
confusion as rumors of my visit to the stables began to cir-
culate. In the meantime, I was able to interview both Little
Pat Connors and Cyrus McGuire while posing as a simple
traveler passing through the community."

Daly moved to pour himself another shot of whiskey while the Sheriff both stretched and tapped his feet. I
yearned for the unconsciousness of sleep myself, something
to blur the memory of the night's painful revelations.

Holmes continued. "The surveillance was successful,
but not quite as effective as I had hoped. The first night I
detected an intruder which subsequent events revealed as
Cyrus McGuire. Unfortunately, Mr. McGuire detected my
presence and made a hurried retreat to the safety of Anaconda's environs before I could catch him." Holmes paused
to shake the burnt wattle from his pipe and returned the
briar to his coat pocket.

"The next day, John and Joe Fitzpatrick came to see me
and reported that Cyrus McGuire had met some 'cowgirl,'
their word, not mine, near the racetrack's grandstand in the
early afternoon. She was described as old, which I interpreted
to mean near thirty, comely with blonde hair and an excellent
rider. She talked with Cyrus for about a quarter hour and, according to the lads, seemed to be scolding Cyrus even though
they couldn't hear the conversation. This meeting puzzled
me deeply because Cyrus is not the most communicative of
individuals and I had a hard time fathoming what he could
be doing talking with an attractive woman."

"Which leads me to ask, Mr. Holmes," interrupted Daly, "now that we're speaking of women, just what is Miss O'Sullivan's role in this whole affair?"

"I'm coming to that, Marcus," retorted Holmes. "Suffice it to say for the moment that Miss O'Sullivan and Cyrus McGuire are brother and sister or, more accurately, he's her half brother. Same mother, different fathers, which accounts for their differing last names."

"And how do you know that?" I asked.

"You told me, Watson, although neither of us knew at the time. Remember the day you met Miss O'Sullivan?"

I nodded in reply. My brief recollection of those hours was vastly more pleasant than what I had just witnessed.

"You mentioned that she came to Montana to be near family," continued Holmes. "Once I began to suspect her of complicity in the matter I had the Sheriff make some discreet inquiries about her family ties, and none were evident. That's when I concluded that the person or persons I was looking for probably had a different last name. Later you mentioned she had a brother."

"And it was Miss O'Sullivan who visited Cyrus at the track?" continued Daly.

"Yes, her hair disguised with a wig and her petticoats replaced by pants, boots and a man's shirt. Save for Dr. Watson, who has had the pleasure of looking directly into her eyes, I doubt that anyone of us here, myself included, would have recognized her as Miss Margaret O'Sullivan."

Holmes' comment cut me to the quick but I remained impassive. It was equal parts exhaustion and curiosity and I wished that Holmes would move the story to conclusion.

Holmes continued. "I was also troubled by the fact

that our surveillance activities at the track were completely unsuccessful. After several days' time, I concluded that someone was watching us and reporting our activities to the malefactors we wished to entrap. Initially, I thought it might be the hotel staff, but quickly reasoned my way out of it. The only person who knew what I was doing was you, Watson, old friend. That's when I dressed up as a preacher and watched you have dinner with Miss O'Sullivan. While you never revealed our plan, your discussion of late nights and little sleep would have been sufficient to instruct her of our activities."

For the second time in under a minute, Holmes had dealt me a blow and I felt myself flush with heat as I realized that it was my own conversations which had stymied the investigation.

"I know that you don't think I pay attention to women, Watson, and you're correct in the sense that I don't pay attention to them in the same way you do." Holmes was about to give my ego yet another blow. I could feel it. "But, when you first reported meeting Miss O'Sullivan, you were vague about her age. I missed it at the time, but on further reflection found that quite interesting because you do have a most discerning eye when it comes to the ladies. When I watched the two of you have dinner, I noticed that she was very artfully made up. So well done was her make-up, in fact, that it would have been the envy of any professional actress. I concluded that Miss O'Sullivan was much older, and more practiced in life than you assumed. It made me even more suspicious."

"But it wasn't until a few nights ago that I learned, or better yet, confirmed Miss O'Sullivan's complicity in the events at the stable when I saw her on East Front Street near the Girton House. I immediately, but erroneously, suspected her of being in league with Billy Farrell, Felix Betancourt's man in Anaconda. Farrell resides in the Girton house, a point Sheriff Fitzpatrick confirmed for me several days ago." Holmes paused for a few seconds to collect his thoughts. Daly had a scowl on his face, the Sheriff yawned again, and Steinbeisser looked agitated, as if his very life depended on Holmes' next few words.

"I found the proprietor on the back step of the building having a nip with one of his tenants and asked the proprietor whether Mr. Farrell had recently enjoyed any female companionship, at which point the tenant replied, 'no, and who, might I ask, is inquiring about me?' So I met Mr. Farrell, a typical Irishman whose charm and loquaciousness increases in direct proportion to the amount of whiskey he has consumed. I took the two of them to the saloon next door and plied my trade while buying them several drinks. In the course of our conversation Farrell told me that if I wanted to talk about horses I needed to go down the street to the Palace Hotel and 'talk to the little guy, Cyrus. He knows more about horses than anyone else in these parts.'"

Holmes continued, "I heeded his counsel, but again talked instead with that building's proprietor who told me that Cyrus had been visited by two women, a blonde who dressed like a man and a most refined lady whose description fitted Miss O'Sullivan most perfectly. The proprietor also commented that the two women appeared to be sisters, sharing a great family resemblance. Sisters indeed. It was Miss O'Sullivan simply altering her appearance with a blonde wig and adopting another persona."

"So you figured out that Miss O'Sullivan and Cyrus were behind the threats . . . ." Holmes never let me finish.

"Two days ago, Watson. That's when I also figured out that I'd never expose the two of them because Miss O'Sullivan had the advantage of counsel regarding the investigation through her blossoming relationship with you. That's why, old boy, I had to unwittingly involve you in a little ruse by telling you that Tammany was to be moved to Sheriff Fitzpatrick's ranch and, more importantly, there would be no night time surveillance at the stables. Mr. Steinbeisser told Little Pat and Cyrus much the same thing. I hoped that information would prompt the confederates to act. The rest is history. We caught them red handed tonight.

"Doing what, Holmes?" I said in exasperation. We'd concluded a manhunt in a stable with the new love of my life showing a most unseemly side, and I still didn't know what for.

"Breeding horses, Watson."

"What?" I retorted in amazement.

"Mr. Steinbeisser, did you not tell Watson here that Mr. Daly's horse breeding program had been a disaster this year?"

"Yes," came Steinbeisser's cautious reply. "And now I know why."

Daly seemed as confused as I was and we both looked to Steinbeisser.

"Pray, please continue," Holmes directed.

"I am sorry, Mr. Daly, truly I am. It was right before my eyes and I didn't see it. Cyrus was putting our mares in with the stallions and then swapping them out for another mare during the night. Our breeding program was no failure, it's just that our stallions were impregnating God knows whose mares."

"Not quite, Mr. Steinbeisser," replied Holmes, at which point the gravity of Steinbeisser's comments registered with Daly.

"Smitham and Betancourt," roared the copper king as he pounded the table in fury. "I've been made to play the cuckold to those two." Daly rose to his feet, his face reddened with hate.

"Sit down, Marcus," said Holmes. "Please sit down. It's far worse than that."

Daly cast his eyes about the room. Holmes nodded toward the chair and Daly shortly sat back down.

"Did any of you recognize that mare which Cyrus planned to mate with Tammany tonight?"

"No," replied Steinbeisser quickly, "and I know every thoroughbred in the northern Rocky Mountains." Daly, the Sheriff, and I likewise concurred.

"Well, I recognized her," answered Holmes. "Her name is Gallant Princess. She's new to Montana, arrived less than two weeks ago from Kentucky where her new owner paid $40,000 to acquire her. The white hourglass blaze on the shank of her left foreleg is quite distinctive."

Daly's eyes met Holmes. "Marcus, I am sorry to have to tell you this, but you've not been victimized by Colonel Smitham or Mr. Betancourt. Miss O'Sullivan and Mr. McGuire were in the employ of Mr. Heinze. I saw that very horse in Heinze's stable a few short days ago."

Suffice it to say the ensuing cacophony could only be described as bedlam. I stayed but a few minutes while Daly raged on, threatening to choke the very life out of his rival from Butte. I headed toward the gate nearest the racetrack expecting to walk the mile or so back to the hotel. There, I found a saddle horse tied to the fence, no doubt the animal which Miss O'Sullivan had used earlier in the evening. I rode it back to the corner of Park and Main and left it free to roam the streets of Anaconda while I tried to extinguish the events of the day in the coma of sleep.

It was nearly 2:00 p.m. before I awoke trapped in a heartsick fog that can only be described as deep melancholy. Holmes was nowhere to be found so I sought the company of my fellow man in a series of taverns starting with the Union Beer Hall down the street from the hotel and ending up at the Northstar Saloon where I made the acquaintance of Fredrick Granger, its proprietor. He was kind enough to see me back to the hotel after the brandy had deadened both the pain in my heart and my legs' capacity to carry me home.

The next morning I arose late and took breakfast, as had become my habit, at Whatley's Café. A copy of the morning's *Anaconda Standard* was on the counter adjacent my stool, its headline screaming "Stables Burn." There were two underlying stories, one from Anaconda and the other from Butte. The first went on to recount the fiery destruction of a horse barn at the Anaconda racetrack. Marcus Daly was quoted at length commenting upon the threats levied against his horses and lamenting the loss of his newly acquired mare, Hourglass, so named because of the unique white blaze on her left foreleg. Hourglass and the stable were both completely destroyed but, fortunately, prompt action by Daly's stable hands prevented further loss of life. Daly urged his fellow thoroughbred owners to be particularly vigilant in protecting their horses until the dastardly villain was caught.

The second story datelined from Butte reported a huge blaze at F. Augustus Heinze's stock farm which resulted in the loss of a large barn containing two stallions, six mares, and four foals.

The Anaconda fire was clearly by Daly's hand, a convenient way of disposing of Heinze's horse, which Cyrus McGuire had brought to Daly's stable. I was sure Daly already had a bill of sale from a reliable friend who would back the copper magnate's version of the truth if ever asked.

The fire in Butte was more troubling. I couldn't see Daly wantonly destroying a small herd of racehorses just to save his pride at being hoodwinked by Heinze. But, copper politics in Montana were rough and tumble by anyone's standards and, perhaps, this was Daly's way of sending Heinze an unmistakably clear message.

My thoughts were interrupted by a light tapping on my shoulder. I turned and found myself gazing into the face of young John Fitzpatrick, the Sheriff's son who first reported the connection between Cyrus McGuire and Miss O'Sullivan.

"Sorry to interrupt your meal, Dr. Watson, but Mr. Holmes asked that I fetch you back to meet with him at the Commercial Hotel."

I thanked the lad, tipped him a nickel, and asked that he return to Holmes with the message that I would be along shortly.

Holmes was in the hotel's small dining room at the rear of the building, sitting at a table next to a window with a sheaf of paper near his left elbow, writing furiously. He welcomed me, offered both coffee and tea, and inquired about my health. I told him that I was extremely distraught by Miss O'Sullivan's complicity in the entire affair but that I intended to go to Daly and ask for her release so that she might build her life anew. Holmes listened patiently for several minutes until I said, "I am sure there are many good reasons why Miss O'Sullivan might be excused her transgressions."

At that point Holmes gave me a steely glare and said, "There might be, Doctor, but I haven't found one yet. Since her arrest two nights ago, the Sheriff and I have both been looking into her background and connection with Heinze."

I was taken aback by the conviction of Holmes' voice and a tone I had only heard him use for the likes of Professor Moriarty, Colonel Sebastian Moran, and other fiends of the worst order.

"Miss O'Sullivan is not an innocent wayfarer in this affair, Watson. I am convinced that she was the mastermind who convinced Heinze of the merit of the plot. I know this troubles you, old friend, but the real Miss O'Sullivan is not the woman you think you know. We've traced her back to New York where she operated a fancy brothel where it appears she first made contact with Heinze. She was also a suspect in the murder of an English industrialist killed while visiting New York. She arrived in Anaconda about a month after the New York murder. I suspect, but obviously cannot prove, that Heinze facilitated her move to Montana and installed her in Anaconda to keep a close eye on Daly. The plan to exploit the stud services of Daly's magnificent stallions came later, simply taking advantage of an opportunity which presented itself, no doubt by Cyrus McGuire's presence in Daly's stable."

I tried to wave Holmes off at this point. I didn't want to hear any more, but he pursued and when we were through, my longing for the grace of her touch and the wistfulness of her smile was completely extinguished. Feebly, I asked, "What's to become of her?"

"A special train car left Anaconda this morning carrying her, Cyrus, and several of the Sheriff's most reliable men, all headed for Seattle. There, Miss O'Sullivan and Mr. McGuire will be placed on a steamer bound for Hong Kong," answered Holmes matter-of-factly. "Daly gave her a choice: prison or deportation. Frankly, I shudder at the prospect of seeing two people of their ilk resident under the Union Jack, but Daly didn't ask my advice."

I nodded slowly, sobered by how close I'd come to making a fool out of myself and a disaster of my life. "And the fire in Butte?"

"I don't know, Watson. I received a telegram this morning from Mr. Heinze asking whether I'd investigate the matter, but I declined. I suspect it was just one of those serendipitous occurrences in life."[16]

"You're probably right, Holmes. You usually are."

---

16 Editor's note: The Butte Police Department investigated the fire and concluded it was caused by arson but no suspects were ever identified nor anyone arrested. The case is officially still open to this day.

The Ghosts of Red Lion

I swear, the crowing of a rooster at the first light of dawn is the most horrific of sounds from the natural kingdom. Who needs to be reminded it's morning? Go away, dumb bird, let me sleep. My thoughts ran riot for a few seconds as I planned revenge on that odious fowl only to be interrupted by the sound of a loud "thrump" from the kitchen below my bedroom. It was the sound of Mrs. Fitzpatrick filling the wood box next to her stove as she started to prepare the breakfast victuals for those of us visiting the Fitzpatrick ranch.[17]

I'd come out with Sheriff Fitzpatrick from Anaconda ten days previously after the conclusion of a sordid adventure I subsequently named *The Tammany Affair*.

---

17   Editor's note: The property which became the Fitzpatrick ranch was first settled in 1872 by Jimmy Isabel, who located several mining claims in the area and built a cabin. Fitzpatrick purchased the place in 1885 and Isabel's cabin was designated the Isabel Territorial Post Office the same year. The State of Montana acquired the property in the 1930s and built a dam across Nevada Creek about a mile north of the ranch buildings, creating the Nevada Creek Reservoir which flooded much of the ranch property. In 2007, ownership of the ranch buildings and Fitzpatrick family home was transferred to Powell County which plans to restore the property and open it as a museum.

The good Sheriff thought I might find some time in the country fresh air invigorating while Holmes looked after another matter for Marcus Daly, President of the Anaconda Copper Mining Company.

The Sheriff and I were accompanied by his three sons, Edward, John and Joseph, who had spent several weeks in Anaconda visiting their father and assisting Holmes as the Montana corps of his Baker Street Irregulars. The five of us had boarded the train in Anaconda. At Durant, a small one-room station about 15 miles east of the smelter city, we abandoned the coach of the Butte, Anaconda and Pacific Railway (B.A.&P.) for a similar accommodation on the Northern Pacific to ride through the Deer Lodge Valley to Garrison Junction. There, we changed trains for the third time and a thirty-minute trip to the community of Avon. Little more than a small cluster of houses, a Catholic church, two saloons, and several shops set in the middle of a broad, treeless valley, the community bore little resemblance to its namesake county in western England.

Mayme Fitzpatrick, the Sheriff's eldest daughter and a spry girl about 14 years of age, met us at the station. We all pitched in to load the buckboard with packages the Sheriff had brought from Anaconda and food stuffs secured at the local mercantile. The ranch was located on Nevada Creek about midway between Avon and another hamlet entitled Helmville. The road was well rutted and it took us through mid-afternoon to reach the ranch.

The ranch house was an imposing, two-story white clapboard structure set against a low hill with a barn, tack shed, and several other outbuildings set to the right. There was also a good-sized chicken coop behind the house, whose leader I'd learn to hate in the morning.

Mrs. Fitzpatrick came down the steps to embrace each of her returning sons. She was a robust woman with dark brown hair and green eyes. I thought I detected just a bit of an English accent in her speech. Holmes would have known for sure.

"Dr. Watson, allow me to present my wife Anna. And this fair lass is my daughter Rose." Pointing past the slender girl beside her mother, the Sheriff went on to identify two younger boys as "Tommy and Gerald."

"Please don't be overwhelmed by the children just yet, Dr. Watson," answered Mrs. Fitzpatrick. "You've still got to meet Tessie and Durnan."

Notwithstanding the torment that rooster put me through each morning, the next several days were among the most idyllic and peaceful of my life. Each morning the sun broke the ridgeline of the pine covered mountains to the east, easing the morning chill as it crossed the southern sky, darting between the white pillows of cloud. The afternoons were warm, but comfortably so, and I only noticed an occasional trickle of sweat as I worked to keep up with the Fitzpatrick lads as they shared their boyhood adventures with me. Joe took me out behind the barn to the tall, yellowed grass and taught me how to catch grasshoppers. They're quick little critters and I repeatedly looked the part of a clumsy fool lunging after them only to come up bare handed. I went fishing with the boys several times on the nether reaches of Nevada, Jefferson and Washington Creeks. I was no stranger to trout fishing given several trips to Scotland, and I held my own in the boys' informal contests to catch the most or largest fish. We caught a species of fish that was unfamiliar to me, the cutthroat, so named because it carried two red slashes on its throat beneath the gills. Its abundance in those Montana streams was truly staggering.

I also tried to earn my keep by assisting with the ranch work. Edward and one of the hired hands had me helping them repair barbed wire fence. Suffice it to say that I had so many nicks and scratches on my hands and arms by the end of the day that I should have been anemic from loss of blood. It was Rose's job to collect eggs from the chicken coop each day and she took me on her rounds one day, all the while regaling me with the happenings of the valley. I hate to sound harsh but I've never met another woman, before or since, who could talk so much and say so little of interest.

As I arose from my bed, I heard Holmes' voice in the hallway outside my door on his way to the dining room, but the voice of his companion was unfamiliar. Holmes had been expected the previous evening but I had gone to bed early. It would do Holmes some good to get away from work for a few days and enjoy the rigor of ranch life as I had. It was good to know that he was safely with us again.

To my surprise, Holmes was not in the dining room. Mrs. Fitzpatrick advised me that he and Mr. O'Flynn had taken their food to the front porch. After loading a large platter with eggs, bacon, fried potatoes and toast, and pouring a large mug of coffee, I bumped the front screen door open with my knee and joined the breakfast party.

Holmes quickly introduced me to Dan O'Flynn. The Irishman was powerfully built and I marked him as a man who had known what it was like to work, and work hard during most of his life. But, given his girth I sensed that he had enjoyed financial success more recently and had substituted a more sedentary life as an overseer. O'Flynn was tall for one of Celtic descent, an inch or two above six feet with a thick, gray moustache and gray hair circling the sides of his head while his hairline advanced back from his forehead to mid-scalp. He wore spectacles which were too small for a man of his size, giving him the look not quite of a scholar, but of a man who was much smarter than he might be judged from the cut of his clothes. O'Flynn was dressed in a worn pair of Levis, a dark green work shirt which was stretched tight in the buttonholes, and heavy work boots with the stain of red mud circumscribed into the leather.

Who would Holmes judge O'Flynn to be upon meeting him for the first time, I asked myself. A life of hard work and dirty boots. It's no contest—a miner, probably a mine owner by now.

"Watson," said Holmes, "Mr. O'Flynn has a problem with ghosts."

"Ghosts," I heard myself mutter in involuntary reply.

O'Flynn nodded in agreement and I found myself thinking, "These Irishmen, you can give them education, fame and fortune, and they still think like peasant farmers in the Mead." Ghosts, oh my God. Instead, I replied with just a touch of condescension, "Wouldn't that be more a matter for the parish priest, rather than a consulting detective?"

"Aye, Dr. Watson, excepting these ghosts are stealing my gold," answered O'Flynn fiercely.

"Mr. O'Flynn owns the Red Lion Mine about 25 miles west of Anaconda," Holmes explained. "He came in search of Sheriff Fitzpatrick late last night."

I flicked a glance toward O'Flynn and gave myself a mental

pat on the back for deducing O'Flynn's occupation before turning back to Holmes to hear the rest of his explanation.

"The Sheriff left early this morning to look into the mysterious death of a logger in one of the camps east of here and asked that I help out Mr. O'Flynn, which I am happy to do if I can count upon your able assistance."

I felt myself pursing my lips and raising my eyebrows in astonishment. Holmes was not given to freely passing out compliments and for the second time in recent weeks he was treating me as a full partner in the investigation. I was flattered. As I dug into the hearty breakfast Mrs. Fitzpatrick had prepared for me, I uttered, "Capital," but with little real enthusiasm. I'd greatly enjoyed my little respite from the detective business on the Fitzpatrick ranch and reasoned that Holmes also could do with some well-needed rest. Nevertheless, Holmes is never more content than when he is pitting wits with some evil malefactor and I could tell by the intonation of his voice that he was intrigued by O'Flynn's travail.

"At the risk of repeating yourself, Mr. O'Flynn, perhaps you could explain the nature of your problem."

"Thank you, Doctor," answered O'Flynn. "I've given Mr. Holmes the whole story. I trust he'll not be wearied by my repetition."

"It began about two months ago. The men working night shift in the mill noticed an orange light coming across the trestle which the cars cross to drop their loads in the stock bins. My night foreman went out to investigate, said he saw a tall figure, maybe eight feet high, with an orange ghostlike body and a grotesque face. It had a garlic smell to it, he said, as it advanced toward him. He didn't stay around to investigate. All the men abandoned their posts and beat it back to the bunkhouse. They rousted a few of their mates and decided to investigate but when they came back outside, the light near the mill building was gone but there were three others on the hillside by the ore tramway. They stayed there for a few minutes while the men watched, then moved up the hill and disappeared."

"How often has this happened?" asked Holmes.

"Six times, Mr. Holmes, and never once when I've been at the mine."

"Your ghosts certainly seem to know your schedule quite well," I observed.

"Aye," responded O'Flynn, "and twice I even tried to trick him into thinking I was leaving and then sneaked back to wait for him to appear."

"What about the ghosts stealing your gold?"

"We scrape the amalgamation plates once a day at the start of the day shift, retort the mercury, and recover the gold that's left behind. On each of the days after ghostly visits we've been short about 100 ounces of gold."

"So about 600 ounces thus far," observed Holmes.

"More or less, about $12,000 worth," replied O'Flynn with anger in his voice.

While Holmes and O'Flynn continued to talk, I tried to visualize the Red Lion Mine as O'Flynn had described it. The mine portal was located near the ridge of a steep hill. Ore removed from the mine was dumped into a series of small buckets connected to an aerial tramway which ferried the rock downslope to the mill site. At the bottom, the tramway buckets were emptied into an ore bin which fed a chute below where ore cars were loaded and pushed across a trestle to another ore bin which led to the stamp mills below.

Stamp mills are constructed in batteries of five stamps, each consisting of a long iron shaft with a heavy hammerhead on the end. A steam engine powers a rotating cam shaft which first lifts and then drops each of the stamps in turn. The ore to be crushed is fed beneath the stamp from the back. The pulverized ore falls off the front of the stamp onto an inclined copper plate covered with mercury. The small particles of gold found in the ore amalgamate with the mercury while the waste rock slides off into a tail race launder and is disposed of in a pool downstream of the mill.

Whenever necessary the mercury, now containing the gold, is scraped off the copper plate and placed in a retort where it is heated. The mercury boils off in a fume and is condensed back into liquid form in a cooling chamber. The sludge left behind after mercury removal is then tossed into a furnace and melted into gold bullion. From the sounds of it, O'Flynn was mining a rich vein with the gold running close to an ounce per ton.

After breakfast O'Flynn saddled up his horse and started back to his mine. Holmes and I readied our belongings to do likewise after promising O'Flynn that we would meet him in three days time.[18]

Three days later Holmes and I were safely ensconced in the passenger coach attached to a short freight train hauling empty ore cars and supplies to the mining camp of Southern Cross west of Anaconda. Our destination, Red Lion, was a further five miles by rough wagon track.

---

18   Editor's note: In the original text Watson noted that once Holmes accepts a case, his customary style is to get started on it immediately. However, Holmes had previously arranged to meet Marcus Daly in Butte on a matter he never divulged to me.

The train, locally known as the Sundown Limited, took us through a most enchanting landscape. To the south were the jagged, snow-capped spires of the Anaconda Range which gave way to the pine forests that rolled across the intersecting ridge lines like a verdant green wave. At Southern Cross we disembarked at a one-room train station at the foot of the mine's ore chutes. O'Flynn was there to meet us and escorted us to the nearby boarding house where we would dine and spend the night.

Southern Cross was no mere mining camp of thrown together log cabins and tents. The buildings were large, several two stories and uniformly covered with a bluish tinged, corrugated tin on both the walls and roof. The boarding house was a most imposing structure, more of a hotel really, with a two-story verandah overlooking a grassy meadow.

"That's Georgetown Flat, Dr. Watson," said O'Flynn as he pointed west toward the meadow. "The creek coming in from the right is the North Fork. It starts up in the mountains above Red Lion. The stream on the left doesn't really have a name. It starts in a spring over by Stewart's mill, over yonder."

I shudder to use hyperbole, but the view from the verandah at Southern Cross was one of the more breathtaking I've ever encountered, certainly comparable to the landscapes of the Alps, and vastly more colorful than the Scottish Highlands.

Holmes, however, would have none of it. He was back on a case and his energy was focused on capturing O'Flynn's gold-stealing ghosts. Holmes' mood swings were such a mystery. There were times when he was so melancholy that you could hardly get him to move from the ottoman in our rooms on Baker Street. And then, literally within minutes, some thought would catch his fancy and he'd be a bundle of energy, not sleeping for days while he pursued his interest. I frequently wondered if medical science might find a way of leveling out Holmes' moods. "Watson! Mr. O'Flynn doesn't have all day."

With Holmes' call I retreated to our rooms for a planning session. In the end, it was decided that I would go to Red Lion in the morning with O'Flynn, posing as an English investor. Holmes, in turn, would follow along on saddle horse separately, so he could privately observe the landscape around the mine for any clues it might offer regarding the origin of O'Flynn's ghosts. We'd meet for supper at O'Flynn's cabin.

By ten o'clock the next morning, I found myself standing before O'Flynn's cabin aside the road, looking out at a small complex of buildings that made up the Red Lion Mine. The mill building was due north of his home about 100 yards distant. Behind it one could see an aerial tramway consisting of a series of ore buckets hanging from a wire rope at regular intervals. The tramway ferried the ore downhill from the mine portal near the ridge and sent the empty receptacles back to be refilled in a slow steady motion.

A blacksmith's shop, assay office, and the miners' bunkhouse were immediately upslope of the mill building. Several other small cabins, most likely occupied by the miners and their families, were to be seen in the forest above and below O'Flynn's home.

After disembarking from the wagon which O'Flynn had used to transport me from Southern Cross I was immediately introduced to his wife Mary. She was a handsome

RED LION MINE

Situated near the crest of Cable Ridge at nearly 8,000 feet elevation, the mine looks down on the North Fork of Flint Creek approximately 25 miles west of Anaconda, Montana.

RED LION MILL

The stamp mill as it appeared in 1910, taken several years after Holmes and Watson visited the property.

woman in the Irish way, medium height, certainly no more than five feet three inches, with dark brown hair and green eyes, and very young. I guessed her to be scarcely past girlhood and O'Flynn, her husband, at least 25 years her senior. When I heard her name was Mary, I had to smile. What Irish woman of Catholic descent isn't named Mary, Ann or a derivative thereof?

"Mary," I heard O'Flynn offer, "this is John . . . ." Then O'Flynn's face went blank. Last night we discussed using an alias but never agreed what it would be. Finally, "Pollard. Excuse me. Mr. Pollard. I hope you'll take no offense at my forgetfulness."

"None, sir," I responded quietly.

"Mary, Mr. Pollard is with the firm of Pollard, Baker and Hines of Manchester. Investors they are, in mines of all types."

"I am so pleased to meet you, Mr. Pollard," answered O'Flynn's wife in a brogue so impenetrable, I guessed she couldn't have been long from the Emerald Isle.

We made pleasant small talk for a few minutes and then O'Flynn hustled me off toward the mill building. I last saw his missus with two pails in her hands headed off to the west from where I'd glimpsed the site of a small stream.

"I take it there's no water in the camp, Mr. O'Flynn?"

"Aye, Dr. Watson, I mean Mr. Pollard. I've got a crew working to bring a ditch from the creek but this portion of the mountainside is all granite."

"Hard digging," I said forcefully as if to emphasize my understanding of his work.

"Not especially," replied O'Flynn. "The rock is well fractured. That helps with the digging but it won't hold water.

It all drains down through the fissures so I have to haul in clay from down in the valley to line the inside of the ditch. It takes forever and is expensive too."

"What do you do in the winter?" I asked quietly, somewhat humbled by O'Flynn's explanation.

"It's tough. We get over six feet of snow and the stream freezes up so we mostly melt the snow. It takes a lot of snow to make a gallon of water, believe me. We get enough to drink but wash water, especially water to wash clothes, is hard to come by."

"You've reminded me of my time in Afghanistan, Mr. O'Flynn, particularly the prison in Kabul."

"Aye, probably a good comparison. I am, myself, loath to go into the men's bunkhouse after Christmas. The stench is overpowering."

The inside of a stamp mill is also an overpowering experience. To begin with, it's dusty. As each stamp hammers down on the rock underneath, a small cloud of dust is ejected and then hangs suspended in the air of the room, gradually settling out in a thin patina of mineral over every available surface. I couldn't help but wonder how much of the reddish, mineral-bearing cloud floating before my eyes stayed in the lungs and gullet of O'Flynn's mill hands.

"I've got two batteries, each with five stamps," explained O'Flynn. To the side of the stamp was a large flywheel hooked to a long camshaft extending through the stamp batteries. As the flywheel rotated, pulled by a wide belt that reached back to the engine room, the camshaft also rotated, lifting and then dropping the pedestal-like stamps. The stamps were made of cast iron and each must have weighed at least a ton.

The ore to be crushed was fed under the stamps from a hopper behind the mill. The crushed rock, now reduced to flour-like consistency, spills onto the inclined table in front of the stamp. I was quite familiar with stamp mills given previous trips to South Africa, California, and Montana as well but O'Flynn didn't know that and he gave me a brief introduction in gold metallurgy.

O'Flynn was practically shouting to make himself heard. Another overpowering aspect of a stamp mill is the noise. The word deafening hardly does it justice. I noticed the mill hands with small pieces of cloth stuffed into their ears. I couldn't imagine what it would be like to work in a big mill where a hundred or more stamps might be employed.

O'Flynn quickly shuffled me from the mill up to the mine portal for a tour underground. I've been in my share of mines over the course of my life and didn't see anything exceptional at Red Lion except the rock. It was the first gold ore I've ever seen that was red or, better yet maroon in color.

"The color is caused by the iron," answered O'Flynn earnestly. "The ore runs 30 to 45 percent iron but that isn't rich enough for iron mining. So we get the gold that's mixed in and forget the rest."

Over the next three hours, O'Flynn showed me every aspect of his property and systematically introduced me to his workers and a couple of the wives as well, when we wandered by their cabins. O'Flynn is genial by nature but I was still surprised by the warmth of the bond between him and his employees.

Following a light luncheon with his wife Mary, and a discussion of both the geology and finances of the mine,

O'Flynn allowed me the use of the table that served as his office so that I might catch up on my correspondence. His wife was busy about me. Later in the afternoon she readied a bundle of laundry while she hummed a tune which I recognized as an Irish folk song, but whose name I couldn't recall. She excused herself saying she needed to wash some clothes, and flashed me a bright smile, her first of the day.

Holmes failed to arrive at O'Flynn's house at the appointed time and I found myself becoming increasingly apprehensive as dinner wore into the early evening. I excused myself to exercise my legs and about a quarter mile below the mine site encountered Holmes sitting on a large boulder next to the road, pipe in hand, as if he expected me to come by.

"Capital, Watson. I suspected you'd stretch your legs after dinner."

"Indeed, Holmes, I am regular of habit, perhaps too regular. How did you know I would walk this way instead of toward another point of the compass?"

"In all other direction, the grade is much steeper and you, dear friend, are a man of some dimension who, I trust, has enjoyed a most filling repast. You want to stroll, Watson, not climb. Here I am to greet you."

"Confound you, Holmes. I hate it when you rationalize my behavior with your smug deductions."

Holmes laughed and, after taking a few seconds to recognize that I was being peevish, I laughed along with him. Holmes was right. Our comfortable lifestyle on Baker Street had reflected itself in my increasing girth. While still modestly fit, I was more attuned to hiking the flat streets of London rather than climbing the mountains of western Montana.

"I trust that you've examined Red Lion in some detail by now, Holmes."

"Most interesting country, Watson. Actually, I was pleasantly detained along the way by Mr. Einar Hansen. His mill is down the road."

"Yes, O'Flynn pointed it out to me when we came up this morning," I replied, somewhat surprised that Holmes had dilly-dallied. He's usually most anxious to get to the crime scene.

"A most interesting gentleman, Mr. Hansen. He saw me traveling up the road, shouted at me to join him for coffee, and afterward gave me a tour of his facility. He's diverted the stream above the mill site and is using a water wheel to power a little, homemade battery with two stamps. It's most ingenious, Watson. Hansen has no fuel cost and no need of an engineer or fireman to operate a boiler. He told me that he mines and mills his ore by himself with just a little help from two sons, who work full-time at O'Flynn's mine."

"What does Hansen have to do with Mr. O'Flynn's problem?" I asked sardonically.

"Nothing, Watson, nothing at all. It was just one of those interesting diversions on the road of life. Mycroft would have been most impressed by his industriousness."

"What did you learn at Red Lion?"

"I've got an understanding of its layout and I made a map of its significant features. On the hillside where the ghostly apparitions were seen, there was some evidence of foot traffic."

"But that means nothing," I interjected. "The miners and mill hands walk all over the site."

"My conclusions as well, Watson, but so far it's the only

thing I've witnessed which allows me to speculate that O'Flynn's ghosts have a distinctly human morphology."

A distinctly human morphology? What is there about being in the American wilderness that prompts an English gentleman to enhance the caliber of his vocabulary? I found myself doing the same thing in Anaconda, particularly in the company of working men.

"Oh, one other thing, Watson. There is a small cabin below the camp perched alongside the stream. I observed three different women enter it earlier this afternoon."

"I suspect that's the camp laundry, Holmes. O'Flynn mentioned it to me as he took me around. He said the women use it as a kind of clubhouse, a place to talk about girl things while they do the clothes."

"Most interesting," responded Holmes as he exhaled a large cloud of smoke and then quietly reflected on my comment for a few seconds. "I guess I had never thought about it, Watson, but women probably need a place where they can meet with their own from time to time."

There were times when Holmes' perspective was truly amazing. He was the world's greatest detective, and yet sometimes his lack of knowledge about the routine aspects of life was truly unfathomable. But, I shouldn't be too hard on my friend. He'd never known domesticity and family the way most men do.

"So what is your plan, Holmes?" I asked to change the subject.

"I'll return with you to the camp and confer with O'Flynn. His mysterious visitor only visits when he's off site. So, we'll publicly plan to get him away from the mine for a day or two and see if the ghosts return."

"So you think someone in the camp aware of O'Flynn's movements is behind the appearances of the nocturnal visitor?"

"Yes, and by the way, are O'Flynn's miners and mill hands Irishmen?"

"I've met several of his men and yes, most of them seem to have Gaelic roots which were only recently transferred to the United States. Why do you ask?"

"The Irish peasantry is a superstitious lot who both believe in and are terrified by ghosts. Recall the Dullahan and Banshee.[19] Someone is using a ghostly apparition to frighten the workmen and then swoop into O'Flynn's mill and steal his gold after the mill hands have run for safety."

"Simple, and yet ingenious, Holmes. Once the ghosts appear the mill hands would be reluctant to go back to the mill until daybreak, which would give the thief more than enough time to collect the gold and slip away into the night."

"That's how I see it, Watson," replied Holmes as he drew on his pipe for a last time before knocking the burnt wattle onto a rock to snuff out the remaining fire with his feet. A half hour later we were in conversation with O'Flynn and his wife seated around a low campfire burning in a fire pit in front of their home. Holmes rarely betrays his emotion and it was just a little flicker of his eyes, but I swear he recognized Mrs. O'Flynn when I introduced him to her as my investment partner. Over coffee, Holmes, who now answered to the alias of Mr. Baker, planned a meeting at Southern Cross between O'Flynn and our third fictional partner, Mr.

---

19   Editor's note: The Dullahan is reported to be a headless ghost that rides a black steed through the Irish countryside at night. The Banshee is a female spirit who wails to mark impending death.

Hines. Holmes explained that Hines suffered from severe arthritis and could not make the rough trip to Red Lion from the railhead.

The next day O'Flynn and Holmes toured the mine site with O'Flynn explaining to his foreman that he would be gone for the next several days. I accompanied them during the visit to the mill building but then retired to a comfortable chair shaded by an immense fir tree near O'Flynn's cabin to catch up on my correspondence. Holmes took a long time in the mill. O'Flynn was getting impatient with my associate, but I understood that he was carefully noting the location of all the doorways as well as looking for every conceivable place where the alleged ghosts might hide.

After a hearty lunch prepared by Mrs. O'Flynn, we saddled our horses and departed for Southern Cross. Holmes and I were going to ride down the wagon road for a short distance, turn off and secretly make our way back to Red Lion to lay in wait for the ghosts. It was a beautiful day for a ride. The radiance of the sun was tempered by a light breeze blowing off the snow-capped mountain peaks to the south. A mosaic of purple, yellow and white wildflowers carpeted the forest floor adjacent the road and a plethora of songbirds seemed to follow our course playing their melodies.

O'Flynn surprised me by commenting on the beauty of our surroundings. I had read him for a miner through and through, not expecting him to take recognition of anything but rock and the metal it yields. I've always found miners to be a curious paradox. As a class they are generally unschooled, hard men who nevertheless are among the most ingenuous souls. Each day they win their living in an unpitying, ever-changing environment, matching their wits against Mother

Earth. Their success or failure is measured in a few cents, more or less, received for each ton of ore mined.

We rode down the wagon track toward Southern Cross, Holmes and O'Flynn engaged in conversation while I lagged behind lost in thought. As we approached Hansen's mill site, the proprietor could be seen cutting wood outside his cabin. He had already accumulated several cords preparing for the long winter ahead that would strike within six weeks. Hansen hailed us as we approached and we exchanged pleasantries for a few moments. He then stepped through the gate and offered me his hand in introduction.

"We've not met, sir. I am Einar Hansen and trust that you're Mr. Holmes' partner."

"Indeed," I replied somewhat disjointedly. "John Pollard. We've come to look into investing in Mr. O'Flynn's mine."

The conversation continued for a few minutes longer with Holmes leaving most of the rhetoric to O'Flynn and myself. On his way to Red Lion, Holmes had mistakenly revealed his correct name to Hansen. We then introduced him around Red Lion as Mr. Baker. The two locations were about two miles apart. I hoped it was sufficient to prevent our little ruse from being discovered but was not optimistic. We were strangers in the area and people were naturally curious about who we were and what we were up to. I suspected we'd be discovered by daybreak. Holmes had a sardonic look on his face and I am sure he had independently reached the same conclusion.

About a quarter mile past Hansen's mill there was a large meadow to the right side of the road. Holmes and I turned off, crossed the stream, and found the facsimile of a trail which O'Flynn said would lead us back to Red Lion hidden from view. An hour later we had worked our way past Red Lion, hobbled our horses, and sat down to wait for darkness and our return to the mining camp.

By my watch it was 9:30 p.m. when Holmes quietly opened the door to the assay office using the key which O'Flynn had given him. We were upslope of the mill building and windows on three sides of the structure allowed us to watch the front side of the bunkhouse, the mill, and the hillside above the mill where the ghostly apparitions were first reported. The sun had set about an hour earlier but it was a clear night and we could see outside quite readily. Holmes opened a cabinet door and recovered some bread, a slab of cheese, and some dried meat which O'Flynn had secreted earlier in the day. We sat down to a simple meal and the hope that the ghosts of Red Lion would soon appear.

The prospect of a long night on watch did nothing for my spirits. Holmes and I had done that repeatedly during the case which I reported as *The Tammany Affair* and I was already getting tired by anticipation. About 11:00 p.m. Holmes suggested that I take a nap. He'd rouse me if I were needed. I was happy to accept his suggestion and stretched out on a long bench beneath a window. It was cool at that elevation high in the mountains but not so cold I couldn't nod off. Holmes would likely ingest some cocaine to keep himself alert throughout the night. He knows that I strongly disapprove of the drug so it's become a matter of convention between us that he uses it privately. I don't ask and he doesn't tell.

The next thing I felt was Holmes shaking my arm and saying, "Wake up, Watson. It's time to go."

My left hip ached from sleeping on the hard bench and

consciousness came slowly, but I managed to ask, "What are we doing?"

"Going back to Southern Cross. The mysterious visitors never appeared. It is coming up on 5:00 a.m. my friend, we need to be out of here before the camp awakens."

We got back to our horses in short order, ate some more of the food given to us the previous night, which Holmes had thought to bring along, and refreshed ourselves in the clear, cold water cascading down the North Fork. Afterward, Holmes begged my indulgence for a few minutes while he took a short nap. That accomplished we carefully made our way down the trail to the meadow below Hansen's mill to rejoin the wagon road.

As we entered the meadow, we encountered Hansen removing a rabbit from a snare. When we drew abreast he offered a surprising greeting. "Good morning Mr. Holmes, Dr. Watson. Beautiful day to be about." Holmes shot me a quick glance. I was shocked. "You seem surprised I know your real names, gentlemen."

"Well, yes," admitted Holmes quietly.

"You didn't register with me, Mr. Holmes," continued Hansen with a broad smile of self-satisfaction. "I know you because of the good doctor. I saw him having a beer with Sheriff Fitzpatrick in the Union Bar in Anaconda a few weeks ago. The barkeep told me the stranger drinking with the Sheriff was a detective named Watson working for Marcus Daly."

Neither Holmes nor I immediately responded to Hansen's admission so, after a brief pause Hansen went on to explain, "I don't read too well but I remember good, real good, and I never forget a face. So I see you two with my neighbor Danny and figure you're here to help him catch his ghosts."

At that point Hansen started to laugh and muttered, "Have to catch some ghosts" several times before regaining his composure.

Holmes then asked, "You find our mission amusing?"

"Aye, I do. Two mortals aren't going to repudiate the will of God."

I shot Holmes a confused glance and he shrugged in reply. Hansen read our befuddlement and continued, "Danny boy must not have told you why he's got hisself a ghost, now did he?"

"No," answered Holmes quickly.

"You must ask him when you see him again, but I'll give the short version. My friend Danny got the Red Lion from John Curtis. Old John staked the claim and brought Danny in as his foreman."

Hansen paused briefly to bite off a large chew of tobacco from a plug he kept in his shirt pocket, loosened it up in his mouth, spat, and then resumed his story. However, the tone of equanimity in Hansen's voice when he first greeted us became bitter as he described O'Flynn.

"Curtis was running short of money so he went to Helena and borrowed heavily from Mr. T.C. Power. He knew he'd be fine because the ore was plentiful and high grade. He didn't count on Danny and his wiles. O'Flynn's up there running the mine and Curtis the mill, but Danny's highgrading and only sending the mill middling ore good enough to pay the miners and their daily operating expenses, but not quite good enough to pay off the debt owed Mr. Power."

Hansen spat again and quietly chewed his tobacco a few minutes to let the weight of his words sink in. Holmes scratched his cheek, more of a nervous tic rather than an itch, and I stepped down from my horse to stretch my legs.

When we were again fully attentive, Hansen explained. "Old John defaulted on his note to Mr. Power. Power took the mine and put Danny in charge, but Power wasn't doing any better than Curtis. So Danny makes a deal to pay Power 50 cents on the dollar for the mine and wouldn't you know, the place begins to pay. Within a year O'Flynn pays off Power and has the place lock, stock and barrel. Now the good lord has sent one of his souls from the nether world to take from O'Flynn, the same way he took from John Curtis and T.C. Power." Hansen spoke with such conviction that were I not an educated man, I am sure to have been convinced.

"A most interesting and cautionary tale, Mr. Hansen," answered Holmes nonchalantly. I knew he was not impressed. "Perhaps I should reassess my relationship with Mr. O'Flynn."

Hansen nodded and cracked a brief smile. "Indeed."

Sensing where Holmes was taking the conversation, I turned to him and added, "Your skills are purely temporal in nature my friend, certainly no match for the divine."

"Mr. Hansen. This has been a most insightful visit. Thank you and good day, sir," answered Holmes. And with that we were back on the track to Southern Cross.

I could tell that Holmes had, indeed, received some insight into the case during our conversation with Hansen, but he refused to divulge his thoughts.

At Southern Cross we met briefly with O'Flynn where Holmes told him that we were withdrawing ourselves from the case. Our presence at Red Lion had caused suspicion and Holmes speculated that the thieving ghosts were unlikely to appear if we were suspected of being anywhere near the property. Holmes told O'Flynn that he would advise Sheriff Fitzpatrick of his thoughts and, perhaps, he could ferret out the intruder we had failed to discover.

Holmes' actions were most irregular and disappointing. This was the man who had exposed the most diabolical schemes of Col. Sebastian Moran and Professor Moriarty, now walking away from a case which appeared to me trifling in comparison. I said nothing to Holmes but excused myself so that I could attend the privy. Temporarily lost to my thoughts in that most private of activities, it suddenly hit me. Holmes has solved the case. It's too mundane to hold his interest and he's turning the matter over to the Sheriff for final disposition. Very politic of Holmes, and justice would be served.

After fastening my suspenders, both body and mind relieved, I returned to the boarding house verandah. Holmes explained that O'Flynn had returned to his mine. The blast of a railroad whistle summoned us to the Southern Cross depot for the return trip to Anaconda. This was a freight train with a cargo of six loaded ore cars. We were to make the passage in the company of the train crew in the caboose.

Two days later the *Anaconda Standard* carried a story regarding our imminent departure. Marcus Daly, Sheriff Fitzpatrick, William Thornton, and several other of Anaconda's notables were at the station the next morning to see us off. I chatted amiably with our well wishers. In contrast, Holmes was preoccupied. He repeatedly crisscrossed the platform and seemed to stare at our fellow passengers. I was about to reprove him for his manners when his mood changed suddenly and he graciously thanked Daly for the opportunity to assist the copper baron with his case. Holmes is not a man given to emotion but I could tell that he, like I, had developed a special fondness for the Sheriff and his brood of children. It was difficult to say goodbye.

In Butte we again changed trains, departing the B.A.&P. for the Northern Pacific. Holmes purchased several newspapers at the station's newsstand and, after settling into the comfort of our seats, lost ourselves in the pages of the *Butte Miner* and *Montana Standard*, our friend Daly's paper.

It was a good half hour later when I looked out the window and saw that we were crossing the Deer Lodge Valley going west rather than east toward England and Baker Street.

"Holmes, if I might discreetly enquire, why are we traveling toward the Pacific coast, and not our lodgings on Baker Street?"

"No particular reason, Watson, except a lot of wanderlust. We've come this far. Why not spend some time exploring more of the American West?"

"Indeed, why not?" I muttered in complete surprise. It was even more astounding that Holmes had not consulted with me. I, for one, was ready to return to the British Isles.

"I've always had a hankering to see California. It sounds like a veritable paradise," answered Holmes more to himself than to me.

"Holmes, if your vocabulary now includes the word 'hankering,' you've been in the American bush for too long. We need to get you back to London with all possible dispatch."

"You may have a point there, Watson," said Holmes as he picked up yet another newspaper, the *Butte Reveille*, and buried his head behind the newsprint.

It was nearing 7:00 p.m. when we pulled into the metropolis of Spokane, Washington. I use the term metropolis advisedly. It was a city of about 30,000 or half the size of Butte. As the train pulled into the depot Holmes removed his suit coat, folded it into a tidy square and said, "I hate to be such a bore, but now that the train has stopped rocking to and fro, Watson, I am going to try and catch a little nap. We'll be all night to Seattle." With that he stretched out and propped his folded coat between his head and the side of the train.

I was puzzled by Holmes' actions but said nothing. Holmes can sleep anywhere. I've never known him to need a train car stationary so that he could rest. Seconds later, however, a young gentleman in the seat before us shot Holmes a quick glance, gathered his things, and departed. I turned to see Holmes open one eye to follow the man's progress up the aisle and then turn his head ever so subtly to observe him cross the platform and enter the station.

"Well, my little ruse appears to have taken root. Be quick about it, Watson. We need to get off as well."

Holmes' rapid action flustered me some but I quickly grabbed my travel valise and followed him toward the exit. "What about our luggage in the baggage car?"

"Not to worry, dear friend. Daly's man took care of them back in Anaconda."

Once again, Holmes had a plan to which I was not privy. No matter, he'd soon explain. Near the door of the terminal, Holmes paused and looked through the window, care-

SHERLOCK HOLMES: THE MONTANA CHRONICLES

ful to scan the room for the gentleman we were following. It turned out we were not following anyone. Instead, I soon found myself in a buggy being driven to the Columbia Hotel on Main Street in the heart of the city. After checking in and ordering some food to be delivered to our rooms, Holmes steered me to the bar and bought us each a snifter of brandy. It was smooth to the taste, and I felt myself flush around the eyes as its warmth drained into my stomach.

"Would you mind telling me what we're really doing? Clearly we're not going to California notwithstanding your hankering to do so."

"Perhaps on another trip, my friend, but right now we're still working on the little matter of Mr. O'Flynn's ghosts."

"I thought you turned that matter over to the Sheriff."

"Publicly, yes. But we're no less involved than we were when we spent the night in the assay laboratory at Red Lion."

"Fine, but then what are we doing in a hotel in Spokane, Washington?" I had been perplexed by Holmes' travel plans from the start and the mystery had only deepened.

"We've accomplished two things today, Watson. First, we appear to have successfully convinced the ghosts who have been robbing Mr. O'Flynn that we have left Montana and reopened the way for them to take advantage of O'Flynn once more. Secondly, we have evaded the individual sent to follow us to insure that we did, in fact, leave Montana."

"You mean the gentleman sitting near us on the train?" I asked incredulously.

"Precisely, old boy. He boarded in Anaconda as we did and seemed most interested in eavesdropping on our conversation. Let me add as well that whoever he is, he bears a striking resemblance to one of the miners working at O'Flynn's operation, a brother most likely."

"And we've slipped his tail," I offered somewhat questioningly.

"It might be more accurate to think he's stopped the reconnaissance convinced that we're on our way to the west coast."

"What's our next move?" I asked more confidently.

"We'll wait a few days, Watson. Go back to Montana and surreptitiously return to Red Lion."

"I am sensing that you think the thief is one of O'Flynn's own men."

"It's the most obvious conclusion, Doctor. The ghosts only appear when O'Flynn leaves the property. There's no telegraph or telephone available in the camp so I have no choice but to deduce that someone at Red Lion is aware of O'Flynn's schedule and mobilizes the ghosts whenever O'Flynn leaves home."

"To frighten the workers into abandoning their posts," I commented in reply, "and gain access to the gold in the mill building."

"A most excellent conclusion, Doctor," said Holmes as he reached into his coat pocket to retrieve his pipe.

"These ghosts don't want to be confronted by O'Flynn," I continued. "The man is fearless, ghost or no ghost."

"I completely concur," answered my detective friend as he put a match to the bowl of his pipe and let loose a great cloud of smoke, so agreeably aromatic.

The few days in Spokane turned out to be a most pleasant respite notwithstanding the disagreeable weather. That first morning we breakfasted with the hotel's proprietor who explained it had been an exceptionally dry summer with numerous dust storms. Around three-thirty in the afternoon, the sky turned an angry black and we were treated to as violent a thunderstorm as I've seen anywhere. The lightning danced through the sky, a veritable electric spider web and, my God did it ever rain, a torrent more akin to a waterfall than a shower. And, twenty minutes later the sun was shining again. The hotel bell captain who watched the storm with me from the hotel lobby called it a "gully washer" and repeatedly expressed his delight at seeing "some rain to knock down the dust." I found that colloquialism "gully washer" most descriptive.

The local informed me that Spokane was a trade center serving both the Coeur d'Alene mining district in northern Idaho approximately 50 miles to the east and the farming country south of the city known as the Palouse. It was certainly a vibrant, though small community. Spokane sits astride a river by the same name whose banks harbored a hydroelectric generating plant, a large flour mill, sawmill, foundry, machine shop, farm implement dealers, and numerous warehouses. The main lines of the Great Northern and Northern Pacific railroads brace the downtown commercial area whose streets hold a variety of mercantiles and smaller shops.

I discovered a most excellent stationer's shop the second day in town and purchased another of Mr. Twain's delightful stories and an English translation of Victor Hugo's well regarded tale, *Les Miserables*. It was a book I'd been wanting to read but never seemed to find the time since I seemingly was always chronicling Holmes' exploits.

On our return to Montana, we exited the train at the little hamlet of Drummond. It was home to a railroad section crew and the families of several saloonkeepers who, judging from the number of taverns in town, did a brisk business catering to the thirst of the cowhands working on the surrounding ranches.

O'Flynn met us at the station and acted as our escort back to Red Lion. The plan was to approach the mine from the north bypassing Anaconda and Southern Cross so that no one might realize we had returned.

It was a difficult, hard ride climbing the mountain single file on a combination of rough roads and steep trails. After several hours we broke out onto a large park covered with wildflowers at the very crest of the mountain.

"Welcome to Fred Burr's pass, gentlemen," remarked O'Flynn. "This little creek is the headwaters of the North Fork. Red Lion is down the road about a mile and a half." We moved to a small alcove in the trees screened from the rough road by a thick stand of fir, in the off chance someone might happen along. O'Flynn then gave Holmes instructions on how to get to Red Lion, dropped a bag of groceries for our dinner, and departed for Georgetown Flats to meet Sheriff Fitzpatrick, who was secretly making his way to Red Lion to help with Holmes' plan. I took a nap anticipating a long night's vigil.

In contrast, Holmes was full of anticipation, pacing around our temporary camp site and repeatedly checking his pocket watch against the angle of the sun. He woke me as the sun reached the ridgeline, a bright golden orb whose rays created a mosaic of red shading to purple in the clouds hanging motionless in the sky. We were soon back at our sentry post in the assay laboratory.

Fortunately, the wait was brief. It began with a piercing screech that was repeated several times, followed by three orange lights slowly climbing above the trees adjacent the tramway. A much larger light moved slowly across the ground toward the boiler room of the mill building as the screeching began anew.

The engineer saw it coming and burst out the side door of the building running toward the bunkhouse and raising the alarm. The other mill hands followed suit, exiting the freight door in the front of the building, their bodies briefly illuminated in the halo of light outlining their escape portal.

"Now, Watson!" yelled Holmes.

I had been previously instructed to take my trusty Webley revolver, enter the mill building, search it thoroughly, detain any ghosts present, and then wait for Holmes near the mercury amalgamation tables. Holmes was going to quietly pursue the ghosts on the hillside. By the time we cleared the door of the assay building, the apparition on the ground had disappeared. It was quite dark and my vision limited. Holmes paused briefly and then turned to chase after the lights on the hillside. I picked my way downslope to the mill building, carefully entering the boiler room through the door left ajar by the retreating engineer. Flattening myself against the wall next to a tool cabinet, I quickly scanned the room seeking my quarry. My heart pumped strongly and its palpitation beat in both my breast and ears. A trickle of sweat ran down my neck.

The engineer had stopped the machinery before abandoning his post. The thump of the stamps, the clanging of the rock moving through the feed hoppers, and the whir of the rotating flywheels was gone, replaced with the soft hiss of steam leaking from a pipe joint.

Quietly, I circled the boiler and then moved into the stamp room searching behind the amalgamation tables and under the ore bins for the presence of a ghost. My final stop was the retort room where the mercury was vaporized to separate it from the gold. All was in order. Per Holmes' instructions I went back to the stamp room and took up residence on a bench adjacent the east wall which gave me a view of the three entrances to the facility.

My excitement gradually receded as I waited for Holmes. He was not long in coming.

"Anything here, Watson?"

"No. It all looks to be in order. Did you capture the ghost?"

"Unfortunately, no, but I watched his three partners drift toward the heavens in their escape. Come quickly now. We've got to get to the mine."

Holmes ran back into the engine room and threw the lever activating the ore tramway. It sprang to life with a loud clatter as the main flywheel began to rotate. The mystery of Holmes' action was quickly dispelled when he urged that I follow him up a steep stairway and across the trestle to the floor above the ore bins where the tram disgorged its cargo.

"The minute that tram bucket clears the chute, climb in, Watson."

Holmes was more adroit about it than I and was soon seated on the side of the ore bucket while I hopped across the floor with one foot inside the car and struggling to find enough energy to allow me to get my other leg aboard. The tram bucket moved closer to the exit portal where my choices became very clear—get into the bucket somehow or fall 30 feet to the ground below. I lunged forward somewhat like a hippopotamus with a sprained ankle. Fortunately, Holmes was there to upright me.

"What in God's name are we doing, Holmes?" I wanted to yell, I was so distraught but, instead, kept my voice steady and low.

"We need to get to the mine, Watson. This is the fastest way."

"The ghost was at the mill site," I protested.

"But, the thief is at the mine," replied Holmes impatiently.

I am sure the view from the tramway would have been stunning but, regrettably, we were wrapped in an impenetrable darkness that rivaled the interior of a tomb. O'Flynn had previously told me that the tram buckets held approximately one ton of ore. Once I got inside, I was amazed at the small size of the bucket, roughly four feet long, three feet wide and two feet deep. Holmes was on the side of the bucket containing the strut which connected the contraption to the cable. I was seated opposite him, my backside on the lip of the bucket wall and my hands clamped on for all their worth. Every time Holmes moved in the slightest, the bucket would start to sway, heightening my anxiety, and prompting yet another prayer for a quick, safe deliverance to the end of the tram line.

We rode in silence, I fearful that if my mouth opened it would be only to exhale a scream of terror. Holmes, to the extent that I could see him, was nonchalant. The ride lasted about 10 minutes, a third of the time it would have taken me to climb the mountain on foot. A lantern was affixed to a post on the loading platform and, following Holmes' lead, my exit from the ore bucket was substantially more graceful than my entrance. Dignity

RED LION TRAMWAY
The remnants of one of the tramway towers and the cable from which
the ore buckets were suspended are shown in this 2002 photograph.
The tram transported gold ore from the Red Lion Mine downslope
about a mile to the stamp mill where the gold was recovered.

restored, I eagerly followed Holmes in pursuit of ghosts or persons unknown.

Holmes grabbed the lantern and led us off the platform to the base of the mine's waste rock dump. There, we found an ore wagon partially filled with rock and three shovels.

"They've escaped, Watson. The sound of the tramway must have alarmed them. This way."

"Holmes, . . ." I wanted to protest but the detective had already started off into the darkness and I had to hurry to catch up. We were following a road into the timber high along the ridgeline of Cable Mountain which sprawled to the south like a huge beached whale rising from the lowlands below.

"Holmes," I whispered, "where does this road take us?"

"To the Golden Eagle and some of the other mines along the flank of the mountain. With luck we'll meet O'Flynn and Sheriff Fitzpatrick."

Holmes had no sooner gotten those words out of his mouth when the light from two lanterns became visible before us in the distance.

"I believe our compatriots are before us, Doctor."

Holmes was correct, of course. But, it turned out to be a party of five, with three men lying face down on the dirt under the watchful eye and pointed pistols of our associates.

"Watson," explained Holmes ebulliently, "you already know Mr. Hansen. I'd like to introduce his two sons, Lars and Caleb."

"Who work the night shift in my employ," injected O'Flynn. "That is, when they're not stealing from me."

"Sheriff, why don't you take these gentlemen back to Hansen's mill and comfortably secure them. Mr. O'Flynn can accompany us back to his mine. There's a fourth conspirator to be captured."

It took about 30 minutes to get back to Red Lion. To my wonderment we did not stop at the miners' bunkhouse but, instead, moved on to O'Flynn's cabin. O'Flynn stepped inside, the glow of his lamp casting the room in a pale yellow hue. I heard him say, "Mary, wake up and get dressed. Mr. Holmes has some questions fer ya."

A muffled reply was made to which O'Flynn replied, "Aye, now hurry."

O'Flynn emerged from the back room, the three of us waiting quietly until Mary O'Flynn appeared. She looked apprehensive, shifting her gaze between the three of us before settling in a chair next to the dining table.

"I am pleased to see that you are wearing your gray robe, Mrs. O'Flynn. It simplifies matters considerably," said Holmes matter-of-factly. He then reached into his coat pocket and pulled out a small swatch of cloth identical in color to Mrs. O'Flynn's robe. He then laid a long piece of orange thread next to it.

Holmes continued very deliberately, "This piece of cloth was found on the corner of the mill building tonight. So was the thread. The cloth would appear to match that rip I see on the left shoulder of your garment."

Mrs. O'Flynn quickly replied, "I tore it there last week."

Holmes steeled his eyes directly into hers and then turned to O'Flynn. "Does your wife make a habit of walking around the camp in her robe?"

"No," said O'Flynn strongly. "Mary's a modest woman."

Holmes turned back toward Mrs. O'Flynn. "I believe that settles the issue of the cloth. Now, for this thread. I believe it came from the item used to create the ghostly apparition which so recently graced the grounds of the camp."

Mary O'Flynn remained impassive, her husband watching intently. Holmes waited a few moments more and then stepped outside and returned a few minutes later with an orange contraption that looked like a Chinese lantern.

"Here's your ghost, Mr. O'Flynn. Just one of many. I originally discovered it in the laundry building several days ago. When you attach a candle to this frame, it functions like a hot air balloon and rises in the air under its own power. Secure it with a length of twine and you can move it at will."

Holmes turned his back on the three of us and walked toward the door. "Watson, please join me. Mr. O'Flynn needs to talk with his wife privately. The Sheriff will be along shortly."

We stepped a polite distance away from O'Flynn's home but the ensuing conversation was anything but restrained. Mrs. O'Flynn upbraided her husband with a tongue I've not heard the like of since I was last on London's docks. A few moments later, Mary O'Flynn emerged from the cabin and said to Holmes, "Take me to the Sheriff. Now!"

Fortunately, Sheriff Fitzpatrick was not long in coming with the three Hansens securely tied to the back of his wagon. Mrs. O'Flynn joined them and the Sheriff departed immediately for Southern Cross.

I asked Holmes for an explanation of the night's events but he warded off my inquiry with a terse "Tomorrow, Doctor. I am exhausted."

It turned out we both were. Taking some blankets from O'Flynn, Holmes and I made camp in the laundry shack.

My next recollection was Holmes shaking me and saying, "It's after ten, Watson. We need to be on our way."

We reached Anaconda late in the afternoon, took up lodgings once again at the Montana Hotel, and left to seek out the Sheriff. Fortunately, we found him preparing for dinner at Whatley's Café. It had been almost 24 hours since I'd last eaten and my appetite was robust.

"Mr. Holmes, Doctor, I want to thank you again for your assistance in solving the case," offered the Sheriff as the waitress set dessert before us and refilled our coffee cups.

"It was our pleasure," replied the detective. "An interesting and yet fairly simple case, now that we have the advantage of hindsight."

"Pray, Holmes, please tell us how you figured it all out," I asked, my mouth at the ready for a piece of apple pie.

"Recall that when O'Flynn came to visit us at the Sheriff's ranch he was distraught but not afraid. Before you joined us that morning, Watson, I quizzed him at length about events at the mine. O'Flynn never believed for a second that he had a ghost problem except for the fact that his men believed it and several had quit his employ."

Holmes paused to drink some coffee while the Sheriff and I waited for him to continue. "Before we left the ranch, I realized I needed several pieces of information. First, I asked O'Flynn to draw me a map of Red Lion so that I could understand how a thief or, perhaps, a ghost could access and move around the property. We'll all agree that Red Lion is in a remote location and typically that implies limited access."

"But that isn't true in this case," replied the Sheriff.

"Correct. There were at least four ways to get to the

mine on passable roads, altogether too many with which to conduct a successful surveillance. O'Flynn's map, by the way, was very accurate as I discovered in my reconnaissance of the mine."

Holmes was in a rare mood, expansive to the point of ebullience, and I recognized that we were in for a long recitation. The Sheriff suspected likewise and took out a cigar.

"When we got back to Anaconda," continued Holmes, "I consulted with Mr. Daly and he referred me to Mr. Reno Sales, the company's chief geologist in Butte."

I gave Holmes a puzzled look.

"It was the same day you went to the races with Messrs. Thornton and Mathewson. I spent the afternoon at the company's geological department."

And an excellent day it was, I recalled, having multiplied my wagering at the track severalfold.

"Daly's geologists not only track the geology and ore production from the mines in Butte, but gather together everything they can on other people's operations in Montana. One room has a series of county maps posted on the walls. Every mining claim registered with the government is plotted on the map and a file opened on it."

"Whatever for?" I asked.

"So that Anaconda can buy them out if they look promising," replied Holmes with just a touch of disbelief in his voice to suggest that I should have recognized the obvious.

"Why would you care about the geology of the Red Lion Mine?" asked the Sheriff, whose puzzlement was even deeper than mine.

"Actually, the geology was of little direct interest," replied Holmes while he raised his coffee cup. "I was interested in seeing who owned property near O'Flynn's and, more importantly, if someone was staking out a land position that might be adverse to O'Flynn's operation."

"And what did you conclude?" I asked.

"That nothing untoward was going on, which only deepened the mystery of the case. My first working hypothesis was that O'Flynn had a neighbor who wanted to take possession of the mine and was using the ghostly apparitions to drive O'Flynn away. Or, at least cause him enough difficulty that he would sell out."

"But that wasn't the case?" answered the Sheriff unsurely, making it sound more like a question rather than a declaration.

Holmes nodded in agreement and continued. "So I decided to investigate the mine site. Watson went ahead with O'Flynn and I spent a full day wandering through the trees looking at the mine from every conceivable angle. Just getting there was, in fact, most informative. I took the upper road along the hillside. What struck me almost immediately is how difficult it would be for an intruder to pass through the area without being seen. There was a crew working the Black Hawk Mine, another on the Sunset, a team building a road on the St. Louis and Mrs. Dempsey was in her cabin on their claim by the same name. From there I passed by the Golden Eagle Mine and Hansen's operation. And, without exception, there were barking dogs everywhere. It wasn't much different on any of the other routes to Red Lion."

"What else did you learn?" asked the Sheriff as he removed his napkin and placed it on the table.

"More than I expected, frankly. When I finally reached the mine site the men were dumping waste rock onto the dump and loading timbers to take back in the mine. Their presence by the portal caused me to work my way uphill to get around them and I ended up following the tramway down to the mill. Just above the clearing north of the mill building, where the ghosts were sighted, I took shelter next to a tree when several of the mill hands came out of the building to have a smoke. There were several small pieces of twine wrapped around the boughs."

"What did you conclude?" I asked primarily to spur the conversation along.

"Nothing right then, other than it was a curious artifact. About an hour later I had worked my way downhill to the North Fork and was moving through the trees near the laundry shed, when I spotted a man and woman aside the building."

"Who was it?" asked the Sheriff quickly.

"It turned out to be Caleb Hansen and Mary O'Flynn but, of course, I didn't know that at the time. They were sidled up quite close to one another. She had one hand on his side, and he was holding the other. It wasn't an embrace, but it was quite clear they were holding an intimate conversation. Before he departed, Caleb reached into a canvas bag attached to his belt and gave Mrs. O'Flynn a ball of orange twine. She went back into the shed and Hansen returned to the camp. Mrs. O'Flynn left the laundry shed a few minutes later without the twine. Suffice it to say my curiosity was piqued and I decided to search the building."

"That's when you discovered those ghostly contrivances," I proffered.

"Indeed," replied Holmes while he stopped momentarily to finish the last of his coffee. "There were three of the contraptions. Each had a light wire framework with a candleholder attached to the bottom of what can only be described as a large, orange Chinese lantern or balloon. But, what really caught my attention was the fabric itself. It was coated with some type of lacquer which rendered the fabric airtight. It would function just like a hot air balloon albeit on a much smaller scale."

"So much for how the ghosts seemed to float in the air above the mill building," I concluded.

"My sentiments exactly, Watson," replied Holmes with a smile on his face. "I then knew how the ghosts were created. We already knew the why – to steal O'Flynn's gold. The remaining question was what were the names of the perpetrators."

Holmes paused briefly as if to take stock and figure out what else to say. Then he motioned to the waitress to refill his coffee cup. The Sheriff ground out the stub of his cigar on the side of a nearby spittoon and I looked covetously at the pie rack on the nearby counter but decided against a second piece.

Holmes continued. "After searching the laundry shed I made my way back uphill to the upper road with the intention of looping back down to the main road where I could meet Watson. It was then that I met the elder Hansen outside his mill. He saw me coming down from the upper to the lower road and he quickly recognized me as an outsider. After I hailed him, I explained that I had become disoriented on my way to Red Lion where I was to meet my partner. Hansen relaxed somewhat and became positively cordial when I explained that we had come to look at Red Lion as a possible investment for our firm. He showed me all about his property and told me how rich the ore was in his mine. It was there that I stumbled. After being with him for close to an hour, he formally offered me his hand and said, 'I am Einar Hansen,' to which I replied 'Holmes.' I thought I saw a flicker of recognition in his eyes, but he said nothing and I quickly departed and met Watson."

"Is that when you figured Hansen to be the thief?" asked the Sheriff.

"No. I didn't really know who was involved save Mrs. O'Flynn and her paramour until the Sheriff and O'Flynn's brother captured them on the road."

"How did you know they were stealing from the mine and not the mill?" It was my turn to play interrogator.

"I didn't, at least, not until later. My next discovery was made after I walked back to Red Lion with you, Doctor. There I met Mrs. O'Flynn and recognized her as the woman I'd seen at the laundry shed. The next day we toured the mill. I spent quite a bit of time talking with the mill hands about how the mercury amalgamation process functions. If you recall, they were stripping off the processed mercury containing the gold and reapplying a fresh coat. There is a decided difference in color with the fresh mercury having a bright silver luster while the processed material has more of a dull gray hue. I was puzzled how a thief could get into the building, strip the amalgamated mercury from the tables, recoat them and it not be noticeable to the mill workers. That's when I deduced that the gold was disappearing somewhere else and that the appearance of the ghosts was merely a diversionary tactic."

"Then we spent the night in the assay laboratory watching for the ghosts to return," I added, recognizing that I was using the term "we" in the royal sense. Holmes watched, I slept.

"Yes, and when the apparitions failed to appear even though O'Flynn had left the mine site, I knew that our real reason for being at Red Lion had been detected. But I didn't suspect Mr. Hansen. I was focused on Mrs. O'Flynn and her lover. It wasn't until the next day when we left the mine and talked with Hansen that it fell into place."

"Because of his vitriolic denunciation of O'Flynn?"

"No. I already knew that story. O'Flynn revealed it to me at the ranch before you joined us that morning for breakfast. When we were in Anaconda, Mr. Daly allowed me the use of his telephone and I called Mr. T. C. Power in Helena to verify if there had been any shenanigans involving himself, Curtis and O'Flynn. Mr. Power was emphatic that O'Flynn had done nothing untoward. In fact, he quoted from a letter in which O'Flynn implored Power to let him mine through the fault zone because he felt the richer ore was behind it. Power refused his request but that's exactly what O'Flynn did once he took possession of the mine."

"Which is where the high grade is located," offered the Sheriff in reply.

"Yes," answered Holmes, "And, as I mentioned before, it was our conversation with Hansen that morning in the meadow that showed me the truth. He claimed that O'Flynn had been highgrading the mine, which wasn't true. But then, it fell into place. Someone was intercepting O'Flynn's best ore at the mine and sending waste rock down the tramway to the mill. The appearance of the ghosts drove off the mill hands, creating the presumption that the gold was stolen at the mill."

"When it never got there in the first place," I said, echoing Holmes' earlier comment. "The Hansen boys were shipping it down to their father's little mill."

"Correct, Watson. Then it just became a matter of us finding out who was involved. I had us watch the mill site last night to see if we could capture the conspirator who created the ghosts. We didn't succeed directly, but once I found that piece of material on the corner of the mill, I knew it was Mrs. O'Flynn. As you know, I had previously arranged with the Sheriff to meet O'Flynn and take up position along the upper road. By then I was sensing that the elder Mr. Hansen was involved but wasn't absolutely positive."

"Until we caught 'em, Mr. Holmes," answered the Sheriff with a satisfied smile.

Late the next afternoon I found Holmes and Daly in the hotel bar, ordered a glass of sherry, and joined them for a conversation. Daly departed soon after my arrival and I was able to ask Holmes my final question regarding the ghosts of Red Lion.

"What became of O'Flynn after that ugly conversation with his wife two nights ago?"

"I saw him in the morning before we left, Watson, and he's a man in grief. The perfidy of his neighbor and employees stealing from him was bad enough, but to discover that one's own wife was a part of the conspiracy was too much to bear."

"The missus didn't mince any words with him. It's hard for me to believe she could marry a man she professed to dislike so intensely."

"It was an arranged marriage, Watson. O'Flynn paid her passage to America but she resented the union from the start. It was but a small step for her to take a lover and look for a way out of her life with O'Flynn."[20]

"A pity."

"In many ways, Watson. In many ways."

---

20   Editor's note: Watson's chronicle concluded with a long postscript explaining that O'Flynn sold his interest in the Red Lion property a few weeks after the successful conclusion to the case. His interest was purchased by a group of investors led by J. R. Joyce, President, and M. J. Fitzpatrick (no relation to the Sheriff), Secretary, with offices at Fitzpatrick's place of business, the Anaconda Real Estate and Insurance Company, 205 E. Commercial Avenue, Anaconda.

The Mysterious Woman

I awoke with a start, my body sensing the chill which enveloped the hotel room where I was resting. My pocket watch, 1admittedly not the most reliable of timepieces, said that it was 2:50 a.m. But, the brightness of the room caused me to doubt the old chronometer and I turned toward the window to confirm the approach of dawn. It wasn't the emergence of the sun that was lighting my temporary abode, but the glow from the street lights below reflected off a million snowflakes traipsing toward the ground. My body shuddered. Suddenly I was freezing. Snow! Cold! Montana! We'd stayed too long.

Now, perhaps, Holmes would take my counsel and agree to go back home to London. We'd been in Montana for almost three months, coming initially at the request of Marcus Daly, the Copper King, to sort out a little matter involving threats to the wellbeing of his prize racing stallion, Tammany. Then we tarried while Holmes solved a case involving theft from one of the nearby gold mines.[21] The

---

21 Editor's note: I've documented these cases as *The Tammany Affair* and *The Ghosts of Red Lion.*

latter affair had been tidied up almost a month previous and Holmes and I had returned to the fair city of Anaconda to enjoy the hospitality of the community. For me, it had largely been a time of relaxation, my mind free to reflect on Holmes' work the past few months and to chronicle several cases which he had solved in England just prior to our departure.[22] I saw little of Holmes during this period. He indicated that he was looking into another matter for our friend Daly and suspected that he was now front and center in the apex battles which were taking place among the rival mining companies in the courtrooms of Butte.[23]

I arose and closed the window, looking down to the street below, and watched the snow melt on contact with the sidewalk. Perhaps it was just an unseasonable event. No matter, it could be dealt with in the morning.

To my surprise and pleasure, Holmes was in the dining room when I arrived at half past seven.

---

22 Editor's note: Watson reported, "Unfortunately for the reading public these cases have never been published. Two involved very sensitive matters of state and, in deference to the Crown, Holmes asked that I destroy both the chronicle I had written and my notes. A third case again involved Major Pendergast in a personally humiliating controversy. Pendergast had been previously involved in a matter I described as the *Incident at the Tankerville Club*."

23 Editor's note: A footnote in Watson's original text noted, "Notwithstanding Holmes' absence, I had enjoyed a most companionable time. Marcus Daly introduced me to John Durston, editor of the *Anaconda Standard* who, in turn, brought me into his little card playing group which included Justice of the Peace Frank Fox; Professor C. E. Taylor, proprietor of the Anaconda Business College; Charles Cress, druggist; Felix St. Jean and his brother Leo, physician and dentist respectively. This group played cards each Wednesday evening and met for coffee and luncheon at other times during the week. I became quite close to the St. Jean brothers who had received their medical training at Johns Hopkins University in Baltimore. The St. Jeans were also bachelors like myself and loved to fish. Together, we often went in search of trout on Sunday mornings, an activity with its own form of religious significance.

THE BOARDING HOUSE—SOUTHERN CROSS, MONTANA
The simple grandeur of the Boarding House can still be seen in this
2004 photograph. The Boarding House is one of five original build-
ings at Southern Cross which have survived into the modern era.

"Good morning, Doctor. I trust that you know your favorite season has arrived."

"I'm hoping it's just a squall. As pleasant as I find Anaconda, I would hate to be snowed in until spring."

At that, Holmes chuckled and commented, "No worry
about that, Watson. I've concluded my work for Daly and
I think we can plan on returning home a week from Monday. But, before we go, I'd like to have you look in on Mrs.
Cameron. She seems to be afflicted by some malady which
the local physicians are at a loss to deal with."

"Certainly, but who is Mrs. Cameron?"

"The wife of Salton Cameron, one of Daly's fellow mine
owners. He owns the Pyrenees near Southern Cross."

"I remember it. Where am I to meet her?"

My snowy expectations were fulfilled. There were eight inches of the white stuff when Holmes and I alighted from the train. Fortunately, the storm had passed and the sun was blazing in the southern sky, its radiance already causing the white blanket to ebb away. We reached the boardinghouse just past noon. Entering the vestibule, we were greeted by a short but powerfully built man who thrust out his hand.

"Dr. Watson, I presume. And you, sir, must be Mr. Holmes. Salton Cameron here. Thank you for agreeing to see us, I mean my wife Amy."

Holmes looked Salton over and quietly observed, "It appears as if your recuperation is going slowly, Mr. Cameron. I trust the pain is manageable."

"Most of the time, Mr. Holmes, but there are days when . . . ." Cameron stopped in mid-sentence and asked, "Did Daly tell you of my accident?"

"No," replied Holmes with a compassionate smile. "Simple deduction, sir. When Watson and I entered the room, you turned to greet us. Your limp is slight, but noticeable. There was also the matter of the mild grimace on your face when you stepped forward with your left foot, which is slightly canted inward. I could hardly but conclude that you had broken your left ankle."

"Very observant of you, Mr. Holmes," said Cameron tersely, his face flushing as if embarrassed. "I stumbled on the steps outside my home about two months past and landed on a rock in exactly the wrong way."

With that our host turned and led us into the dining room, a large area approximately 40 feet long and filled with tables covered by heaping platters of meats, potatoes, bread and butter, all occupied by hungry miners and mill hands.

Cameron proceeded to a small table in the far corner where we were introduced to his wife Amy. She had a husky build for a woman, with short brown hair, dark eyes sunk deeply into her skull and a complexion with a yellow cast to it. I could understand her husband's concern. Mrs. Cameron did not look healthy. She was also quite reserved and resisted both Holmes' and my efforts to engage her in conversation. I suspected her reticence may have had something to do with her husband's presence at the table so, after completing our luncheon, suggested that Cameron join Holmes for a walk about town while I examined his wife. She visibly brightened at my offer and we moved to a second floor sitting room which the proprietor graciously provided.

Mrs. Cameron took a seat in a large, overstuffed chair and leaned forward, clearly more anxious than she had demonstrated in the dining room a few minutes earlier.

"Do you mind if I smoke?" she asked while pulling a small cigar from her purse. "It helps calm my nerves."

"Your husband allows you to smoke?" I asked in disbelief.

"Of course not," she replied casually as she set the match to light.

I was startled both by her audacious behavior and by the complete transformation of her character seen at the lunch table just a few minutes previous where I couldn't decide if she were meek or melancholy.

"That's better," Amy Cameron exclaimed after exhaling.

Unlike Holmes, I can't type tobacco from either the composition of its ash or its aroma, except to conclude that the tobacco was low grade, akin to that used in the cigarillos fancied in Latin America.

Regaining my composure, I asked, "I have been led to believe that you are suffering from a perplexing malady. What are your symptoms?"

"There's nothing perplexing about it at all, Doctor," answered Mrs. Salton. "I go to bed and awake exhausted. From time to time I seem to slip into a trance. After coming back to my senses I often feel like I've traveled somewhere."

"Could you give me an example, Mrs. Cameron?"

"Please call me Amy, Doctor. I grew up in the home of a livery hand and I am not well schooled in formalities."

"If you prefer," I answered, both my puzzlement and exasperation with this woman increasing by the minute. "Describe one of your trances."

"I had one, three days ago. I had just started the washing in my kitchen. It was a little past 8:00 a.m. My next conscious recollection was me sitting on the bed with the clock on the dresser chiming four times. When I walked into the kitchen my washing was still there, not done, and I had this sensation that I had been climbing the hillside behind our home."

"For eight hours?" I interjected with a note of disbelief clearly detectable in the tone of my voice.

"Evidently," answered Mrs. Cameron demurely. "I've never had a trance last that long before. At least, not that I know of. They seem to last a few minutes. I'll be in the kitchen and the next thing I know, I am in the privy or another room of the house with no recollection of having done anything between. But then I'll see something, like my husband's business records on the table, when I know they were in his desk."

"Has your husband witnessed this behavior?"

"I am not sure, Doctor," answered Mrs. Cameron. She drew on her little cigar, exhaled, and continued, clearly less anxious now. "He's never said anything about me being in a trance, but then he'll talk to me about something as if we've discussed it before, and I've no recollection of such a conversation whatsoever."

"My departed wife frequently complained that I did the same thing, Amy. It's not uncommon to get lost in thought and not hear what someone is saying."

"Judging from the strength of Salton's reaction, I don't think he viewed my action as just a little inattentiveness. He claims, for example, that we discussed a forthcoming trip to St. Louis and the arrangements he was making to bring my sister over from Helena so I would have some company when he was gone. I don't remember it, and believe me, that's not something I would forget. These memory lapses are causing us a lot of trouble. Salton's become increasingly angry and I regret to admit it, but I've responded in kind. We're barely speaking to one another."

"So that was the cause of your reticence at lunch," I observed offhandedly.

"Lunch," replied Mrs. Cameron. "We had lunch?"

I can only say that as perplexed as I was soon after meeting this woman, the mystery only deepened. I talked with her for another two hours, completely baffled by the incoherence in her story and by the shift in her mood. The remark questioning whether we had lunch together was followed by a period of quiescence, which suddenly metamorphosed into a state of assurance, if not ebullience, during which time she smoked another cigar.

I rose to open the window and clear the room of its

smoky haze and mentioned that I could see her husband and Holmes walking back toward the boardinghouse. When I turned back toward Mrs. Cameron I caught but a brief sliver of her brown shawl as the door closed behind her. Today's interview was over.

A few moments later, Mrs. Cameron walked down the steps from the front verandah and climbed aboard the buckboard parked next to a watering trough in front of the building. Mr. Cameron joined his wife, and after shaking hands with Holmes, turned the wagon south toward their home at the Pyrenees mine about a mile away as the crow flies.

Holmes looked toward the building, saw me standing in the window, and motioned that I should join him. The snow was melting rapidly, its spawn dripping from the eaves to the ground below counting cadence like a battery of snare drummers. The sky had cleared as the sun moved toward the western horizon, burning back the start of winter.

Holmes and I soon found ourselves keeping company with a raucous group of Cornishmen in a small establishment simply described by the word "Saloon" above the door. The men were ordering "ditches", a term I'd previously heard in Anaconda but paid no heed. My curiosity aroused, I tried one for myself and discovered it was nothing more than whiskey mixed with water. Just a waste of good whiskey in my mind.

Cornwall is the heart of the British copper, tin and lead mining industry. When Daly and his fellow mining magnates needed skilled miners, they looked to that rocky peninsula on the southwestern coast, renowned for both the strength of its gales and the heartiness of its miners.

When I casually mentioned that Holmes and I would be returning home the following week, a robust fellow by the name of Chadwick, who hailed from a small village near St. Austell, looked me squarely in the eye and asked, "Are you daft, Doctor Watson?" I looked at Chadwick dumbfounded, but quickly recovered my tongue and started to explain my reasons for wanting to return home. Chadwick interrupted. "In America a working man can easily make five dollars a day. That's six quid a week. We couldn't do that in a month in the old country."

Chadwick's mates chimed in agreement, and I reluctantly struck the Union Jack and gracefully retreated back to the boardinghouse with Holmes quietly chortling at my embarrassment. It had never been put to me quite so forcefully as it had by these miners, but to the poorer classes, America was truly a welcoming land that offered opportunity beyond anything they could envision in Europe. As near as I could tell, no one shared my desire to return to England. Even Holmes seemed irresistibly drawn to the United States. While we might soon return to London, I was certain that Holmes would be back to this hither shore.

We had dinner at the boardinghouse, sharing our table with two young men from Sweden who worked as shaftsmen in the Southern Cross Mine. Neither spoke English very well, but it was clear from the conversation that they shared the same view of the United States previously expressed by the Cornishman. Afterward, Holmes and I sat on the second floor of the verandah adjacent our sleeping rooms and discussed Mrs. Cameron's condition. When I had finished recounting my meeting with her, Holmes offered a quiet, "Most interesting, Watson, most interesting," and faded off in thought. I momentarily excused myself to refill my glass of brandy. When I returned, Holmes was ready to resume our conversation.

"Mr. Cameron was not quite as forthcoming as his spouse, Doctor. All he wanted to talk about was mining."

"Have you ever known any miner who didn't?" I interjected.

Holmes smiled at that remark and shook his head no and continued, "But I managed to pull a few bits and pieces about her behavior from him. Cameron said the problem began back in late June while his wife's sister from Helena was visiting the couple. Cameron had committed to escorting them both to a dance over the hill at Gold Coin. But he got busy at the mine and completely forgot about it. Cameron returned home expecting dinner but instead found an empty house. The two women had gone to the dance without him."

"What little I've seen of Mrs. Cameron, I am not surprised. She's a saucy lass to be sure, and apparently, not well schooled in the feminine refinements," I added.

"That might describe her manner, but according to Cameron, not the way she acted before the incident involving the dance. Cameron blames the situation on his sister-in-law, Abigail, who is well schooled in the writings of Elizabeth Cady Stanton and Susan B. Anthony, the suffragettes."

"Oh my God, Holmes, and this Abigail has corrupted Mrs. Cameron."

"So it would seem, Watson. After the women returned home, Cameron and his missus got into a 'helluva row.' His term Watson, not mine. She accused him of being completely insensitive to her needs, treating her as little more than another one of his mining machines."

"And what was the sister-in-law doing?" I asked.

"Encouraging Mrs. Cameron and, at one point, even taunted Cameron directly by saying that her sister could leave home and as long as there was someone wearing a skirt in the kitchen Cameron wouldn't likely know his wife had departed for days."

"I am surprised Cameron didn't strike her dead on the spot."

"I think he might have wished it, but instead left the house and slept in the miners' bunkhouse. That turned out to be faint comfort, for the men regaled him with tales about how the two ladies had comported themselves at the dance. Supposedly, Amy was somewhat reticent to begin with, but Abigail had no such reservations and by the time the night was over had danced with every single man in the place. Abigail also encouraged her sister to try some hard cider and once it had found its way into her veins, demonstrated her own skill on the dance floor."

"My heavens, Holmes, this is far more serious than I thought."

"I am not finished, Doctor."

"Pray, forgive me."

"When Cameron returned home the next day, he was advised that Abigail had departed. He then apologized to his wife for his previous night's anger, but she was not in a forgiving mood. He described the next several days as 'walking on eggshells' before she relented and began to converse with him again. But it didn't last. Cameron felt the need to release the energy that had been building in his loins and when he swept his wife into his embrace, she said no, quite forcefully, and pushed him away. He then tried some force of his own during which time his wife caught her foot on a table leg, fell, and struck her head on the floor. He put her to bed and called a physician out from Anaconda. She slowly recovered, but her character changed and she began to physically deteriorate."

"Finally!" I said with considerable animation. "Mrs. Cameron undoubtedly experienced a concussion, and I am sure that if I could open her skull, we would find one or more lesions on her brain."

"You've seen this condition before, Watson?" asked Holmes while he drew his briar from his left-hand coat pocket and searched the right for matches.

"Yes. Twice, actually, not with exactly the same behavior pattern, mind you, but sufficiently similar to prompt my diagnosis." I paused to collect my thoughts while Holmes lit his pipe.

"The case most like the present situation occurred in Afghanistan. We were on bivouac north of Kabul. A young leftenant[24] with the 142nd Scottish Fusiliers was thrown from his horse, his head striking the barrel of a cannon."

"I am surprised he did not snap his neck," answered Holmes.

"My observation at the time as well, Holmes, but it must have been a glancing blow because his neck was not broken. The leftenant was unconscious for four days and when he awoke everything appeared to be normal. He slowly convalesced, but then one day he started to talk like a child.

---

24 Editor's note: The American spelling is lieutenant.

Within a matter of a few weeks he regressed to the mental state of a boy six years of age. Preparation had been made to return him to England when he tangled with a viper outside his billet and died."

"And the lesions?" asked Holmes.

"His commanding officer was quite perplexed by the leftenant's condition and requested that I do an autopsy. I discovered two lesions on his cerebrum. Neither was very large, but I was in no position to do further study and had little choice but to bury the lad. Nevertheless, the experience convinced me that there are specific parts of the brain which control one's character."

"Franz Joseph Gall and Cesare Lambroso would appear to share your point of view, Doctor."[25]

"Blast you, Holmes, I am a medical man, not a soothsayer. Biological theories to explain crime is the stuff of hobgoblins, and you know it."

---

25 Editor's note: Franz Joseph Gall writing in the early 1800s posited that the structure of the human skull was indicative of the brain's "faculties." The faculties are, in turn, related to various character traits such as aggressiveness, greed, etc. and it was therefore possible to determine a person's character by reading the bumps on a person's skull. Gall's theory came to be known as "phrenology." Lambroso, a contemporary of Watson's, was an Italian anthropologist who believed that there was a biologically determined "criminal type' that can be discovered from various physical anomalies present in the criminal's body.

While Gall and Lambroso enjoyed a wide following in both Europe and the United States, particularly among those members of society which had little direct contact with the criminal classes, to their credit the senior hierarchy at Scotland Yard thought such theories absolute nonsense. As Holmes was quick to point out, Professor Moriarty completely repudiates the notion of biological determinism as a cause of crime. Application of either Gall's or Lambroso's theory to Moriarty's body would quickly lead one to conclude that he was of noble birth, rather than an arch villain.

"And the other time?" asked Holmes eagerly.

"What other time?" I replied, confused by the direction of the conversation.

"You said that you had seen brain lesions twice, once in Afghanistan. What about the second case?"

"Sorry, old boy. Your needling me about my philosophical kinship with Lambroso and Gall disoriented me. Yes, the other case. It occurred when I was taking my surgical training at the University of London. A navvy from the east end docks was brought to us in a coma. He keeled over in the road outside his home. His wife said that he had been in the best of health except for an accident at work where he was lashed across the left side of the head by a rope, which had broken free of a winch."

"No other symptoms?"

"None that she reported. He passed away that same day. When we opened his skull as part of the post mortem, there was a massive lesion about the size of a robin's egg on the left side of the brain."

"It could have been there before the accident," Holmes commented skeptically.

"I agree. The cause of his death was listed as unknown. Even more perplexing to me was the complete absence of other symptoms. The size of the tumor alone suggested to me at least that he should have been experiencing a lot of pressure in his skull. He should have had headaches."

"Did Mrs. Cameron report headaches?" asked Holmes, changing the subject on me.

"No, just forgetfulness and trancelike states, but to be truthful with you, Holmes, I never really got the chance to ask her about physical symptoms. We talked extensively about her behavior and her relationship with her husband."

Holmes rose from his chair and leaned against the balustrade surrounding the verandah, watching the sun seek its repose behind the western mountains. After allowing him a few minutes of solitude, I asked, "What have you deduced thus far?"

Holmes turned to me, his body a silhouette backlighted by the ever-diminishing sunlight, and said, "I am pleased to hear that Mrs. Cameron's affliction may be organic in nature. From what I've seen thus far, I was beginning to think we might be dealing with the female counterpart of Dr. Jekyll."

I was astounded by Holmes' observation. Between 1883 and 1885 he had assisted a reluctant Inspector Newcoman discern the truth about Dr. Jekyll and his evil alter ego, Mr. Hyde. But Holmes' role in the affair had never been publicly acknowledged. To my recollection, he had only discussed the case once following its successful conclusion and that was to observe how fortunate he had been to destroy the doctor's writings lest they fall into the hands of someone like Moriarty.[26]

"I find your opinion unfathomable, Holmes," I replied casually. "Mrs. Cameron has experienced a shift in her character balance, but there is nothing sinister in her actions. Besides, the woman has no background as either a physician

---

26 Editor's note. Watson's reference to Holmes' involvement in the Jekyll/ Hyde case here is interesting and unique inasmuch as there is no other mention of the case in the Canon. Watson never formally chronicled the case until 1917. See *Dr. Jekyll and Mr. Holmes,* by John H. Watson, M.D. as edited by Loren D. Estleman, Penguin, 1979.

or chemist to suggest that she might independently concoct Dr. Jekyll's evil brew."

"I daresay that you're right, Watson. But we'll know more in the near future. Cameron has asked us to be his dinner guests tomorrow evening."

The next morning Holmes and I breakfasted with Charles Brostrom, Superintendent of the Southern Cross mine. He seemed most interested in showing us his handiwork, and soon the three of us were stepping into a man cage for a ride 400 feet below ground.

The mine sits on the western edge of a bluff overlooking a large meadow to the west. In contrast, the southern horizon is etched in bold relief by the Anaconda Range whose bluish spires reach toward the sun through a patchwork of ice and snow crusting their flanks. The mine consists of a headframe, popularly known as a gallows frame, squatting over a vertical shaft, a portal to the nether world. Atop the headframe are three large sheave wheels, each with a wire rope running over its top and tying back to a large circular hoisting drum. The cylinder rotates to raise or lower the man cage and skips (ore buckets) to the depths below. The hoist is powered by steam produced in the powerhouse boiler. Large mines, like these owned by our friend Marcus Daly, now use electricity to operate their hoists. It's much faster and more economical than steam.

To the uninitiated, when a man cage starts to descend it's as if the floor has literally dropped out from under one's feet, the cage in freefall. The hoist operator counts the rotations of the hoisting drum to know when to pull back on the brake and stop at the correct level. A system of bell signals allows the miners below ground to communicate with the hoistman.

I braced myself against the side of the cage knowing what to expect. Holmes did not, but seemed unruffled by the experience when we stepped out of the cage in the shaft station at the 400 level. A string of ore cars were lined up on a side track, and the minute we cleared the cage, the trammer wheeled one about to start its ascent to the surface. The cage we were riding in had three compartments stacked one atop the other. Each would be filled with a small ore car carrying a ton of the gold-enriched rock.

From the shaft station we worked our way along the haulage drift (tunnel) to a stope where the miners were mining the ore. A stope is driven upward from one drift to another.

The only light we had was carried on our forehead created by the flickering flame of a carbide lamp perched there. The miners also had candles to illuminate their workplace. They were double jacking, drilling a hole in the face of the vein where dynamite would be placed. One miner held a pointed shaft of steel in the drill hole while his partner swung a 16-pound sledgehammer striking the end of the drill shaft. With each strike of the hammer the miner holding the drill bit rotated it a quarter turn. Their work moved with a steady rhythm, the clang of the sledge followed by a soft grinding sound as the drill bit rotated, over and over again.

When we reached their work station, I recognized the miner swinging the sledgehammer as Chadwick, the Cornishman who lectured me on the American way of life. He was a skilled workman, each blow of the hammer accomplished with measured efficiency translating the immense strength of his shoulders and arms into a powerful stroke on the tip of the drill bit, which penetrated the rock as if he were driving it into a snowdrift.

The miners ignored our presence and moved on with their work. Miners are paid on a piecework basis for each cubic foot of ore they excavate. It's called 'working on contract' and their take home pay is a direct reflection of their effort and skill with a little luck tossed in.

"Chadwick's a working fool," commented Brostrom. He told me he's saving his money so he can get out of the mines and open a business.

"Laudable goal," responded Holmes.

"He'll make it too. In this section of the mine, the rock's a lot softer. It's good digging. Chadwick and young Raymond, his partner, made over nine dollars a day last week and they never earn less than five dollars."

"My God, no wonder the man thinks the streets of Montana are paved with gold," I offered in retort.

"Make no mistake, Doctor, he earns his money," answered Brostrom. "If I could get the same amount of work out of my Irishmen, this would be the most profitable mine in Montana, but the harps like their whiskey and beer too much. It takes them three hours every shift to work the drink out of their veins."

Brostrom showed us every nook and cranny of his underground world, and Holmes responded in kind with enthusiasm, asking questions of every sort about its operations, maintenance, and finance. I knew my friend would catalogue everything in his encyclopedic brain, but I wondered why. His practice in London was with another sort of people.

When we again reached the surface, Brostrom led us to the mill building to show us how the gold was recovered from the ore. Along the way, he quietly inquired, "I've heard you gentlemen have been spending some time with my friend Salton Cameron. I take it, it's about his missus?"

Holmes gave me a questioning look and I shrugged in return. After a pregnant pause of several seconds, I replied, "Mr. Cameron asked me to examine his wife in conjunction with a medical ailment."

"She certainly needs your help, Doctor. Amy has become the talk of the mountainside, particularly among the women. My wife, Ingrid, told me that her behavior has become so bizarre that it's like another person stepped into her body."

"Has she described any other symptoms?" I probed. It would be good to get another perspective regarding Mrs. Cameron, even if the information was merely anecdotal in nature.

"Her self has changed."

"Her self," I repeated. "Oh, you mean her nature."

"Aye. Before, Amy was a spirited but gentle and loving woman and she doted on Salton. According to Ingrid, she now speaks of her husband with contempt. Says he oppresses her, but I am not sure I know what that means in this case. Salton's a fine man, earns a good living, and doesn't bother Amy with how she runs the house."

With that, Brostrom shook his head in dismay and was reaching out to open the door to the mill building when Holmes asked, "When she talks to the other women now, what does she talk about?"

"Voting, mostly. That's new as well. I am told her sister in Helena is an ardent suffragette. Never met her myself."

"Sounds like the sister has rubbed off on Mrs. Cameron," I said.

"Is there anything else you can tell us about Mrs. Cameron, or is there anyone else who may have had dealings with her who might give us some more insight into her character?" Holmes asked.

Brostrom thought about that for a while before answering. "There's two. Murphy, who runs the general store behind the boardinghouse. He deals with all the women from the camps. And there's old Gordon, the night watchman. He told me he's seen Amy Cameron walking around the camp at night on at least three occasions. Once he caught up with her and asked if she needed any help. He said she just looked at him with a blank stare, kind of shook her head no, and went on her way."

"Was Mr. Cameron told?" asked Holmes.

"I don't know. Gordon and Cameron aren't too keen on one another. They had a dispute over the ownership of a claim some time back and the dust has yet to settle."

Brostrom started our tour of the mill on the floor above the stock bins where the ore cars from the mine discharge their cargo. The stock bins have sloped floors made of heavy planking. Gravity pulls the rock down the slope to a chute which is periodically opened to meter the rock into a ball mill. The mill is a conical drum about half full of two-inch diameter iron balls. Water is added as the mill rotates. The balls inside cascade down on the ore, crushing and grinding it into a fine slurry.

The ball mill serves the same basic function as the stamp mills we saw earlier at the Red Lion mine, namely to crush the ore into a fine powder and liberate the gold.

Brostrom explained that the mill at Southern Cross was a "wet mill," that is, it uses a cyanide solution to recover the gold versus the mercury amalgamation process typically used at a stamp mill.

The gold-bearing slurry discharges from the ball mill into a large wooden vat containing the cyanide solution. A large wooden agitator slowly stirs the brew. Cyanide is one of a very few chemicals with the ability to dissolve gold. The gold-bearing cyanide solution is decanted from the top of the tank while the undissolved portion of the slurry discharges from the bottom into another vat where the process is repeated.

THE SOUTHERN CROSS MINE—CIRCA 1915

This photograph, which was taken almost 20 years after Holmes' and Watson's visit, shows the great mine and some of the Southern Cross town site. The Boarding House, so frequently mentioned by Watson, was located to the immediate left of the photo. The large expanse of water seen in the background is Georgetown Lake. It was created in 1901 when the Anaconda Copper Mining Company constructed a masonry dam to replace an older earthen facility built in 1885. The new dam led to the complete inundation of Georgetown Flats.

The gold-bearing solution is fed into another tank where zinc dust is added. There, the gold collects on the zinc and falls to the bottom of the tank where it is later collected, dried, and then smelted in a furnace to produce gold bullion. In the meantime, the cyanide solution is recirculated back to the first tank and reused over and over again.

Holmes seemed enthralled by the whole process. I doubt that he's ever seen so much poison concentrated in a single location, yet nary an injury to behold. As a consulting detective Holmes thinks of such materials as occurring in apothecary quantities capable of being concealed in a small vial or envelope. In our respective professions, cyanide is more commonly known as Prussic acid, its presence in the human being noted by a faint almond smell and a bluish cast to the skin caused by oxygen starvation, which is medically referred to as cyanosis. As is often the case, a human artifact which we see as deadly in one context is immensely beneficial to mankind in another.

I was momentarily distracted by one of the mill hands, who joined us on the catwalk perched above two rows of cyanidation vats running along both sides of the building. When I turned back to my party, I heard Holmes comment, "And you've never had a man killed by the cyanide."

"Never," replied Brostrom. "Cyanide is quite safe to handle if you keep the solution strongly alkaline. We mix burnt lime with water, then add the cyanide. The alkalinity keeps the gas from forming. It's the gas that's deadly."

I must have given Brostrom a blank stare because he asked me, "Doctor, you don't detect the almond smell, now do you?"

"No," I replied, somewhat embarrassed.

"The smell is carried by the gas. Put cyanide into something acid, in water, or the human body which is mostly water, and you'll evolve the gas. We're quite safe here, even though there are thousands of gallons of cyanide solution in the building, because the alkalinity in the solution keeps the gas from forming."

Suffice it to say, Holmes and I spent almost four most instructive hours with Brostrom. After lunch, Holmes excused himself to give some thought to a little issue that has been of concern to Mycroft, Holmes' brother who handles the most sensitive matters of state for the British Crown. I was feeling both energetic and curious, and given the warmth of the September day we were experiencing, decided to go exploring. I rented a saddle horse from the livery stable and headed down toward Georgetown Flats. We were expected at Cameron's house for dinner at 6:00 p.m.

I enjoyed an invigorating ride touring between the mine sites and watching a group of woodcutters pursue their craft. When Holmes and I reached the Cameron household just before 6:00 p.m. our host was pacing back and forth on the front porch, clearly distraught. Upon seeing us, he motioned for us to be quiet and pointed toward a stable to the west of his home. We met him there.

"I am so thankful you've arrived," said Cameron with a tone of exasperation in his voice. "I've been sick with worry."

"Please, calm yourself, Salton, and tell us what troubles you so," replied Holmes.

"This!" exclaimed Cameron as he moved a bag of oats. He then reached down and pulled out a small paper box of the type used by millinery shops and opened it for us to see.

"What you called Prussic acid, Mr. Holmes, and what we Americans call cyanide."

"I take it that you suspect your wife of hiding this material here."

"Indeed. I recognize the box. She brought it back from Anaconda last spring. There's enough cyanide in the box to kill an army, and to be candid with you, I don't know whether she plans to do in herself, or some other party."

"When did you make this discovery?" asked Holmes calmly.

"This afternoon. I had gone over to the Cable mine to meet with Frank Ballard, the manager, about some equipment he wants to buy. When I returned Captain to his stall, I bent down to fetch the water bucket and spotted the corner of the box behind that sack of grain."

"She must have gotten it at Southern Cross," I added. "It has the only wet mill in these parts."

"But how?" asked Salton with a perplexed look on his face. "It's not the kind of thing that's available for the asking."

"But perhaps for the taking," replied Holmes thoughtfully.

Cameron gave the two of us a look of disbelief, started to say something, and rolled his eyebrows in a furrow as if he were deep in thought. Then he started to shake his head no, when Holmes observed, "Perhaps at night when you're deep in slumber. There aren't many men working the night shift. I think it would be relatively easy to steal into the mill building and procure some cyanide crystals. I don't recall the storage area being locked."

With Holmes' observation Cameron became visibly

agitated. His neck and face both flushed to a deep crimson. Holmes paused for a few minutes and then added, "Is there something more you can tell us about Mrs. Cameron's behavior?"

Cameron nodded almost imperceptibly. "That could be, Mr. Holmes." He said it very quietly, and I was perplexed by his demeanor. "Amy could be leaving the house at night and I'd not know it." At that point Cameron's voice deepened as he quietly admitted, "I've not slept in my marital bed since Amy fell and injured her head. The guest room has been my bed chamber these many months."

"So your wife would be quite free to move around the house or the neighborhood without your knowledge," commented Holmes casually.

"Aye. And I am a deep sleeper to boot. Is that what you think she's doing?"

"Indeed," answered Holmes. "I've been fearful that something sinister might be in the offing and your discovery seems to confirm the point. I trust that you can safely dispose of that toxic stash."

"Aye, that's no problem," answered Cameron more calmly.

"As for joining you for dinner this evening, I think Watson and I will defer your gracious invitation and join you and Mrs. Cameron a bit later for conversation."

"Oh, my God, I'd forgotten about Amy cooking dinner. I don't dare eat it either," replied Cameron.

"It never portends well for equanimity about the house by insulting a woman's cooking, Mr. Cameron, but given the alternative, facing her wrath may be the prudent thing to do." With that, Holmes led us out the side door of the stable and promised that we'd return at 7:30 p.m.

When we returned the Camerons were sitting on their porch, he reading the newspaper and she mending a dress. They both greeted us warmly and Cameron excused himself to get us a drink.

"How have you been feeling, Mrs. Cameron?" I asked after Holmes moved down the porch a distance to light his pipe.

"More rested, Doctor, thank you. I took a nap this afternoon and, well, I am loath to admit it, I completely slept through the dinner hour. Your delay in reaching our home has saved me profound embarrassment."

"Think nothing of it. Mr. Holmes' profession rarely allows him a regular schedule and it's frequently difficult for us to keep our commitments, as was the case today. I hope you'll accept our apology."

"Thank you, Doctor. You're most kind."

"Tell me, Amy, have you experienced any more of your forgetful spells since yesterday?" I asked as Holmes rejoined us.

"Not that I am aware of, Doctor. They seem to occur most often at night or in the morning."

"I see that you're a most accomplished seamstress, Mrs. Cameron. Was that your profession before marriage?" inquired Holmes.

"No, Mr. Holmes. I worked in an apothecary and had I not met Salton, I would have opened a shop of my own."

"So you're a trained chemist?" I asked.

"Very much so," added Mrs. Cameron matter-of-factly and with a smile.

I noticed Holmes' left eyebrow shift every so slightly, his signal to me that we may well be dealing with a feminine version of Dr. Jekyll.

The evening wore on quite congenially. We talked about their home, life in Montana, politics, and inevitably, mining. Actually, Cameron talked with me about mining while Amy engaged Holmes in a long discussion about politics. When not distracted by Cameron's talk about the mine, I managed to overhear snippets of their conversation and it was clear that Mrs. Cameron was well read and, frankly, far more knowledgeable about such issues than her husband. She also demonstrated great courage in her conviction that women should have the right to vote. Holmes sparred with her on that matter and Amy was more than equal to the challenge. When Cameron turned and brought Holmes into our conversation about mining, Amy was obviously bored. Her head began to nod and she completely distanced herself from the conversation. When I asked her a question about her sewing, I was met by a blank stare as though she were deaf. Holmes was otherwise engaged with Cameron at that point and didn't notice her behavior, but it was clear to me that Amy was having one of her spells. I continued to visit with her quietly until she started to converse, answering me in an automatic way, her voice flat and without inflection. At that point, I stood up and thanked Cameron for his hospitality and insisted to Holmes that we needed to get back to Southern Cross and let the Camerons get off to bed.

It was well past sundown and Cameron gave us a lighted lamp to guide the way back to the boardinghouse. When we had moved far enough along the trail so that we would not be visible, I said to Holmes, "Let's turn off the lamp and return to their home. I saw her enter a trance while you and Cameron were discussing ground support systems for the mines. If we get back there and take up vigil we may well discover the meaning to all of this."

"So you're telling me that the game's afoot, Watson. Is that it?" asked Holmes with a chuckle.

"Pray, please forgive me, but yes, Holmes, yes."

Fortunately, we did not have to wait long. Around 11:00 p.m. the back door of the house opened and Mrs. Cameron emerged carrying a candle lantern, its soft white light leading her toward the railroad grade below her home. To our collective surprise, she turned east toward Anaconda and not toward Southern Cross. I wondered where she was leading us. Holmes and I followed at a comfortable distance. Fortunately, the moon was nearly full and we were able to find our footing without needing to relight the lantern.

We followed Amy for more than an hour. She walked briskly and it was difficult to stay apace traveling in the dark. As we neared the Gold Coin mine, about three miles distant from her home, Mrs. Cameron departed the rail bed and proceeded upslope on a wagon road toward the mine buildings. One structure was made of stone and looked remarkably like a powder magazine. I shuddered at the thought and quietly gave vent to my fears. Holmes responded by quickening his step.

Moments later we lost sight of the light from Amy's lantern as the road curved around a copse of aspen trees. When we rounded the bend she had disappeared. Holmes and I struggled forward slowly, caught in the deep black of a shadow caused by the trees warding off the moonlight. I didn't even see the building looming up on my left until I cracked my skull on something hanging from its side. We soon discovered that the something was Amy's lantern, which she'd hung on a peg jutting out near the doorway, its metal casing still warm from the candlelight that had radiated inside but a few moments before.

We paused for a quick consultation and decided that she was either inside the building or had made her escape in the surrounding darkness. Holmes relit the lantern and slowly opened the door of the stone building before us. It was, as I had feared, a powder magazine. Next to the wall across from the door were better than a dozen cases of Mr. Nobel's gift to the mining and construction industry, dynamite. One case on the top of a pile was open and several sticks had been removed.

Holmes didn't tarry. "Watson, come quickly. I fear the worst." Holmes stepped out the door while I fiddled with its latch in a futile effort to secure it tightly.

"There's our quarry, Doctor," Holmes exclaimed behind me.

I turned just in time to see a figure cross the final few feet of a clearing and disappear into another stand of trees. "I know the road, Holmes. I was here yesterday on my ride. It crosses the ridge near the Luxemborg mine and leads right to Cameron's house. Amy is going home."

I retrieved her lantern from the peg beside the magazine door, lit it, and guided by our respective lights, we made our way toward Cameron's home with all possible dispatch. Holmes' breathing was a bit labored when we reached the gate in Cameron's back fence, and frankly, I was exhausted and had to steady myself at the gatepost while gasping for air.

The part of the American experience which I had come to best appreciate was its diet, especially the thick steaks and rich breads which were so readily abundant. My appetite had, of late, shown itself in the snugness of my trousers and waistcoats and now, in my lack of stamina. Privately, I vowed to lose weight when we returned to Britain, a task I figured would be easier there given the blandness of English food. While I could never admit this to the English-reading public, the truth is, the Americans set a much finer table than the British.

While I rested, Holmes circumnavigated the house, being careful to stay in the shadows where he wouldn't be observed. Upon his return we quietly conferred, with Holmes suggesting that we wake Salton and confront Amy. I didn't share his point of view and pointed out that all we knew for sure was that Mrs. Cameron had taken a late night walk. I could see him purse his lips in the moonlight and, after rubbing his jaw simply said, "I believe you are quite correct, Doctor. Let us gain some rest for ourselves and revisit this matter tomorrow."

With that comment, Holmes turned about and together we hiked back to our rooms at the boardinghouse without another word between us.

The next morning I slept well past my usual breakfast hour and, in doing so missed Holmes, who is fastidious about his meal times. The serving girl in the dining room gave me a note which said:

> *Meeting Cameron and looking after other matters.*
> *Holmes*

Holmes' message left me free to look after my own affairs for several hours and after a light breakfast, I took a cup of coffee out to the front verandah to commiserate about the matter of Amy Cameron. The sun was rising upward in the sky, its face hidden by the billows of clouds punctuating the azure dome that spread from mountaintop to mountain-top. It was cool and I needed the warmth of my waistcoat. I spotted two squirrels in the tree just past the railing, work-ing methodically to collect pine cones which they carried beneath the verandah floor. Their haste convinced me that the full onset of winter could not be far away. I certainly hoped that nothing else would capture Holmes' imagina-tion and prevent us from our departure. Notwithstanding the quality of American victuals, I was ready for the com-fort of our lodgings on Baker Street, the challenges that presented themselves with Holmes' work, and the more genteel quality of British culture.

I puzzled over Mrs. Cameron's case for a considerable period, looking at it from several different perspectives, and was convinced my assessment was correct. I decided to tell Holmes of my opinion on the matter when he returned but thought it advisable to meet again with Mrs. Cameron.

She was hanging some washing on the clothesline be-side her house as I entered the gate whereupon she greeted me formally and, with little apparent enthusiasm, a simple, "Good morning, Doctor."

"And the same to you, Mrs. Cameron," I said with a broad smile and jovial voice. "Did you sleep well last night?" Her weariness was readily apparent. Women aren't constitution-ally geared to taking five-mile strolls over hill and dale in the middle of the night and then facing the tasks needed to manage a household.

"I slept just fine, Doctor," came her monotonic response. "Why do you ask?"

"Because you look exhausted. If I didn't know better,

I would swear you went mountain climbing last night after dinner."

"I certainly don't have the energy for pursuits of that type, Doctor, not with a husband to look after, and I . . ."

At that point Amy paused for several seconds, looking inwardly as if she were trying to search the deep recesses of her memory.

"I am sorry, Doctor," came an almost embarrassed reply. "I am tired, very tired, and it shows in my lack of hospitality. Even worse, I don't know why, although I can tell you that I had another bizarre dream last night, one of many these past several months."

Mrs. Cameron motioned for me to follow her into the kitchen where she set out and filled two huge mugs of coffee. This I didn't need having just drunk my fill at Southern Cross, but accepted her offer and the conversation which would inevitably follow.

"I must have thrashed about all night, Doctor. My legs, here in the thighs, are sore."

"Did you dream?" I interjected.

"Oh yes, the dream. I dreamt that I was out under the night sky walking on a dark road. I've had that dream on several occasions, by the way, but last night was different. Last night, two men were following me. One carried a lantern and they just about caught me but I turned into a deep shadow and they ran by me."

"Do you recall carrying anything in your hands?" I asked gingerly.

"No," came Amy's quick reply. "There was nothing in my hands."

"What happened to the two men?"

"They just disappeared."

It was clear to me that Mrs. Cameron had partial recollection of our respective walks through the forest last night but as I probed further, discovered that her memory was quite limited. It was also evident to me that she was quite sincere in her answers. I concluded that she had again entered one of her trances and spent almost three hours leading Holmes and me on a walkabout with little memory of her act. Cameron's comment about the deteriorated state of Amy's health also came to focus. If she was taking these midnight strolls with any frequency, she couldn't help but be exhausted.

Our conversation turned to more pleasant topics and I was about to leave when Cameron came back from the mine in search of his luncheon. I deferred the opportunity to eat with them, no mean feat for a man of my character, particularly when Amy opened the cake box and pulled out a thick white cake with butter frosting. As I departed, Cameron commented that Holmes had been by his office and that we'd all see one another in Anaconda the next evening.

My initial reaction to hearing that was one of irritation. We had undertaken this little venture so that I could examine Amy Cameron to determine the cause of her infirmity, a matter which I had resolved to my satisfaction, although I had yet to tell the patient, her husband, or Holmes of my diagnosis.

Upon further reflection, my anger dissipated. Meeting the Camerons in Anaconda would allow me to acquire some medication to alleviate Mrs. Cameron's condition and get me closer to my goal of returning to 221B Baker Street.

On my way to the Cameron home that morning the wind had chilled. I needed the warmth of my topcoat. Unfortunately, it was hanging in my room at Southern Cross, which I now hurried to reach. Another thing I'd come to understand about Montana, even if I couldn't appreciate it, was that it could be cold any day of the year.

After returning from my visit with Mrs. Cameron I spent the balance of the day catching up on my correspondence and reading through several back issues of the *Anaconda Standard* next to the stove in the dining room. Around 4:30 a handsome young man, who the proprietor later identified as John Ferkin, one of the shaftsmen from the mine, came in and picked up a basket of food from Ida, the serving girl. She was obviously quite smitten by him, and he with her. Young love is the same the world over, a mixture of excitement and embarrassment. Out of the corner of my eye, I saw Wong, the Chinese cook, watching the two and giving his nod of approval.

Holmes did not return until dinner but he was in a reclusive mood, little interested in conversation. I spent the dinner hour visiting with several of the mill hands who lived in adjacent cabins but took their meals at the boardinghouse.

Holmes excused himself before dessert and asked that I stop by his room later. I arrived just past 7 p.m. and found him hunched over the desk writing furiously, the room enshrouded in a cloud of pipe smoke, and he completely oblivious to the majesty of the sunset unfolding outside the window glass before him.

"Sit, Watson. There's brandy in my portmanteau if you're interested." Holmes then tidied up a pile of papers, secured them with a ribbon, and placed them in a folio.

"That has the look of a new manuscript, Holmes," I stated, more to get the conversation started than with any real interest.

"Indeed, Doctor. I expect to call it *The Uses of Plant Pollen in Crime Detection*," came his confident reply.

"Surely you jest, Holmes. What possible use could pollen play in solving crimes?"

"Elementary, my dear Watson. Pollen is ubiquitous in the environment. It's everywhere, in house dust, on the ground, in the air. We're constantly immersed in it and yet each location has pollens which are unique to it, and it alone. If I were to scrape the mud from your shoes, we'd find pollen unique to this area, and quite distinctive from that of the English countryside, the American Midwest or the streets of London."

I didn't reply immediately. The general principle Holmes had just articulated was obvious, but its value as a crimefighting tool was lost on me. I was about to voice my skepticism when Holmes thundered on. "The thought occurred to me during our last trip to the United States. Unlike England, the country is vast with great variations in its climate and, accordingly, its flora. But, the principle works equally well in Britain, particularly between major regions of the country. Cornwall, for example, versus the Scottish highlands or East Anglia."

I was about to respond, but Holmes gave me a big smile and exclaimed, "And it's been an amazing learning experience as well. The staff at the University infirmary allowed me the use of their microscopes and, suffice it to say, it's been a most fascinating journey into the world of micro-botany."

"Is that what you've been doing on these days when you seem to disappear for hours on end?" I asked skeptically.

"Precisely. But now that I've tested my theories, I'll be less mysterious."

Holmes waxed eloquent about his new interest while I listened politely, waiting for the opportunity to discuss Mrs. Cameron's condition.[27]

Perhaps lack of exuberance for the subject matter revealed itself because Holmes soon dropped the topic and asked me about Mrs. Cameron. I explained my diagnosis and a possible course of treatment.

"So you've abandoned your theory about lesions on her brain?" asked Holmes when I had finished.

"Not necessarily. A brain lesion may well be the cause of her affliction, but there is no way of knowing that short of a post mortem."

"Has her affliction stabilized?"

"I don't know that either, Holmes. It's been almost three months since her accident and, based upon what we've learned to date, it doesn't appear as if her mental condition has worsened even though she's deteriorated physically. I don't know for sure."

---

27 Editor's note: Watson's manuscript contained several passages regarding people that he and Holmes met in Anaconda. The passage below is illustrative. "Holmes attributed much of his interest and success in the study of pollen as a potential crime fighting tool to Dr. Jasper Spelman, a physician in Anaconda and the county health doctor whom we'd both met at a dinner party sponsored by Marcus Daly following successful resolution of the case I've chronicled as *The Tammany Affair*. Dr. Spelman was both an avid arborist and apiarist. He and Holmes spent considerable time together during our stay in Montana. I had assumed the relationship was purely social and discovered, only later, their mutual professional interest."

"Frankly, Watson, I am relieved to hear your diagnosis. Upon further reflection, my concern about a female Dr. Jekyll in our midst seems increasingly farfetched. I think we should move forward along the line you've suggested."

Together, we drew up a plan to apprise the Camerons in a way that would make it impossible for Mrs. Cameron to equivocate. I've learned through my years of medical practice that when the ailment is influenced by the functioning of the brain, the patient is usually reluctant to accept the diagnosis and often will try to rationalize or deny their condition.

I went to bed full of expectancy. Tomorrow night we should resolve this mysterious woman's condition and, by the grace of God, be on an eastbound train Monday morning, destination London.

The following evening found Cameron, Holmes and myself sequestered together in Holmes' room across the hallway from the elevator in the Montana Hotel in Anaconda waiting for Amy Cameron to take one of her nocturnal expeditions. Holmes had positioned a small mirror in the transom above the door so that he could keep track of traffic in the hallway without being seen.

Ten o'clock merged into 11 and then on to midnight. Cameron was a working man used to being up at the crack of dawn and was dozing in the overstuffed chair by the window while Holmes and I alternated reading with conversation. The night dragged on, time passing even more slowly as both my anticipation and bodily fatigue deepened.

"Finally, Watson," I heard Holmes say. He then motioned for me to be quiet. Soft footsteps could be heard in the hall. They passed our door.

"She's making for the stairwell. Roust Cameron, if you will, Doctor, and meet me in the lobby. I don't want her to get away from us."

With that Holmes quietly slipped out the door and I tried to waken Cameron. I soon understood how his missus could get up at night and roam the countryside without his knowledge. The man slept like he was dead. Calling to him and shaking his arm had no effect. In exasperation I gave him a good slap on the cheek and hauled him to his feet as he finally shook the slumber out of his eyes.

Holmes was in the hallway near a side door of the hotel. He waved frantically and we redoubled our pace.

"Amy's got a good start on us, gentlemen," said Holmes as he pushed through the door. "She's on Third Street, heading west."

The three of us quickly made our way through an alley behind the adjacent Commercial Hotel, emerging on the sidewalk across from Anaconda's commons. Mrs. Cameron was walking briskly, like she did in the mountains two nights previous. She turned south on Hickory Street heading uphill toward Anaconda's mansion district, which might be overstating the case significantly. Perhaps I should just say the area of town where Marcus Daly and a number of the town's more prominent citizens resided.

Holmes led us in a diagonal across the commons and soon we were stealing along the sidewalk just a few feet behind Mrs. Cameron, she oblivious to our presence.

When Amy reached the corner of Sixth and Hickory, just a few feet from the steps leading to Marcus Daly's home, Holmes quietly said, "Now, Doctor."

With the steep gables of Daly's three-story, red brick

mansion looming over my head, I took four long strides, reached out and grabbed Mrs. Cameron by the shoulder, turned her toward me, and said, "Amy, wake up!"

She stared at me blankly, and then started to turn and walk away. By this time Holmes and Salton Cameron had reached her side. Holmes grabbed her by the shoulders while I opened a vial of smelling salts and thrust it beneath her nose.

It took several minutes to shake Mrs. Cameron out of her stupor. Meekly, she finally uttered, "Salton, Dr. Watson, what are we doing here?"

"Solving the problem of your trancelike states, Mrs. Cameron," I said in reply. "You suffer from a severe case of somnambulism."

"What's that?" injected Cameron before his wife could reply.

"Sleepwalking," answered Holmes matter-of-factly. "Let's go back to the hotel so we can put this mystery to bed, and then, perhaps, we can do likewise."

We returned to the Camerons' room at the hotel and I quickly apprised them of the reasons for my diagnosis.

"I've never been a sleepwalker before, Doctor. Why would it develop now?" asked Mrs. Cameron.

"Medical science doesn't know why the condition is triggered, Amy, but it's much more common in children than in adults, and most of the time it simply goes away. In adults it's more commonly seen in people who are overwrought and full of distress."

Mrs. Cameron didn't respond to my remark about emotional distress, but her husband did. "Maybe that's it, Doctor. Things have not been good between us, and I realize now my anger must have put a special burden on Amy."

Cameron then turned to his wife, gently took her hand into his own and said, "Amy, I am sorry. I can't tell you how ashamed I am for anything I may have done to upset you. Please forgive me. I care for you so much."

Mrs. Cameron remained speechless, a slight blush appearing on her neck and slowly climbing to her cheeks, apparently overcome by her husband's apology and expression of endearment.

Cameron turned to me and asked, "What can we do to treat her ailment, Doctor?"

"She needs rest, real rest, not sleep while she walks all over the mountains above Georgetown. Amy's exhausted because she works all day managing your household and then walks several country miles each night."

"What about her trances during the day?" asked Cameron quickly.

"They're not trances at all. Amy just falls asleep while appearing to be awake. It's just a slightly different form of her somnambulism. I've had the local apothecary prepare this compound of laudanum. Amy should take a quarter ounce with water before bed. It should help her sleep through the night. Will you do that, Mrs. Cameron?"

Amy nodded in reply.

"We also need someone to help her around the house and watch for her at night. When Amy rises she must be wakened and then put back to bed, and you sleep much too soundly, Salton, to be the watchman. Is there a neighbor woman you could bring in, or family member nearby?"

Before either Salton or Amy could answer, Holmes interjected, "I know Doctor Watson thinks that your head injury earlier this summer was the catalytic event which triggered your condition, but I am not sure I share his opinion, Mrs. Cameron. I am not a medical man, but there are certain facts about this case which suggest to me that the cause of the malady is deep emotional distress."

Holmes paused to light the pipe he'd been filling with shag while he talked. Both Camerons looked at me with questioning glances and I could offer little in return except a shrug of the shoulders and a puzzled look of my own to indicate that I had no idea what the world's greatest consulting detective was about to say.

After exhaling the smoke of his Turkish blend, Holmes looked squarely at Mrs. Cameron and, with an accusatory tone to his voice, exclaimed, "Deep emotional distress caused by pretending to be something that you're not!"

Holmes' remark caused Amy to shrink back into the chair and her head to droop.

"My God, Mr. Holmes, what are you talking about?" asked Cameron in a loud, angry tone.

"Excuse me, and I'll show you," Holmes replied.

Holmes disappeared through the door leaving it ajar. I heard him tapping on another door down the hallway, followed by some muffled conversation and two sets of footsteps coming back toward the Camerons' room. He entered with a woman dressed in a dark blue robe, the mirror image of Amy Cameron.

"Watson, may I present to you the real Mrs. Salton Cameron. Mr. Cameron, I am sorry to have to tell you this, but the woman you've tried to live with these past three months as husband and wife is not Amy, but Abigail, her identical twin."

Cameron looked first at the woman in the chair next to him whom he assumed to be his wife. She nodded yes in a meek reply. He then turned to the woman adjacent Holmes, who did likewise. He paused, turning his head from one woman to the other, his complexion changing from pale to a deep hue of crimson, a volcanic cataclysm imminent.

Standing up, Cameron bellowed, "Abby, you're behind this, I know!"

At which point the real Amy standing next to Holmes stepped forward and said, "No, Salton. It was my idea. You spend all your time on business and never have a moment for your wife. I asked Abby to switch places with me, to prove to you that you didn't know your own wife from another woman."

The color drained out of Cameron's face quicker than it had blossomed. He was dumbstruck, turning first toward one woman and then the other. Finally, he sat down and looked at the real Amy, shook his head in dismay and said, "What kind of a man am I to not know his own wife?"

"You're a good man, Salton, and I love you. I just wanted you to appreciate me, like I do you, that's all," answered Amy as she stepped forward and wrapped her arms around Cameron.

Sister Abigail climbed out of the chair she was occupying and moved quickly to the doorway with Holmes and me in pursuit. The Camerons needed time for two.

Despite the lateness of the hour when I finally reached my bed, my sleep was fitful and I arose early, my mind full of questions regarding the previous night's discovery. I especially looked forward to seeing Mrs. Cameron's imposter sister Abigail, but the hotel desk clerk informed me that she and the Camerons had already departed.

In the confusion following Abigail's unmasking last night, I had failed to again impress upon her the need to take the pharmaceuticals I had prescribed. I was certain that being relieved of the burden of posing as Cameron's wife would have a salutary effect on her health but profound stress, even when relieved, requires the passage of time for full recuperation.

Holmes was nowhere to be seen and I knew better than to seek him out. He moved so frequently in the pursuit of either business or his own intellectual pursuits that all I was likely to obtain for my effort was an extensive walk about town. I busied myself drafting a letter to Miss Abigail outlining my medical concerns for her condition and urged her, in the strongest terms, to consult with a qualified physician in Helena. Then, once again I began packing for our departure to England, which was scheduled two days hence, momentarily distracted from that endeavor by a trip to the stationers where I replenished my writing supplies and purchased a book with the fascinating title of *Ben-Hur: A Tale of the Christ* by Lewis Wallace. I didn't recognize the name.

That afternoon I was reading through a stack of day-old newspapers in the hotel lobby when I heard the tap of boots on the marble floor behind, recognizing Holmes' gait in an instant. "Holmes," I said as I turned to face him.

"You've questions, no doubt, my friend," came his quick reply.

He sprawled in the chair beside me, his fatigue evident.

"So you didn't go to bed last night, my friend. You're getting too old for that."

"True, old chap, but I thought it my only chance to talk with Miss Abigail about her charade. It was a remarkable performance, but then she's a remarkable woman."

"Does she measure up to Miss Adler?"[28] It was a provocative little thrust on my part. Irene Adler was the only woman Holmes had ever considered his intellectual equal and it was the standard by which he measured all members of the fair sex, although he would never admit it.

Holmes ignored my inquiry and asked in reply, "I trust that you would like the background to this story?"

"Indeed, I am particularly curious about how this plot against Cameron was launched and how the women thought they could succeed."

"It all started, as was reported last night, by Amy, who was feeling quite lonely and neglected by Salton. If you'll recall, Salton Cameron mentioned an argument with his wife during which time sister Abigail taunted Cameron that any woman could stand by the stove and he would accept her as his wife."

"Yes, I remember the conversation."

"That idea took root with Mrs. Cameron. The next morning she talked Abigail into cutting her hair and stepping into Amy's clothes. Amy then departed for an overnight visit with a friend who lives a few miles away. Cameron came home, saw the woman he thought was Amy working about the kitchen and simply assumed it

---

28 Editor's note: Holmes encountered Irene Adler in a case titled *A Scandal in Bohemia*. Impressed by her cleverness, thereafter Holmes always referred to Miss Adler as *the* woman.

was his wife. She explained that Abigail had decided to cut her visit short and had returned to Helena. The ladies' ruse was helped along at this point by Cameron himself. His vision isn't the best and he left his spectacles in the office at the mill."

"And that night?" The scandal of a woman offering her marital bed to her sister was more than I could fathom.

"Amy wasn't too worried about it, according to Abigail. She told Abby 'just go to sleep, that's all I do. Salton thinks about nothing but the mine. He hasn't touched me in months.'"

"Astounding, Holmes. If I was living with a woman so fair, it would be hard to think of anything else."

"A most reasoned observation, Doctor, but mining isn't in your blood as it is among men of Cameron's type. You've met several of them since we've come to Montana, O'Flynn most recently. To them, mining is life itself."

I recognized the wisdom of Holmes' words but I couldn't help but feel dumbstruck that there were men about this world whose manhood was secondary to their occupation.

Holmes continued. "The next day the ladies met, laughed at Cameron's gullibility, and decided to continue the experiment for a few days with Amy actually going back to Abigail's home in Helena to enjoy the attractions of the city, a respite from the toil of marriage."

"Did she try and pose as Abigail?"

"For a few hours, but the effort was in vain. Abigail is a school marm by profession and her apartment is in a building where several of her lady friends and coworkers reside. Amy was discovered by noon but instantly adopted by Abigail's friends, whereupon she started to have the time of her life, freed from the responsibility of looking after a husband and household."

I couldn't help but smile. I could picture Amy looking through the shops in downtown Helena and feasting on the intellectual diversions that were not present in the rough mining camp she called home.

"Guess what happened next," said Holmes quietly.

I quickly replied, "Amy was in no hurry to come back."

"Very perceptive of you, Doctor, and back at the mine, Cameron rekindles a little energy in his loins, which leads to his confrontation with Abigail and, ultimately, to Abby's head injury. Her sleepwalking appears to have started after that, perhaps as a result of the blow itself as you suggested or, as is my theory, to the internal strife Abby must have felt trying to live as Amy."

"I still think the most profound aspect of this case is how Abigail could pose as Amy for what was it, six weeks?"

"Seven," replied Holmes?

"Seven weeks," I continued, "and not be discovered, pretending to be someone she was not. From what I saw, it doesn't even appear that she was ever suspected as being fraudulent. I can certainly sympathize with the real Mrs. Cameron about feeling unloved and taken for granted by her husband."

"Incredible, I agree, Doctor. But I think we all do that to some degree, particularly men."

"There is no question of that, Holmes. Women have an instinctual sense for people and it's particularly acute for the members of their family, especially children."

"We men are creatures of the world, Watson; women of the home. I suspect that our friend Cameron will have far greater appreciation of the latter in the days to come."

"Indeed, Holmes, indeed. I am also somewhat puzzled by why Abigail let the matter go on for so long, particularly after she was injured. I would think that once the somnambulism started she would have tried to contact Amy and have her come back home."

"That's odd, I admit," answered Holmes as he started to fish through his coat pockets for his pipe and tobacco pouch. His eyebrows furrowed as they frequently do when he's thinking so I took the liberty of removing my coat and folding it over the arm of my chair. After he had put his pipe to fire Holmes continued. "I suspect it was lack of opportunity, Doctor. Abigail was isolated at Georgetown. The only telegraph was in the depot at Southern Cross and she may not have wanted to risk saying something in a message to her sister which the telegrapher might report back to Cameron. And, she was only in Anaconda twice during that period, both times to consult with physicians, and I doubt that Cameron ever left her side."

"Plausible, entirely plausible," I answered and then countered by observing, "but there is always the postal system. She could have sent a letter to her sister."

"Your logic is impeccable, Doctor, but we are, after all, nothing more than two men speculating at the inner workings of a woman's mind. That's an unfathomable task, I am sure you'll agree."

I wasn't pleased by Holmes' answer but, after mulling it over for a good minute or two, couldn't dispute his reasoning. I decided to drop the subject inasmuch as I had other questions of a more factual nature. "Pray, Holmes, how did you discover Abby's substitution for Amy?"

"I hate to confess it, Watson, but I was focused on something sinister, something akin to a reprise of that ugly incident involving Dr. Jekyll."

"Well, I was starting to see it that way myself, old friend, particularly after Cameron discovered that box of cyanide in his stable."

"Which, by the way," interrupted Holmes, "turned out to be nothing. Amy reminded Cameron that she obtained the poison last spring to kill rats."

I took advantage of Holmes' momentary pause to summon the bellman and give him an order for some liquid refreshment.

"As I was saying, Watson," continued Holmes after the bellman had departed, "I was headed off in the wrong direction until that evening when we visited with the Camerons at their home."

"I remember. Cameron talked to me incessantly about the mine while you explored politics, art, religion, and philosophy with whom we thought was Mrs. Cameron."

"Indeed, Watson, and I was most impressed by her grasp of those issues, particularly by one living in a remote camp where a newspaper is a rare treasure and whose household contains few books. In the course of that conversation she quoted Ella Knowles. Now, there is no reason in the world whatsoever why the real Amy Cameron would ever know Ella Knowles, a point Cameron subsequently verified for me."

"Who is Ella Knowles?"

"She's an attorney, the first woman admitted to the Montana bar, and currently serving as deputy Attorney General of the State of Montana. She is also an active suffragette. I met Miss Knowles in Butte not long after we arrived in

Montana, while we were looking into that little matter involving Daly's racehorse. I didn't have any answer for the infirmity, which was affecting the woman we thought was Mrs. Cameron. You provided that, but I knew Mrs. Cameron was an imposter. A telegram to the Pinkerton office in Helena resulted in a few discreet inquiries being made and my theory was confirmed."

"And then you contrived a reason to get Amy back to Anaconda."

"Yes, another telegram, this one under Cameron's name indicating that her sister was gravely ill.

The bellman returned with two brandies on a silver tray.

"Let us drink to your health, Watson."

"And to the successful conclusion of another case, Holmes. I think I will chronicle it as *The Adventure of the Substitute Sister.*"

Holmes shook his head in disagreement.

"Too revealing, Doctor. Your readers will know the outcome from the title page. You need something more mysterious."

Holmes was right.

About the Author

John Fitzpatrick is a native of Anaconda, Montana.
For the past thirty years he has worked as a lobbyist for the metal mining, telecommunications, and utility industry.
He resides in Helena, Montana.